James Roberts Gilmore

John Sevier as a commonwealth-builder

A sequel to the rear-guard of the revolution

James Roberts Gilmore

John Sevier as a commonwealth-builder
A sequel to the rear-guard of the revolution

ISBN/EAN: 9783337234324

Printed in Europe, USA, Canada, Australia, Japan

Cover: Foto ©Raphael Reischuk / pixelio.de

More available books at **www.hansebooks.com**

AS A COMMONWEALTH-BUILDER

A SEQUEL TO

THE REARGUARD OF THE REVOLUTION

BY

JAMES R. GILMORE

(EDMUND KIRKE)

AUTHOR OF "THE REAR-GUARD OF THE REVOLUTION,"
"AMONG THE PINES," ETC.

NEW YORK
D. APPLETON AND COMPANY
1887

PREFACE.

THE materials from which this volume has been constructed have been, in part, the same as those I employed in writing a preceding book upon the same subject, under the title of "The Rear-Guard of the Revolution." But this work goes over later and more thoroughly tilled ground than that, and hence I have had for it a wider range of authorities.

Briefly stated, my sources of information have been, first and primarily, lengthy conversations with Dr. J. G. M. Ramsey, of Knoxville, Tennessee, during which his "Annals of Tennessee" was used somewhat in the manner of a text-book—Dr. Ramsey pointing out its inaccuracies, amplifying its narrative with interesting details, and relating to me such additional facts as he had gathered during the nearly thirty years since the writing of his history. He was a man of rare culture and trained intellect, and, by the character of his mind, was peculiarly qualified for historical investigation. When I knew him, he had given fifty years of his life to the study of this subject.

Next in importance as authorities, I rank the traditions which I gathered, during the years from 1880 to 1884, by a systematic inquiry among the descendants of the men whose deeds I have recorded. The descendants whom I met numbered half a hundred, and nearly a score of them were aged men, who, in their boyhood, had personally known Sevier and many of his compatriots. Their accounts I have compared carefully with one another, and verified by all the means at my command. It is my sincere conviction that—in the form they are stated in this book—they may be safely accepted as authentic history. Among many there is a prejudice against tradition as a foundation for historical writing; but it should be borne in mind that most history is, and was, originally tradition. By tradition I do not mean rumor, but those carefully treasured accounts of striking events and heroic exploits, in the lives of our forefathers, which are handed down with religious care from father to son in all families having a proper pride in their ancestry. Upon some such traditions were undoubtedly based all but one of the biographies we have of the greatest character in history; and my investigations into the present subject have given me a singular light upon the manner in which at least two of those histories, and the introductory portion of another, must have been constructed. The three synoptic gospels accord wonderfully in their reports of the spoken words of Christ, but they differ considerably as to the circumstances attending some of the important events which they relate. In a similar manner, striking speeches, which in this and the previous volume I have put into the mouths of Sevier, Shelby, and Robertson, have been repeated to me alike, word for word, by half a dozen separate narrators, while the same persons have differed widely in their narrative of events—in some instances so widely that the accounts can not be reconciled, and I have been obliged to discard them all.

I have also been aided in my understanding of events by visits to all the principal localities I have mentioned, and by mingling freely with the men who are descendants of the early settlers, and have inherited many of their great qualities.

Of written authorities I have, I think, consulted all that bear upon my subject. Among other books, I have carefully examined Albach's "Western Annals"; Monette's "Valley of the Mississippi"; Haywood's "History of Tennessee"; A. W. Putnam's "History of Middle Tennessee"; Prof. W. W. Clayton's "History of Davidson County, Tennessee"; Francis Baily's "Journey through the Unsettled Parts of North America in 1796–1797"; the Rev. T. W. Hume's (Knoxville) "Centennial Address"; the volumes of the "Columbian Magazine" from 1785–1797; a file of the "Knoxville Gazette" from 1791–1796 (kindly forwarded to me, across a thousand miles of country, by the Tennessee Historical Society); and, in addition, through the courtesy of Prof. Johnson T. Platt and Addison Van Name, Esq., I have had access to the very complete collection of Colonial and Revolutionary newspapers contained in the library of Yale University.

I have also received essential aid from Mrs. William O'Neil Perkins, of Franklin, Tennessee, who has furnished me with very many letters from John Sevier to his son, George Washington Sevier; various written statements of fact by her father, the historian of Middle Tennessee; and other documents that have helped to make the present volume more full and accurate. This lady has the peculiar honor to be the great-granddaughter of General John Sevier, the hero of King's Mountain, and also of General Israel Putnam, the hero of Bunker Hill. She is also the granddaughter of Colonel George Washington Sevier, and the daughter of Colonel A. W. Putnam, of Nashville—a pedigree more to be valued than a descent from kings. To her my acknowledgments are strongly due; and also to the Hon. John M. Lea, the President, and to Anson Nelson, Esq., the Secretary, of the Tennessee Historical Society, for their hearty interest and co-operation in my work; as well as to the Society itself, for its public indorsement of the accuracy and value of my previous volume.

And now I beg to say a few words of an explanatory character. In the course of this volume I speak in condemnatory terms of two enemies of Sevier, Joseph Martin and John Tipton. I have quoted some of Martin's letters; and they are enough to show that he was a treacherous friend and a self-seeking demagogue. My characterization of Tipton is based upon the facts I relate of him, every one of which is abundantly authenticated. My opinion of him accords with that of Dr. J. G. M. Ramsey; but it is not universal among Tennesseans. To be assured that I was correct in my estimate of the man, I have sent my manuscript to one of the first jurists of Tennessee, who is, no doubt, better acquainted with the history of the State than any one now in it; and his reply shows that he does not take my view of Tipton's character. He writes: "Tipton was always regarded as a rough and uneducated, but a brave and honorable man. I know many of the family, and to a man they are courageous and true; but self-willed, impulsive, and imperious. You may be correct in your conception of his character; but, if anybody else than one who had investigated the subject were to write of Tipton as you have done, I should think he had misconceived his character, or, rather, had magnified its objectionable features." I regret that I can not make my views of Tipton accord with those of this gentleman. I differ from him with much reluctance, and only after much questioning of my own judgment; but, while I would "gently scan my brother man," I can not, in the face of incontestable facts, come to any other conclusion about Tipton than the one I have stated in this history. However, if my judgment upon him is too harsh, it will not stand; and, also, new facts may yet be discovered to compel a more favorable view of his character.

Before I began this book I intended to include in it

an account of the remarkable career of James Robertson; but I soon discovered that I could not so condense my material as to make that possible. That work, therefore, I have to reserve for another volume.

This is all I have to say, except that I wish my book were worthier of my subject. It is only as good as my poor ability and the limited time at my disposal have enabled me to make it; but, just as it is, I commit it to public scrutiny, in the hope that it may awaken an interest in the great character it attempts to delineate, and lead other and abler historical writers to investigate his career, and do more efficient justice to his memory.

JAMES R. GILMORE.
(EDMUND KIRKE.)

CONTENTS.

CHAPTER I.

CHAPTER II.

2

CHAPTER XI.

CHAPTER XII.

CHAPTER XIII.

JOHN SEVIER.

CHAPTER I.

THE ACTORS IN THIS HISTORY.

THE thirteen United Colonies, which in 1783 achieved their independence of Great Britain, were composed of as heterogeneous elements as ever came together for the forming of a nation. Among them were men of every class and nationality, every rank and character, and every variety of political and religious opinion. Writing of them in 1750, the Rev. Hugh Jones, chaplain to the Honorable Assembly of Virginia, and minister of Jamestown, said : "If New England be called a receptacle of Dissenters, and an Amsterdam of religion, Pennsylvania the nursery of Quakers, Maryland the retirement of Roman Catholics, North Carolina the refuge of Runaways, and South Carolina the delight of Buccaneers and Pyrates, Virginia may justly be esteemed the happy retreat of true Britons, and true Churchmen, for the most part, neither soaring too high nor dropping too low ; consequently, it should

merit the greater esteem and encouragement." History fully confirms the worthy chaplain's characterization of the various colonies, and it records also the
singular fact that early North Carolina, the "refuge of
Runaways," was the first-born daughter of Virginia,
that "happy retreat of true Britons, and true Churchmen."

Though the Lords Proprietors of the Carolinas introduced into the northern colony prior to 1670 several
ship-loads of respectable English settlers from Barba-
does, and considerable numbers of Swiss, German, and
French Protestants came in soon afterward, and some
small colonies of Scotch Jacobites directly following
the Stuart rebellion of 1745, a large majority of the
early settlers of North Carolina were "runaways"
from Virginia—either criminals, escaping from justice
in the older colony, or "worthless trash," expelled from
it because disorderly, and altogether unprofitable in a
civilized community. These last were the remnants or
descendants of the servile class who had in former
years been imported to work the plantations, and in-
dentured to the planters to pay their passage across
the ocean. They were Englishmen, but, for the most
part, Englishmen who could trace their lineage no
further than the prisons and slums of London. Their
indentures expired, they found themselves shut out from
respectable society by the prejudice entailed by their
antecedents ; and the consequence was that the meaner-
spirited among them became outcasts, herding together

in the backwoods, and gleaning a wretched subsistence from hunting and fishing; or, hanging upon the outskirts of the plantations, living there in filthy cabins, and preying upon the planters' henneries and smoke-houses. The better and more enterprising portion—those who retained some lingering traces of manhood, and had some aspirations for a higher life—emigrated at once to North Carolina, where, being joined by such of the outcasts as were from time to time expelled by the planters, they formed the principal element in what soon came to be known in the vernacular of the period as the "Tar-heel Commonwealth." From a people of such antecedents a model community could not be expected; and we shall see that the tree bore its legitimate fruit if we glance for a moment at the condition of North Carolina at the time of the Revolution.

Bancroft asserts that at this period there was neither law nor lawyers in North Carolina. This, though substantially true, was not so literally; for lawyers might be found there of the order of Andrew Jackson, who varied a two-years' reading of Blackstone by intense application to horse-racing and cock-fighting; and courts could be discovered sitting in taverns and log-hovels, with judges knowing nothing of law or precedent, and coming to their decisions only after close consultation with a whisky-bottle. Judge Lynch was the popular magistrate, and his decrees were usually those of a crowd of hooting and drunken ragamuffins. Until 1703 there

was not a clergyman in the entire colony, and the first
school was opened and printing-press established just
on the eve of the Revolution. As a consequence, the
people were densely ignorant, few among them could
read or write, and disorder and lawlessness everywhere
abounded. To a few towns along the sea-coast a mail
came once a month from Virginia, but the post-rider
never penetrated into the interior. There the people
dwelt in thick darkness, having from year's end to
year's end no more intelligence from the outside world
than could be gleaned from the few travelers who had
the hardihood to venture into their wooded solitudes.
There was next to no town life. New Berne and Wil-
mington, the principal towns, had each a population of
less than six hundred. A vast majority of the people
occupied small, scattered farms—often unfenced clearings in the midst of wide forests, from which the trees
had been removed by girdling, and which were cultivated by negro-labor in a most primitive and wasteful
manner. For the farmer himself, however poor he
might be, was either too proud or too lazy to work.
His time he spent in lounging at taverns, drinking
poor whisky, and indulging in "manly encounters"
with his neighbors, in which noses were broken, and
eyes gouged out by the long finger-nails which he allowed to grow, and pared to a point for that express
purpose. In aspiration and instinct he was generally
but a little above the brute ; and yet he did know
enough to dodge his taxes. Law and religion were to

him unmeaning terms, and the chief end of man was to live without work, and keep down the expenses of government. Owing to a coarse diet and brutish habits, these people were poorly developed physically, and they regarded with astonishment the uniformly tall and athletic over-mountain men who marched over their wretched roads to fight the battle they should themselves have fought at King's Mountain.

But there were a few grains of wheat in this big bushel of chaff—a few brave spirits, "studious of their rights, bold to avow, and brave to maintain them," whose patriotic acts have cast a gleam of sunlight over the dismal history of Revolutionary North Carolina. These men were mostly of the foreign element which had settled in Orange, Wake, and Mecklenburg Counties. In resistance to the tyranny of Tryon, they in May, 1771, fought the battle of the Alamance, and in May, 1775, they issued what is known as the "Mecklenburg Declaration of Independence." These two acts have given North Carolina the name of being the first of the colonies to make organized resistance to British oppression; while in truth the credit belongs to but a small fraction of the population. A large proportion of the people were what I have described; and many of them were Tories in the Revolution; and Tories not from any intelligent idea of the issues at stake, but because all of the better class among them were patriots, and their instincts led them to oppose the law and order element. Impartial history has to record the fact that at this period the masses of North Carolina were the pariahs of American society, and the State itself little better than a Botany Bay for the American continent.

The men who planted civilization beyond the Alleghanies were a different order of people. Though settled on the soil, and within the jurisdiction of North Carolina, they were not North Carolinians. They were mostly Virginians, belonging either to the gentry or to the sturdy Scotch-Irish and English yeomanry who worked their own plantations. Of this latter class was the body of immigrants whom James Robertson led over the mountains in 1770 to form the first civilized settlement west of the Alleghanies. They were Virginians who had only shortly before settled in Wake County, and they supposed, when they built their cabins beyond the mountains, that they were again upon the soil of the Old Dominion ; and this was the impression of all the settlers till a number of years afterward. For nearly ten years the immigration continued to be of this class, and almost altogether from Virginia, for no road had yet been opened into Eastern North Carolina, and the hunters' trace across the mountains was well-nigh impassable ; whereas, from Virginia there was, following the southwestern trend of the valleys, a broad, beaten trail which had been the Indian war-path for many centuries. When a passable road was finally opened over the Alleghanies in 1778, a tide began to set in from North Carolina, but it was of the better class—for it goes without saying that a man must be possessed of very manly qualities who will deliberately set up his abode where he has to take his life in his hand and face death daily. Still, the larger number of new-comers continued to be from Virginia, and the dominant sentiment was always Virginian, alike on the Holston and Watauga and on the distant Cumberland. With but one exception the trans-Alleghany leaders were all native Virginians—Sevier, Donelson, and the two Bledsoes being from the ranks of the gentry, Robertson and Cocke from that yeoman class which has given some of its most honored names to English history. The one exception was Isaac Shelby, who was of Welsh descent, but born and educated in Maryland.

The over-mountain settlers were not fugitives from justice, nor needy adventurers seeking in the untrodden West a scanty subsistence which had been denied them in the Eastern settlements. And they were not merely Virginians—they were the culled wheat of the Old Dominion, with all those grand qualities which made the name of "Virginian" a badge of honor throughout the colonies. Many of them were cultivated men of large property, and, though the larger number were poor in this world's goods, they all possessed those more stable riches which consist of stout arms and brave hearts, unblemished integrity and sterling worth. They were so generally educated that in 1776 only two in about two hundred were found unable to write their names in good, legible English. No body of men ever had clearer ideas of civil polity or more highly valued the blessings of good government. Order-loving and God-fearing, they lived together for twelve years without so much as one capital crime among them. Shut out by wide forests and high mountain-barriers from civilized law, they made their own laws, and framed for themselves a government which was, with the sole exception of the "Fundamental Agreement," entered into by the "free planters" of New Haven on June 4, 1639—the first absolutely " free and independent " constitution that existed in this country.

The ruling motive of many of these men—as it is generally of those who seek new fields of enterprise—was, no doubt, the bettering of their worldly condition ; nevertheless, I think it true that much the larger number sought in their Western homes not so much worldly wealth as political freedom. They would be beyond the reach of the "red-coated minions of tyranny"; they dreaded less the war-whoop of the savage than the stinging insult of the British oppressor. But their leaders were far-seeing men, and they had higher aims than a mere escape from political tyranny. They sought to found in those Western forests a great empire of freemen, and they knew they were clearing the way for a civilization which should overspread the continent. Said Robertson, while yet the navigation of the Mississippi was controlled by Spain, and all the vast region beyond that river was fast-locked by her mediæval bigotry, " We are the Advance Guard of Civilization, and our way is across the continent"; and to Governor Caswell, Sevier wrote, when the settlers were but a handful, "However inconsiderable the people of this country may appear at this day, reason must inform us that the time is not far distant when they will become as consequential in numbers, if not more so, than most of the Eastern States."

Under these two leaders, John Sevier and James Robertson, these people had developed a boundless courage, a constant fortitude, a self-devoted patriotism, worthy of the most heroic ages. When only a handful of thirty men able to wield an axe or handle a rifle, they ventured beyond the Alleghanies, and in the mountain-girt valley of the Watauga built their cabins and tilled their fields, encompassed by twenty thousand armed savages, and shut off by a trackless wilderness from all civilized succor. There for five years they held their ground, till they grew to number about two hundred riflemen, and then, under John Sevier, they began a career for which it is hard to find a parallel in history. Outnumbered more than twenty to one, they held for six years the gateways of the Alleghanies against the savage horde which Great Britain had enlisted for the destruction of the colonies. Time and again they met the savage onset, and time and again they beat it back, and carried havoc and death into the very heart of the Indian country. And so well did they guard the mountain-passes that in all these years not one savage band broke through to carry the torch and the tomahawk to the homes of Eastern Carolina.

3

Their own cabins went up in flames, their own firesides were drenched in blood, and their mothers and wives and children fell before the merciless scalping-knife of the Cherokee, yet they never shrank and never wavered, but stood, from first to last, the immovable rearguard of the Revolution. And not content with this, when the day was at the darkest, when seaboard Carolina was trodden under foot by the red dragoon, and the young republic seemed in the very throes of dissolution, they left their own homes well-nigh unprotected, and, mustering their best and bravest, rushed over the mountains to the rescue of their distant countrymen. Making an unexampled march of two hundred miles, they hurled themselves, only nine hundred and fifty strong, against the almost impregnable defenses of King's Mountain, and, in one hour, annihilated the left wing of the army of Cornwallis! The result, in logical sequence, was Yorktown and American independence.

Doubtless, the great achievements of the over-mountain men were largely due to the remarkable qualities of John Sevier, who was both their civil and military leader. He knew how to achieve great results with slender means, and before Napoleon was born had discovered that principle of dynamics by which a small body, driven with immense force, will deal a heavier blow than a much larger one having only the ordinary momentum. He was a man of great natural endowments, and of a training that peculiarly fitted him to be what he became, the rearguard of the Revolution, and the guardian and defender

of the newly planted civilization beyond the Alleghanies.
No other man of equal talents and equal achievements
has been so little noticed in American history, and hence
it is not amiss to devote a few pages to a consideration of
his life and its influence in founding and developing the
great empire which has grown up west of the Alleghanies.

He was not of the ordinary type of backwoodsman.
He was a gentleman born and bred; and in his veins
flowed some of the best blood of the French and English
nations. He had the force and fire of the Navarre Hu-
guenots combined with the solid Anglo-Saxon elements
which have had here, perhaps, their highest expression
in our venerated Washington. This peculiar blending
of qualities was seen even in his face, which, while in
contour and lineament strikingly like that of Washington, had the mobility of feature and delicacy of expression which belong to the French physiognomy.

He was born in 1745, in the Shenandoah Valley of
Virginia, where his father had established himself a few
years before as a considerable planter. The place was
then on the confines of civilization, and had few educa-
tional facilities; but John was taught the rudiments of
learning by his mother, and, an Indian war soon break-
ing out, which forced the family to Fredericksburg, he
had there the advantage of a good school for several
years. The family returned to their frontier home when
John was twelve years old, and then he was sent to an
advanced school at Staunton, where he remained, an apt

and ready but not very industrious student, until he was sixteen years of age. From these few years of tuition he acquired as much of an education as was common to young gentlemen of the period—enough to enable him in after-years to be a ready and effective speaker and writer, and to associate on equal terms with the leading men of the country. But he was always better acquainted with men than with books. Study was irksome to his active nature, but the knowledge of men came to him by intuition.

Leaving school before he was turned of seventeen, young Sevier struck out at once in life for himself by marrying a wife, and laying out a township about half a dozen miles distant from his father's plantation. This town, still bearing the name he gave it, is now the beautiful village of Newmarket, in the valley of the Shenandoah, about one hundred and fifty miles northwest from Richmond. Here young Sevier erected a log warehouse and dwelling, much in the style of a fort, for security was the prime requisite in backwoods architecture; and in the warehouse he opened a store for the vending of dry-goods and groceries, thereby making his town what its name indicated, the market-center of a wide agricultural region.

Among the young trader's customers were many of the red dwellers of the forest, who came to him for powder and lead and the long-barreled rifle. Their eyes were dazzled by the bright array of "stroud," beads, scarlet cloth, and looking-glasses, with which the warehouse was adorned, and they longed to possess the gorgeous wonders. To their untutored virtue, a few discharges of powder and shot seemed an easier mode of payment than a tiresome getting together of peltries, only to be procured by long and tedious hunting. So, one dark night, they descended upon Newmarket, and attempted to take forcible possession of young Sevier's business establishment. The young gentleman had only a half-dozen men with him, but he made such effectual resistance that the baffled savages soon scattered into the adjacent forest. In the morning, a trail of blood through the trodden undergrowth told the route they had taken; and, gathering a score of his friends together, young Sevier followed in pursuit of the marauders. After a toilsome march through a pathless forest, he came up with them at their wigwam village, and, not stopping to count their numbers, made so furious an assault upon them that they speedily fled in all directions. Their village was reduced to ashes, and a number of their braves were left unburied among the cinders.

Thus did this born soldier, when a youth of scarcely eighteen, inaugurate a new system of Indian warfare. Thenceforth, wherever his influence went, it was attack and not defense: not a skulking behind trees and log-fortresses; but an open forest, a wild halloo, and then the onward rush of the hurricane! It was by such tactics that Sevier became the victor in thirty-five battles, and the most renowned of Indian fighters.

The Indians naturally objected to a bonfire being

made of one of their villages at the whim of a white stripling, and they attempted to enforce upon him their law of retaliation. They descended again upon New-market in largely augmented numbers; but this the young soldier had anticipated, and he was ready to receive them. At the head of about a hundred hardy borderers, he put them again to flight, and he followed up his success by again invading the Indian country, burning their villages, destroying their standing corn, and often defeating bodies of five times his own number.

His exploits attracted universal admiration, and in time reached the ears of Lord Dunmore, the last royal Governor of Virginia. The Governor at once sought out the young volunteer who had thus taken off his hands the business of chastising the unruly savages. He expected to find him an uncouth backwoods youth, of rustic ways, and the rude speech of the border; but, instead of this, he met a young man of refined aspect, easy and prepossessing manners, and an air of natural dignity that bespoke the born gentleman. The courtly Englishman was fascinated with the backwoods youth, and took him at once into favor, showering upon him many marks of distinction, and, among others, in 1772, a commission as captain in the Virginia line—the same corps in which Washington then held the rank of colonel.

Thus, for about half a dozen years, Sevier fought the Indians with one hand, and with the other dealt out dry-goods and groceries from his warehouse at New-

market—doing the last so successfully that, by the time
he was twenty-six, he had accumulated what, for the
time and place, was an ample fortune.

Then, one spring day in 1772, he was invited by one
of his fellow-officers—Captain Evan Shelby, subsequently
General Shelby, of the Revolutionary army—to visit him
at his cattle-farm of King's Meadows (now Bristol,
Tennessee), on the southwestern border of Virginia.
Sevier went, and there he heard of a body of adventurous pioneers, who, under the lead of James Robertson,
had, less than two years before, built their cabins at Watauga, on the western slope of the Alleghanies. Curious
to see this handful of settlers, who had thus ventured
upon the hunting-grounds of twenty thousand warlike
savages, Sevier rode on to the settlement with Evan
Shelby and his son Isaac, who afterward became the
first Governor of Kentucky. The visit brought him in
contact with Robertson, and that fixed his earthly destiny. On the instant he decided to cast in his lot with
that feeble community beyond the mountains.

Viewed in the light of human prudence, this act of
Sevier's seems the extreme of folly. With wealth already acquired, with devoted friends who were among
the most influential men in Virginia, and with every
avenue of distinction wide open to him in the older settlements, he had within his reach every object that usually attracts the ambition of a young man conscious of
commanding talents. But he deliberately turned his
back upon this brilliant future, and chose instead a life

remote from cultivated society, and amid an unexplored
forest, where he was sure to encounter hardship and pri-
vation, and every peril that waits on civilized man when
he comes in daily contact with untamed barbarism.   It
would be idle to seek his motive for thus throwing away
the most coveted objects of ordinary ambition; but, looking at him and events through the lens of a century, it is
easy to see that he had found his appropriate life-work;
and that he had been fitted for this work by an exceptional training—such a training as probably came to no
other cultivated man of his generation.   There may
have been, among the three millions who then peopled
the Thirteen Colonies, some other man who could have
done what he did, but no such man came to the surface of affairs, and hence it is reasonable to conclude
that he was a "providential man," as have been all other
men who have executed great tasks in pivotal periods of
human history.

I have conversed with a number of aged men who
knew Sevier well in their boyhood, and they all agree in
describing him as possessed of a personal magnetism that
was nothing less than wonderful.   It was potent with
both his friends and his enemies; felt alike by the courtly Dunmore and the untamed savage.   He fought the
Cherokees for more than twenty years, but they never
came within the sphere of his presence without casting
aside their grievances and grasping his hand as their
brother.   Once, when he had reduced their nation to the
very verge of starvation by burning every stalk of corn

and ear of grain in their country, their king wrote to the Governor of North Carolina, "Send us John Sevier, for he is a good man, and he will do us right." Though they recognized in him the Nemesis of their nation, they conceived for him a fanatical admiration, which at last deepened into a superstitious belief that he was the special representative of the INVISIBLE. Fighting with him was therefore a struggle with Destiny, and this thought did more for Western civilization than a thousand Deckard rifles.

His magnetism being thus potent with his enemies, we can easily conceive how it came to be irresistible with his friends — those people whom he had now settled among ; for whom he poured out his wealth like water ; whose homes he watched over with sleepless vigilance ; and whom he soon led in many a desperate battle, crowned always with victory. This magnetism sprang from his overflowing kindliness and goodness of heart, and this it was, with his commanding abilities, which caused him to be recognized from the outset as their leader by these people, and made him, during a long life, the very soul of the Western commonwealth.

In a previous book * I have tried to trace the career of this remarkable man from his first appearance at Watauga to the close of the Revolutionary struggle. In the present volume I propose to take up the narrative where

---

* "The Rear-Guard of the Revolution," D. Appleton & Co., New York.

it is there left off, and to follow, as well as I can, his course from the Peace of 1783 to the end of his life; during which period, opposed by North Carolina and unaided by the General Government, he built up a great commonwealth in the very heart of the Western wilderness.

CHAPTER II.

THE FIRST SECESSION.

BETWEEN two such peoples as are described in the preceding chapter, there could be no community of feeling; and this lack of sympathy grew into antagonism, when the western settlers witnessed the indifference of North Carolina to their security, her parsimonious refusal of all appropriations for their benefit, and the grasping eagerness with which she enforced upon them taxation, and availed herself of the proceeds of their unoccupied lands. They had unwittingly settled upon her territory, and from the outset had regarded her as a step-mother; and this she proved herself to be by exacting all of a mother's rights, and discharging none of her duties. To this antagonism is mainly to be attributed the first secession which occurred in this country.

Like all the Thirteen Colonies, North Carolina came out of the Revolution not only impoverished but loaded down with debt. She owed vast sums to her soldiers, and also her proper share of the national obligations, which now amounted, in round figures, to forty-two million dollars, with an addition of about three millions for unpaid interest. A considerable part of this sum was due to France, whose government was then asking for some adjustment which would in time provide for the principal, and at once secure the prompt payment of the interest. France had befriended the country in its utmost need, and the general conscience demanded that something should be done to satisfy its just claims. But what could be done with an empty treasury, and the few worthless cannon and worn-out muskets, which comprised the total resources of these United States, then just embarked on their great career among the nations? Various plans were proposed and expedients suggested, and among them was one that the individual States should cede their unoccupied lands to the General Government to create a fund to meet the common liabilities. The demand for such lands was active, owing to a large influx of immigration; and it was calculated that they would speedily yield sufficient avails to expunge the national obligations.

North Carolina at this time held about twenty-nine million acres beyond the Alleghanies—all that region which is now comprised within the great State of Tennessee. She had acquired this vast domain without the expenditure of a drop of blood or an ounce of treasure, for all that portion of the Henderson purchase which was south of latitude 36° 30' she had unceremoniously confiscated on the George III theory that none but a sovereign

State has any natural right to buy lands of the Indians; and the remainder, which was not in actual occupation by the Cherokees, had been bought or wrested from those savages by John Sevier and his riflemen, who had fed, clothed, and equipped themselves without a dollar of aid from North Carolina. As the State contained about one ninth of the population of the Union, she was in equity bound for a like proportion of the national debt; and now was presented to her legislators the opportunity to execute a brilliant financial feat—to discharge her share of this vast indebtedness without withdrawing a dime from her treasury or imposing a dollar of tax upon her tax-loathing people. This her legislators proceeded to do by passing an act in June, 1784, which ceded the whole of what is now Tennessee to the General Government; and this they did without so much as consulting one of the thirty thousand or more loyal citizens who occupied this territory, and had freely expended their blood and treasure to secure her independence. Without a word, she thrust them ruthlessly from her door, and consigned them to a distant Congress, which could afford them neither shelter nor protection.

For Congress at this time had none of the powers that are requisite for efficient government. The Union was merely a rope of sand; the thirteen States were thirteen small republics, each one exercising nearly all the functions of sovereignty. The cementing principle between them was mutual protection; but they had separate and antagonistic interests that might at any moment

4

rend them asunder. When threatened by a common
danger, they had stood shoulder to shoulder ; but, that
danger passed, there was little to hold them together.
Nor was there any general sentiment of nationality
among the people. The traveler through the country
met a great many Virginians, South Carolinians, and
New-Englanders, but very few Americans. To Congress
these little republics had delegated a few powers, just
enough to entitle them to the name of United States, but
not enough to enable the General Government to preserve order at home or command respect abroad. Congress could contract debts, levy armies, and make agree-
ments with foreign powers ; but it could not collect an
impost, or force a State to observe a treaty or to contrib-
ute a single soldier for the common defense. It had a
head, a body, and about ninety bodily members, but the
breath of life was not in it. It did not even possess the
power to protect itself from indignity and insult by its
own soldiery, as had been shown a year previously, when,
in its "own hired house" at Philadelphia, it was surrounded by two hundred and eighty mutinous soldiers,
clamoring for the pay which was unrighteously withheld
from them by the thirteen little republics. To this inert
and powerless body North Carolina bade her over-mountain citizens look for security and protection, at the very
time when they were in daily danger from a savage
enemy, and when she was thrusting upon them a host of
her own Tories—desperate, lawless characters, thieves,
house-burners, cut-throats, and woman-violators, whom

nothing but the strong arm of omnipotent law could hold
in civilized subjection. Can it be wondered at that,
when the tidings crossed the Alleghanies, it aroused a
universal feeling of indignant consternation ?

News in those days traveled slowly. The State capital was more than five hundred miles from Watauga, and
the road to it over the mountains was in places so steep
and rugged that none but a backwoods horseman would
attempt its passage. Nearly thirty days were usually
consumed in the journey, and thus it was far into July
when tidings of the cession act came to the western
settlers. They had no printing-press, and so all news
passed among them by word of mouth ; but this flew
with the rapidity of lightning. From man to man, from
cabin to cabin, from hamlet to hamlet it sped, and everywhere it went it kindled a flame of angry excitement.
With stern faces but anxious hearts they came together
to deliberate upon the situation. They had, they said,
asked North Carolina for a Superior Court, to deal with
the criminals she was driving among them, and for a
general officer with power to rally their militia for the
common defense against the daily increasing danger from
the Creeks and Cherokees ; and, while the ink upon their
petition was scarcely dry, she had answered it by unceremoniously turning them over to a distant body, composed of men whose interests were upon the seaboard,
and who knew no more of their condition and necessities
than they did of the geography of the moon—nor half so
much, if they had chanced to listen to Professor John

Winthrop, of Harvard, who was then the supreme authority on earthquakes and lunar mountains. Whenever before did Watauga so much need a strong government? It was idle to say that the settlers had hitherto governed and defended themselves. They had done this: preserved order at home when every man was law-abiding; subdued the Cherokees when small forces would do the work; and fed and equipped their volunteers when men like John Sevier had full granaries from which to draw their rations. But now a disorderly element was coming among them, and this element, driven out by the settlers, was herding with their enemies, augmenting their strength, and increasing their hostility. Larger armies were now needed for their protection, and Sevier and others like him had become so impoverished by frequent generosity that they could no longer feed and equip large numbers at a moment's warning. And, if they could, what power had Sevier to call the men together? His old companions would respond to him promptly; but would the new-comers answer his summons with the same alacrity? Had they for him a similar sentiment of fealty? Would they follow where he led when the foe was twenty to one against them? It was not likely they would, for he had never marshaled them to victory; never carried them unscathed through the savage fire, nor saved their homes from burning, and their wives and children from the midnight tomahawk. He had been this people's law as well as leader, and that he would continue to be; but with this large influx of strange and dangerous elements the time had come when even he could not rule without all the forms of civilized government. North Carolina had cast them off, but they would form a government of their own, and apply for admission to the Union. With these thoughts stirring in their minds, the settlers came together at Jonesboro.

They were sober-minded, judicious men, and they determined to do nothing in haste, or without the assent of the whole body of the people. Consulting now together, they decided to recommend the meeting of a convention of forty delegates, who should have power to decide upon the course of action to be taken in the circumstances. These delegates should be elected from the three counties into which the district had been divided, and they should not meet until thirty days had passed, that they might have full time to deliberately consider the situation.

The delegates were elected, and they assembled in convention at Jonesboro, on the 23d of August following. Among them were John Sevier, Charles Robertson, John Bean, Stockley Donelson, Judge Campbell, and others—as true patriots and as worthy men as were to be found in the country; and there is no question that they represented correctly the popular sentiment. They sat with open doors and windows in the log court-house, which—according to the builder's specifications, still preserved—was of "diamond corners, hewn down after being built up, with plank floor, neatly laid, and a justice's bench, a lawyer's and clerk's bar, and a sheriff's box to sit in," and was the first seat of justice erected beyond the Alleghanies. This stately structure is now crumbled away, only one solitary log remaining, which a grand-nephew of Sevier has preserved with "pious care" by building it into the wall of a stable! "To what base uses may we come at last!"

There was scarcely room within the little building for the forty delegates; but the outside audience suffered no sort of inconvenience from the cramped condition of their quarters. They had "all out-doors," carpeted with a luxuriant greensward, and roofed with wide-branching oaks and poplars. Fully two thousand had come together, mounted on fleet horses, and clad in linsey trousers and the universal buckskin hunting-shirt; for the country was aflame with excitement, and such another gathering had not been seen there since the never-to-be-forgotten ten hundred and forty rendezvoused at Sycamore Shoals, to be led by Sevier and Shelby on the long march to King's Mountain.

The convention organized with John Sevier as president, and then appointed a committee to consider the cession of the Territory to Congress by North Carolina. This committee reported that, inasmuch as North Carolina had thrust Watauga out into the cold, it should at once form a State government, and apply for admission to the Union. No precedent existed which these men could follow, for Vermont had not yet been admitted, but had been kept standing, hat in hand, at the door of Congress since 1776. This was poor encouragement for Watauga, but the report was unanimously adopted by the convention, and then read from the court-house steps to the outside auditory, not all of whom could hear through the open door and windows. It was received with shouts that made the woods ring, and therefore may fairly be considered the voice of the people. The convention then adjourned, after recommending that the people should elect fifteen deputies to decide upon a Constitution, and organize a government for the new State.

This election took place on the 14th of December, but before it occurred the people over the mountains heard of the steps being taken by Watauga for self-government. The North Carolina Legislature came together in November, and it made haste—at this distance of time, it appears an unseemly and undignified haste—to repeal the act of the previous session. It also gave to the Watauga settlers a Superior Court, having jurisdiction over capital offenses; and it formed the militia into a brigade, giving the command to John Sevier as brigadier-general. In other words, the horse being stolen, these sapient legislators locked the stable-door. Requests long refused they suddenly granted, and granted so promptly as to show that they were actuated by a reluctance to losing their grip upon the western counties, and not by any desire to promote their welfare and security. This was apparent to the dullest intellect, and it was also seen that this action conveyed no guarantee of any favorable legislation that might be called for by the exigencies of the future. The concessions came too late. Had they come earlier, they would

have met general acceptance; but now they only served
to deepen into contempt the dissatisfaction that had been
long growing up toward the older counties. With one
solitary exception, this was probably the feeling at this
time of every settler upon the Watauga and Holston.

That one exception was John Sevier. He had been a
member of the convention that formed the Constitution
of North Carolina, and had himself caused the insertion
in its Declaration of Rights of a provision for the creation of a separate State beyond the Alleghanies. This
fact shows that he thus early contemplated the creation
of an independent commonwealth; but he now saw that
the time for it had not yet arrived. The Watauga District was not yet strong enough in numbers and wealth
to properly sustain a separate existence. The concessions
which had been granted by North Carolina would enable
the settlers to restrain the disorderly among them, and to
promptly meet their enemies the Cherokees. These were
the evils of the moment, and, these provided for, Sevier
thought it wisdom to let things go on in their accustomed way. He wrote to his friend Colonel Kennedy,
who had been a member of the convention, under date of

"*2d January*, 1785.

"DEAR COLONEL : I have just received certain information from Colonel Martin that the first thing the Assembly of North Carolina did was to repeal the Cession
Bill, and to form this part of the country into a separate
district, by name of Washington District, which I have

the honor to command, as General. I conclude this step will satisfy the people with the Old State, and we shall pursue no further measures as to a new State. David Campbell, Esq., is appointed one of our judges."

Sevier also wrote to prominent citizens of Greene County, advising them to take no further action in respect to a new government, and he used his personal influence to that end in his own county of Washington. But revolutions, it is said, never go backward. The elections were held in the three counties at the appointed time for the fifteen deputies who were to form the new government. The polls for Washington County were opened at Jonesboro, and, it being the most populous district, a large throng gathered there to participate in the election. Sevier addressed them, stating what had been done by the Legislature of North Carolina, and advising that no further steps should be taken toward erecting a separate government. These men were accustomed to follow his lead almost blindly, and they would have done so on this occasion had there not "happened to be there a man of Belial, whose name was Sheba, the son of Bichri," who said : "We have no part with North Carolina. Every man to his tent, O Israel !"

This man was one of those restless spirits who seem never entirely happy unless they are in the midst of strife and discord. Profane, foul-mouthed, turbulent,

and of an irascible, domineering temper, he lacked every
quality of a gentleman except personal courage, and that
nameless something which comes down in a man's veins
from an honorable ancestry.   He had the ambition but
not the ability to lead, and he could not understand why
men should give to Sevier such unquestioning allegiance.
He did not know that there is a "divine right" in commanding talents, exercised unselfishly in a people's service.   He was greedy for office, and a born demagogue,
and he had the natural jealousy of Sevier that men of
low and yet ambitious minds feel for their moral and in-
tellectual superiors.   This feeling was deepened into enmity when he saw himself shut out from positions to
which he felt entitled by his own abilities, and the prominence of his family ; for he was of good lineage, and
bore a name that is honorably mentioned in Southwestern history.   A younger brother, named Jonathan Tipton,
had been second in command to Sevier at King's Mountain, and was badly wounded at Boyd's Creek.   Two
others of his family have given names to counties in Tennessee and Indiana.   One of the next generation emigrated to the latter State, and, when but a stripling, was
an ensign at the battle of Tippecanoe.   Of him it is related that, in the heat of the action, General Harrison,
riding by, inquired of the boy, whose features were so
begrimed with blood and powder that he could not be
recognized, "Young man, where is your colonel ?"
"Dead, sir," was the answer.   "Your major, then ?"
"Dead, sir."   "Your captain ?"   "Dead, sir."   "Then

who commands this regiment?" "I do, sir—Ensign Tipton, Fourth Indiana."

This black sheep of the flock—Sheba, the son of Bichri—saw now that the sentiment of the whole community was unmistakably opposed to any further connection with North Carolina, and quickly he seized upon the opportunity to step into the leadership which seemed about to be vacated by Sevier. In an impassioned harangue he urged the people to go on with the election. They did so ; but they did not throw their beloved Nolichucky Jack overboard. Whether he would or not, they were determined that Sevier should go with them. They elected him one of the delegates to organize the State government ; but, unfortunately, they joined with him this same John Tipton and the Rev. Samuel Houston—men of totally opposite characters, but destined, by acting together, to be largely instrumental in overthrowing the Watauga commonwealth.

And now Sevier made the one mistake of his lifetime—the one to which may be traced all his subsequent misfortunes. Seeing that he could not stem the current, he allowed himself to be borne along with it. Had he been Robertson, he would have quietly stepped aside, and let the torrent waste itself in its own wild fury. The force of their passion having once spent itself, these people would have returned to him and to reason. In the absence of any express statement from Sevier, it is difficult to determine why he did not pursue this course, for he did not lack the moral courage to stand alone, and he

must have seen that in the changed attitude of North
Carolina any further action would be actual rebellion.
An easy way to account for his course would be to say
that, seeing power about to slip away from him, he
promptly changed front and went with the multitude in
order to retain his ascendency over them. But we are
to judge of character not by one act, but by a whole life,
and during his entire career Sevier never sought office.
It was always thrust upon him ; and for nearly ten years
he persistently set Robertson—a man much inferior to
him in ability—above himself in the councils of Watauga. He was pre-eminently disinterested and unambitious
—one of the least self-seeking of those great men to
whom the world owes the establishment of civil and religious freedom in America. And, had Sevier been ambitious, he must have known that he was in no danger of
permanently losing his control over the men of Watauga,
for his ascendency was founded in the very nature of
things. From the first they had recognized in him
the qualities that made him their natural leader. They
knew that he, and only he, could carry them safely
through the dangers by which they were environed, and
that deserting him would be throwing overboard their
pilot when the ship was riding storm-vexed amid the
breakers. Moreover, their feeling for him forbade any
separation. They had for him a personal attachment,
an almost blind devotion, which has seldom been accorded to any popular leader. I know of nothing like it in
American history. Washington and Jackson were greatly

beloved, but their popularity waxed and waned, while that of Sevier never knew a moment's diminution. For forty-three years, alike when he was at the head of a great State, and when, a hunted outlaw, fifteen hundred armed men sprang spontaneously to his rescue, he was the idol of the frontier people. Of all this he must have been conscious, and, therefore, we have to seek some other motive for his present action than a fear of losing his hold on power and popular favor.

Doubtless Sevier felt contempt for the ruling element in North Carolina, and disgust at the uniformly selfish and now vacillating policy of its Legislature; and he may have thought that a firm stand would bring about the separation so much desired by the Watauga settlers. This idea may have had weight with him; but still I think the main reason for his course is to be found in his strong sympathy with the Watauga people. They were to him as the "bone of his bone and the flesh of his flesh"; for twelve years he had shared with them storm and sunshine, peril and victory; and now, when he saw them encompassed with dangers from which only he could extricate them, and heading recklessly upon a dangerous coast, begirt with sunken rocks and treacherous quicksands, he determined to stand by the ship and guide it, if possible, into a secure haven; and, if that were not possible, then to go down in the wreck with those he loved and who so loved him. No other supposition seems consistent with his character, or sufficient to account for his now going against the convictions of

5

his cool judgment, as expressed in his letter to Colonel Kennedy, and freely announced by him to the people, prior to the election of the deputies.

The deputies came together, organized a State government, and then adjourned, after calling, for the ensuing November, another convention to frame and adopt a permanent Constitution. A Legislature was then chosen, which unanimously elected John Sevier as Governor; and then the wheels of the new State were set in operation. John Tipton's intemperate advocacy of the new order of things had failed to convince the people that he would fitly grace an official position. Consequently, he was left out in the cold, and denied even so much as a seat in the lower branch of the Legislature. A like fate befell one Joseph Martin, another blatant denouncer of North Carolina. These apparently insignificant events had important consequences, as will appear further on in this narrative.

Sevier had hoped to guide the ship in safety through the breakers; but could mortal hand do this, when she was storm-beaten from both east and west, and her own crew was in mutiny?

CHAPTER III.

THE ABORTIVE COMMONWEALTH.

THE territory that was termed in legislative documents "Washington District" comprised the whole of what is now Tennessee, except the country around Nashville, at which remote outpost of civilization the heroic Robertson was at this time holding his ground against a horde of savage enemies. But the larger portion of this vast region had in 1784 no other inhabitants than wild beasts and wilder men, and the white settlements in it were restricted to an irregular parallelogram, bordering upon the Holston, Watauga, and Nolichucky, and extending southwesterly from the Virginia line at King's Meadows (now Bristol) to Southwest Point, near the confluence of the Clinch and Tennessee Rivers. And this settled district was but thinly peopled. It contained no large towns, and but few villages. Knoxville was not yet in existence. Greeneville was little more than a log court-house and a log tavern; and Jonesboro an insignificant hamlet of some fifty or sixty log cabins, clustered around the unpretending temple of justice which has been mentioned. The people dwelt mostly in isolated farm-houses, in the midst of wide forests, or in close vicinity to log "stations"—block-houses encompassed with palisades, in which were a few cabins to house the women and children in case of a hostile invasion from the Indians. Scattered as they were, it is wonderful with what speed the men came together on occasions of sudden danger, either to Jonesboro or to the home of Sevier on the Nolichucky, the usual places of rendezvous. As many as two thousand are known to have assembled within twenty-four hours after Sevier's couriers had sounded the alarm through the territory—so perfect was his system for conveying intelligence, and so fleet were the animals bestrode by those tireless riders. The total population of the district (exclusive of the Cumberland settlements) at this time can not be given with decided accuracy, but, estimating it by the force with which Sevier soon afterward offered to march to the aid of Georgia, it could not have been far from twenty-five thousand. A handful, truly, to set up an independent existence, when surrounded by hostile savages, and opposed by the great State which then ranked as the third in the Union!

It was no easy task that Sevier assumed when, on the 1st of March, 1785, he took oath to well and truly administer for three years the office of Governor of the new State of Franklin. He had to evolve order from rank disorder, and to erect a stable government with the most unstable materials. He had to create a currency when even the wealthy had not enough money to pay their taxes, and the North Carolina "promises to pay" were not worth one cent on a dollar. He had to provide facilities for education, when nothing above a cross-road school-house existed in the country. He had to establish courts and enforce law, when a lawless element, pouring in on the heels of the Revolution, had flooded every settlement, and was stalking unchecked upon every highway. And he had to organize and discipline a militia, with which to meet the ten thousand Creeks and Cherokees, who, armed and backed by Spain, were preparing to swoop down upon the territory. In short, he had to enforce law, establish good order, and foil the murderous designs of a great European power, when he was himself acting contrary to law, and in defiance of the constituted authorities of the country. It was a herculean task, but in an incredibly short period, and without the loss of a single life, Sevier accomplished it; and, in doing so, he displayed a fertility of resource and a wise statesmanship that entitle him to rank very high as an administrator; and we are forced to conclude that, if his course had been obstructed by none but outside foes, he would have then established a stable government.

Within sixty days from the coming together of his Legislature, Sevier had reduced internal affairs to a satisfactory order. He at once established a Superior Court, with David Campbell as chief-justice—the same who had been named for that office by North Carolina; and he reorganized the militia—now over four thousand strong—placing over it William Cocke and Daniel

Kennedy as brigadier-generals, he himself being com-
mander-in-chief.   Having thus provided for the enforcement of law and the defense of the country, Sevier
directed the attention of his Legislature to subjects of
less pressing importance.   At his suggestion it incorpo-
rated an institution of higher education, to be presided
over by Parson Doak, the pioneer preacher.   It was
named Martin Academy, in compliment to the Governor
of North Carolina, but its title was subsequently changed
to Washington College.   It was the first institution for
classical learning west of the Alleghanies.   He also
caused acts to be passed levying a tax for the support of
the government; "to determine the value of such gold
and silver coin" as was in circulation; and "to ascertain
the salaries" to be allowed the Governor and other State
officials.   These were fixed at the following magnificent
sums: For the Governor, £200; for the Judge of the
Superior Court, £150; for the Secretary of State, £25
and the fees of his office; and members of the Legislature were to receive four shillings per diem.   The appointment of all the minor officials was left in the hands of
the Governor, and he continued in office all those who
held commissions under North Carolina.   Thus the
passage from the old to the new State did violence to no
one, and produced no convulsion.   There was, in fact,
no alteration in form; but there was a total change in
spirit—an infusion of life into a lifeless machinery,
which made it at once a conservator of order and a
terror to evil-doers.

But no civil government has existed within historic times without a circulating medium, and some standard of value by which to regulate exchanges. Among civilized nations the standard is gold and silver, but the North American Indians regarded wampum as money, and Pontiac issued letters of credit upon birch-bark, which were redeemed by the French in hard currency. But gold and silver are sometimes scarce commodities even in civilized communities; and at such times, while they have remained the measure of value, other articles have of necessity been resorted to as a circulating medium. In 1631 it was enacted in Massachusetts that corn at current prices should be received in payment of debts, and in 1656 "musket-balls, full bore," were made a legal tender at a farthing apiece. As late there as 1680 the town of Hingham paid its taxes in milk-pails; in South Carolina at about the same period the currency was corn, and in North Carolina as late as 1738 it was hides, tallow, and furs; while in Maryland and Virginia for more than a century the standard of value, as well as the circulating medium, was tobacco. In the latter State it was enacted that the marshal should be paid, for "laying by the heels," five pounds of tobacco; "for duckings," ten pounds; "for pillory," ten pounds; and during a long period the market value of a wife—good or bad—ruled in that colony with wonderful regularity at one hundred and fifty pounds. At the time of the Revolution the currency of nearly all the colonies was poorly lithographed "promises to pay," printed on dingy paper, by which the government treasurer did not so much as agree to pay the sum that was called for by the "shinplaster." One of these, issued by North Carolina, is now before me. It reads simply : " N. Carolina Currency. Half a Dollar. By authority of Congress at Halifax, April, 1776," and in one corner are the figures of a man and a dog, the man discharging a leveled musket, with the motto, "Hit or miss." The thing certainly "hit" somebody, or it would not now be in existence ; but it as certainly made a "miss," if it ever attempted to draw its face value from the treasury of North Carolina.

It may be questioned if Sevier, or any of his legislators, ever so much as heard of the musket-ball and milk-pail currency of Massachusetts, or of the Virginia mothers who, perhaps, were dear bargains at one hundred and fifty pounds of tobacco. These men had probably none of these precedents before them ; but, there being next to no gold or silver in Franklin, they felt the need of some other circulating medium, and they adopted one which had intrinsic value, inasmuch as it could be either worn or eaten, and was, moreover, within the reach of every one who had a strong arm and a good rifle. In the law levying a tax for the support of the government, they inserted this clause :

" *Be it enacted*, That it shall and may be lawful for the aforesaid land-tax, and all free polls, to be paid in the following manner : Good flax linen, ten hundred, at three shillings and sixpence per yard ; nine hundred, at three shillings ; eight hundred, two shillings and ninepence ;

seven hundred, two shillings and sixpence; six hundred, two shillings; tow linen, one shilling and ninepence; linsey, three shillings, and woolen and cotton linsey, three shillings and sixpence per yard; good clean beaver-skin, six shillings; cased otter-skins, six shillings; uncased ditto, five shillings; raccoon and fox skins, one shilling and threepence; woolen cloth, at ten shillings per yard; bacon, well cured, sixpence per pound; good, clean tallow, sixpence per pound; good, clean beeswax, one shilling per pound; good distilled rye whisky, at two shillings and sixpence per gallon; good peach or apple brandy, at three shillings per gallon; good country-made sugar, at one shilling per pound; deer-skins, the pattern, six shillings; good, neat, and well-managed tobacco, fit to be prized, that may pass inspection, the hundred, fifteen shillings, and so on in proportion for a greater or less quantity."

"And all the salaries and allowances hereby made shall be paid by any treasurer, sheriff, or collector of public taxes, to any person entitled to the same, to be paid in specific articles as collected, and at the rates allowed by the State for the same; or in current money of the State of Franklin."

It will be noticed that the closing paragraph provides that taxes might be paid in "current money of the State of Franklin," which shows that this "coon-skin currency"—as it was termed—was merely a temporary expedient, designed for the present relief of tax-payers; and that Sevier looked forward to the possession of a more civilized circulating medium. This the State soon had—thirty thousand dollars, in silver, issued from the mint of Charles Robertson—but, nevertheless, the articles enumerated did for a time pass current as money. It was at first confidently asserted that this currency could not be counterfeited. But in this its advocates were mistaken. It was mostly of skins, which passed from hand to hand in bundles or bales, from the ends of which the caudal appendages were allowed to protrude, to designate the species of the animal. Before long, acute financiers affixed the tail of the otter to the skin of the fox and the raccoon, and thus got the better of the receiver in the sum of four shillings and ninepence upon each peltry.

The rapidity with which the above-named acts were passed shows not only great unanimity among the legislators, but the remarkable ascendency which Sevier had over the frontier people. His word was literally their law, and their absolute devotion to him was what had enabled him to conquer his greatly superior savage enemies. Now, with a strong militia organized and embodied, he had no fear of the Creeks and Cherokees; but he preferred peace to war, and, when internal affairs were once set in order, he lost no time in dispatching messengers to the Indian capital, inviting the principal chieftains to a conference, to arrange terms on which the two races might live together in "perpetual amity."

In doing this, the new State was about to exercise one of the highest functions of sovereignty; but it was no more than had been done by nearly every one of the Thirteen Colonies. They had now delegated the treaty-making power to Congress, but at that very moment

North Carolina was arranging to hold a treaty with these same Indians. Sevier had no confidence in the ability of its present Governor to secure from them terms that would be advantageous to the Watauga settlers, and he very naturally thought that what would be lawful for North Carolina could hardly be deemed unlawful for Franklin. But, lawful or unlawful, some action had to be taken at once, for the attitude of the Cherokees threatened immediate hostilities. It was better to incur the displeasure of Congress than to invite the midnight torch and tomahawk to every settler's dwelling. A frank explanation might appease the wounded dignity of the Central Government; but no apology would restore wasted fields and burned farm-houses, or gather up the blood that might be spilled in a conflict with the savages. It was these considerations that now induced Sevier to make overtures of peace to the Cherokees.

The Creeks were in secret league with Spain for the extermination of the settlers, and their allies, the Cherokees, had been in a chronic state of dissatisfaction since 1782, in consequence of the locating of the whites upon lands south of the French Broad and Holston Rivers, which had never been formally ceded to North Carolina. Their king, Old Tassel, the wary but wise and pacific successor to Oconostota, had addressed frequent protests to the Governor of North Carolina against these encroachments; but they had been practically unheeded, though his Excellency, as far back as February 11, 1782, had written to Sevier: "Draw forth a body of your militia on horseback, pull down their cabins, and drive them off, laying aside every consideration of their entreaties to the contrary." Sevier had not laid aside these considerations, for some of the encroaching settlers were his old companions in arms, who had fought by his side at King's Mountain, and, time and again, protected the settlements from the midnight raids of these same savages. Though an officer of North Carolina, he had given little heed to the Governor's arbitrary command. He had not driven the people off, but had dissuaded them from any further encroachments, and given assurance to Old Tassel that none would be permitted. But this, though the settlers were some miles distant from the Indian hunting-grounds, did not satisfy the Cherokees, who rightly regarded every forward movement of the whites as merely another step toward their own final expulsion from the country.

This dissatisfaction among the Indians had been but recently inflamed to the pitch of hostile action by the unfortunate killing of Untoola, of Citico, one of their principal warriors, by Major James Hubbard, of the Watauga riflemen. The evidence was that the killing was entirely justifiable, being done strictly in self-defense; but Hubbard was known among the Cherokees to be the implacable enemy of their race and nation. His whole family had been remorselessly butchered by the Shawnees in Virginia, and, ever since, the one business of his life had been the slaughter of Indians. Though but a young man, he was reputed to have killed more Cherokees than any two men upon the border; and, inflamed by a spirit of vengeance, he did not always wait for what would be deemed justifiable provocation. Knowing this, the Cherokees had no difficulty in believing that he was the aggressor in the rencounter which had resulted in the death of Untoola. Revenge—blood for blood—was with them a religious principle, and the whole nation now cried out for vengeance upon the slayer. The infuriated braves were only restrained from going at once upon the warpath by the promise of Old Tassel to lay the matter before the Governor, and by his assurance that his Excellency would now not only listen to their complaints, but would speedily take steps to redress this and their other grievances.

In this the Cherokee king was not mistaken. Without so much as asking for the evidence against Hubbard, Governor Martin gave orders for his immediate arrest and conveyance over the mountains; and he also, to appease, it would seem, the wrath of this Indian chief, issued a proclamation commanding the instant removal of all settlers upon the lands south of the French Broad and Holston. At the same time he wrote to Old Tassel, stigmatizing these settlers as "bad people," willing to disobey "any law for the sake of ill-gain and profit," and "caring not what mischief they do between the white and red people if they can enrich themselves"; and he closed by entreating the wily old savage to be "patient, and not listen to any bad talks which may disturb our peace and good-will: for you may be certain your elder

6

brother of North Carolina will do everything in his power to give your minds satisfaction."

This language Governor Alexander Martin addressed to untutored savages, who would be sure to mistake kind words for weakness; and his proclamation he directed against several thousand law-abiding citizens, who had settled on those lands in reliance upon a special promise of protection made to them by an ordinance of the North Carolina Legislature in May, 1783. Moreover, the men whom the Governor branded as lawless and "bad people" were among the best in the territory—men whose daily lives exhibited some of the noblest traits of American character, patient industry, indomitable energy, manly resolution, and heroic courage.

The Governor's language was regarded as an outrageous insult, his proclamation as a flagrant injustice; and both were deplored because calculated to render the Cherokees more unreasonable in their demands. The Indians were thus assured of the sympathy of their "elder brother of North Carolina," and this might lead them to reject any terms that should provide for the peaceable retention of their homes by the intruding settlers. This Sevier well knew; but he also knew that his name was a terror among the Cherokees, and he counted upon the dread the old king would have of a collision with him, to counteract the effect of the Governor's proclamation. In any event, he should protect the French Broad settlers, and not permit their removal.

The council was held on Dumplin Creek, near the

north bank of the French Broad River, and about ten miles east of the present city of Knoxville; and it began on the 31st of May, 1785, only a few days after the adjournment of the Franklin Legislature. It lasted three days, and was attended by a numerous body of chiefs and warriors. When all had assembled, Sevier addressed them. He did not tell them that his old comrades had wrongfully intruded upon their lands, nor did he make any apology or offer any reparation for the killing of Untoola. But he assured the Indians that he desired to live in peace with them, and, says the old historian, "in a speech well calculated to produce the end in view, he deplored the sufferings of the white people; the blood which the Indians had spilled on the road leading to Kentucky; lamented the uncivilized state of the Indians; and, to prevent all future animosities, he suggested the propriety of fixing the bounds beyond which those settlements should not be extended which had been imprudently made on the south side of the French Broad and Holston, under the connivance of North Carolina, and could not now be broken up; and he pledged the faith of the State of Franklin that, if these bounds should be agreed upon and made known, the citizens of his State should be effectually restrained from all encroachments beyond them." *

The fearless and manly attitude of Sevier had the desired effect upon the Indians. The Cherokees ac-

---

* Haywood.

cepted the situation, and not only ignored the killing
of Untoola, and waived the removal of the settlers, but
made a cession of a much larger territory than had been
already occupied, establishing as the boundary between
themselves and the whites the high ridge which divides
the waters of the Little Tennessee from those of Little
River. For these lands Sevier promised compensation in
general terms, dependent, however, upon the good behavior of the Cherokees, and their faithful observance
of the treaty. Thus, by a few spoken words, and the
magnetism of his presence, did he reduce the refractory
Cherokees to reason, and undo the evil effects of the ill-
advised "talks" of the North Carolina Governor. But
the wily Old Tassel absented himself from the conference, and was not therefore a party to the treaty. He
knew from Governor Martin of the rupture between
North Carolina and Franklin, and he sought, by staying
away, to keep in a position to repudiate the treaty in
case circumstances should render such a course advisable
or profitable to the Cherokees.

As Sevier was about setting out to negotiate this
treaty, an angry blast came from over the mountains.
It was wind, empty and loud-sounding, but in it was
an articulate voice, which gave warning of "breakers
ahead" on the course the new State was pursuing.
Before the adjournment of the Legislature, Sevier had
dispatched an official letter to the Governor of North
Carolina, apprising him of the secession of Franklin;
and now came in reply a manifesto from that function-

ary, addressed "To the Inhabitants of the Counties of Washington, Sullivan, and Greene." The document is too long to be here quoted, but a few extracts will give its essential features. It began by saying, "Whereas, I have received letters from Brigadier-General Sevier, under the style and character of Governor; and from Messrs. Landon Carter and William Gage, as Speakers of the Senate and House of Commons of the State of Franklin, informing me that they, with you, the inhabitants of part of the territory lately ceded to Congress, had declared themselves independent of the State of North Carolina, and no longer consider themselves under the sovereignty and jurisdiction of the same, stating their reasons for their separation and revolt, among which, it is alleged, that the western country was ceded to Congress without their consent, by an act of the Legislature, and the same was repealed in the like manner." The Governor then went on through four closely printed octavo pages to arraign the western leaders for high treason, and to warn the people of the direful consequences that would attend a defiance of the Tarboro Legislators. "The State of North Carolina," he said, "could not suffer treaties to be held with the Indians and other business transacted in a country where her authority and government were rejected and set at naught. . . . Far less causes had deluged states and kingdoms with blood. . . . There is a national pride in all kingdoms and states that inspires every subject with a degree of importance—the grand cement and support of every government—which must not be insulted." His people had been grossly insulted, the honor of his State "particularly wounded," and "Congress could not countenance such a separation, wherein the State of North Carolina hath not given her full consent; and, if an implied and conditional one hath been given, the same hath been rescinded by a full Legislature. Of her reasons for so doing, they [who?] consider themselves the only competent judges."

After much of this high-sounding verbiage, the Governor resorted to threats, as follows: "I know," he said, "with reluctance the State will be *driven to arms;* it will be the last alternative to *imbrue* her hands in the blood of her citizens; but, if no other ways and means are found to save her honor, and reclaim her headstrong, refractory citizens, but this sad expedient, her resources are not yet so exhausted, or her spirits damped, but she may take satisfaction for this great injury received, regain her government over the revolted territory, or render it not worth possessing." The italics are the Governor's own.

These threats were ill-advised, and the whole document was poorly calculated to win back the western people to a government which had never afforded them either aid or protection. However, the paper did contain a single paragraph which, had their minds not been inflamed by passion, might have led the western settlers to more fully reflect upon the consequences of their action. This paragraph was as follows: "By such rash and irregular conduct a precedent is formed for every district, and even every county of the State, to claim the right of separation and independency for any supposed grievance of the inhabitants, as caprice, pride, and ambition shall dictate,.at pleasure, thereby exhibiting to the world a melancholy instance of a feeble or pusillanimous government, that is either unable, or dares not restrain the lawless designs of its citizens."

Copies of this manifesto were freely circulated in manuscript among the people; but it appears to have made no general impression. At the moment every one west of the mountains was too much infatuated with a new-born sense of freedom from a hated connection, or too much engrossed with thoughts of the pressing danger from the Creeks and Cherokees, to give heed to what seemed idle talk from North Carolina. Sevier paid no attention to the document so long as Martin continued Governor; but in a few weeks Martin was succeeded in office by Richard Caswell, a far abler man, and to him Sevier addressed a letter, controverting the positions of his predecessor. In it he denied that he and his people were in revolt from North Carolina. That State, he said, had by the act of cession invited the western settlers to the course they had pursued; and they had taken it from the necessity to prevent anarchy, and provide against their enemies the Cherokees; and they fully believed that the acts of North Carolina tolerated the separation.

And he added : "The menaces made use of in the manifesto will by no means intimidate us. We mean to pursue our necessary measures, and with the fullest confidence believe that your Legislature, when truly informed of our civil proceedings, will find no cause for resenting anything we have done. The repeal of the cession act we can not take notice of, as we had declared our separation before the repeal. Therefore, we are bound to support it with that manly firmness that becomes freemen."

Throughout the letter Sevier is dignified, but conciliatory. By brief, pointed sentences he overthrows the wordy ranting of Martin—that is, where it can be overthrown—but he takes no notice whatever of the latter's allusion to the danger of secession. This he did not attempt to answer; probably, because he felt that it could not be answered. That he appreciated the evil that might result from the precedent he was trying to establish, is evident from a reference he made to it two years later—in a letter he wrote to the Governor of Georgia, wherein he styles secession an ulcer which, if allowed to spread, may at last infect the whole body politic.

It was fortunate for the Watauga settlers, and fortunate also for the country, that Richard Caswell was now Governor of North Carolina. He was one of those rare men—not over-plentiful at any period, and least of all when society has been but recently upheaved by the strong passions of a revolution—who can look on both

sides of a question, and, while not forgetting his own
rights and obligations, can fully appreciate the circumstances and necessities of an adversary. Had Martin
continued in office, and attempted to enforce his policy
of coercion, the most disastrous consequences would
probably have followed. North Carolina outnumbered
the settlers more than twenty to one, but she had no
military leaders, and her wretched "sand-hillers" were
no match for the over-mountain men, who would have
fought behind their mountain fastnesses, and under the
lead of Sevier, who was incarnate victory. The proba-
bilities are that Watauga would have been successful;
and her revolt, occurring so early, while the Central
Government was as yet but a rope of sand, and the
various States were drawn apart by conflicting interests, other revolts would doubtless have followed. Thus,
what Sevier termed the "ulcer" of secession would have
spread, till the Union was rent into fragments, and
there had been to-day a dozen little republics instead
of our one vast and united nation. So, on what seems
to us insignificant events hang often great results, which
are felt far along the course of time, and over the whole
of a continent. In reply to Sevier's letter, Governor
Caswell wrote as follows :

"KINGSTON, N. C., 17th June, 1785.

"SIR : Your favor of the 14th of last month I had
the honor to receive by Colonel Avery. In this, sir, you
have stated the different charges mentioned in Governor

Martin's manifesto, and answered them by giving what I
understand to be the sense of the people and your own
sentiments with respect to each charge, as well as
the reasons which governed in the measures he complained of.

"I have not seen Governor Martin's manifesto, nor
have I derived so full and explicit information from any
quarter as this you have been pleased to give me. As
there was not an Assembly, owing to the members not
attending at Governor Martin's request, the sense of the
Legislature on this business, of course, could not be had ;
and as you give me assurances of the peaceable disposition of the people, and their wish to conduct themselves
in the manner you mention, and also to send persons to
adjust, consider, and conciliate matters (I suppose) to
the next Assembly, for the present things must rest as
they are with respect to the subject-matter of your letter,
which shall be laid before the next Assembly. In the
mean time, let me entreat you not, by any means, to consider this as giving countenance, by the Executive of the
State, to any measures lately pursued by the people to
the westward of the mountains."

Being thus left unmolested by North Carolina, Sevier
had time to attend to the consolidation of the new government. Law was at once effectually administered, a
few notorious criminals were properly punished, the disorderly element was awed into good behavior, and the
militia was thoroughly drilled, to be in readiness at any

moment to repel an attack from the treacherous Creeks
and Cherokees. Under Sevier's mild but efficient rule
everything soon went well ; and now for several months
it seemed that Watauga had entered upon an unbroken
career of peace and prosperity. So successful was Sevier's administration of affairs that it was not long before the Scotch Presbyterians of the Backwater settlements, some of whom had fought by his side at King's
Mountain, took steps, under the lead of Arthur Campbell, to sever their connection with Virginia, and enroll themselves under the new Franklin government.
Strange as it may seem, the first ripple that disturbed
this placid state of things was raised by the distant Central Government, which now was in session at Philadelphia. It had thus far turned a deaf ear to the application of Watauga for admission to the Union ; and it was
now to exercise its treaty-making power in a manner
both embarrassing and dangerous to the nascent commonwealth.

On the 19th of September, 1785, not much more
than half a year after the launching of the State of
Franklin by the over-mountain Legislature, one Joseph
Martin, Indian agent for the State of North Carolina,
held a conference with the principal Cherokee chieftains, in the grand council-house of the tribe at Echota.
Squatted on a buffalo - robe by his side was the Old
Tassel, while around him, on the ground, or on the
cane benches which encircled the dingy but spacious interior, were gathered the "head-men" of the Ottari and

Erati Cherokees. These warriors had come together from far and near to hold what in Indian parlance is styled a "talk" with this "head-man" of North Carolina; and this talk, reduced to writing, and dispatched over the mountains, was first to stir the stagnant atmosphere of North Carolina, and then to arouse a breeze in the great council-house of the Union at Philadelphia— a breeze which should bode no good to the government of Sevier, and to the "bad people" who now, by right of treaty, were peacefully gathering their crops on the south side of the French Broad and Holston.

This Martin, though an official of North Carolina, had been one of the earliest and most active promoters of the new State; but somehow, when it came to be organized, he had, much to his chagrin, found himself, like Tipton, left without any official position whatever. This, had he been greedy of emoluments, could not have been a very sore affliction, but he probably cared more for position than profit, for the reason that in the backwoods the possession of money is not a sure passport to influence and consideration. Luckily, however, he had not been so unwise as to cast away an old coat before obtaining a new one; and now he resumed his former office, and left the new State to go on its own way to destruction. But in these early days of September there arose an occasion when, to preserve what little of official position he had, it seemed to Martin necessary that he should help the new government on to its pre-destined consummation. This might involve the betrayal of his friends, but that were better than the loss of office under North Carolina.

Martin had passed the most of the summer among the Cherokees, listening to the grumblings of Old Tassel and the smothered curses of the warriors upon the fast-incoming settlers, who were rapidly filling up the lands recently ceded to Franklin ; but he had uttered not one word of sympathy, encouragement, or remonstrance. The affair he deemed none of his ; he was an officer of North Carolina ; and, as yet, he had no definite intimation of how the recent secession was regarded by its new administration. But early in September there came to Echota the same Colonel Avery who had borne Sevier's letter to Governor Caswell, and he brought to Martin a missive from his Excellency, which he had carried in his pocket ever since the date of the Governor's letter to Sevier. The Governor had heard of Martin's activity in the formation of the new State, and he now asked the Indian agent the pertinent question, if he intended to serve two masters—or rather, in backwoods phrase, if he was attempting to ride two horses at once, barebacked, after the Indian fashion.

The Governor's question alarmed Martin, and he deemed it necessary to do something at once that should assure North Carolina of his zealous allegiance. So, suddenly, he became sympathetic with Old Tassel, and told him that the existence of Franklin had not yet been recognized by North Carolina ; that, consequently, the treaty which Sevier had lately made with the Cherokees

7

was no better than waste paper; and that, if Old Tassel should petition the Governor of North Carolina, his Excellency would doubtless order the removal of the "bad people" from the lands south of the French Broad and the Holston. This it was which had led the Cherokee king to call together the "head-men" of the whole nation, who now were assembled in their great council-house, eagerly listening to this white man, who was telling them by what treacherous diplomacy they might evade the sacred obligations of a treaty, and involve in ruin several thousands of his own race and kindred. The "talk" which resulted from this council, and was dispatched from Old Tassel to Governor Caswell, was as follows:

"BROTHER: I am now going to speak to you; I hope you will hear me. I am an old man, and almost thrown away by my elder brother. The ground I stand on is very slippery, though I still hope my elder brother will hear me, and take pity on me, as we were all made by the same Great Being above; we are all children of the same parent. I therefore hope my elder brother will hear me.

"You have often promised me, in talks that you sent me, that you would do me justice, and that all disorderly people should be moved off our lands; but the longer we want to see it done, the farther it seems off. Your people have built houses in sight of our towns. We don't want to quarrel with you, our elder brother. I therefore beg that you, our elder brother, will have your disorderly people taken off our lands immediately, as their being on our grounds causes great uneasiness. We are very uneasy on account of a report that is among the white people, that call themselves a new people, that live on French Broad and Nolichucky. They say they have treated with us for all the lands on Little River. I now send this to let my elder brother know how it is. Some of them gathered on French Broad, and sent for us to come and treat with them; but, as I was told there was a treaty to be held with us by orders of the great men of the Thirteen States, we did not go to meet them; but some of our young men went to see what they wanted. They first wanted the land on Little River. Our young men told them that all their head-men were at home; that they had no authority to treat about lands. They then asked liberty for those that were then living on the lands to remain there, till the head-men of their nation were consulted on it, which our young men agreed to. Since then we are told that they claim all the lands on the waters of Little River, and have appointed men among themselves to settle their disputes on our lands, calling it their ground. But we hope you, our elder brother, will not agree to it, but will have them moved off. I also beg that you will send letters to the Great Council of America, and let them know how it is; that, if you have no power to move them off, they have, and I hope they will do it."

Of his own personal knowledge, Martin knew that

this "talk" was a tissue of duplicity and downright falsehood, calculated and intended to deceive, and designed to induce such action on the part of Congress as would render homeless, or expose to the tomahawk and scalping-knife, some thousands of men, women, and children of his own nation and kindred; and yet he not only permitted this false paper to go forward to the Governor of North Carolina, without contradiction or remonstrance, but himself sent it to his Excellency; and there is good circumstantial evidence that he inspired its lies, and intrigued with Governor Caswell to get himself appointed by Congress upon the treaty commission, in order the more effectually to accomplish his end, which was the infliction of a vital blow upon the government of Sevier, a man with whom he had served, and for whom he then and afterward professed the warmest friendship. With the "talk" Martin dispatched to Governor Caswell the following epistle:

"CHOTA, 19th September, 1785.

"DEAR SIR: Your Excellency's favor of the 17th June, by Mr. Avery, never came to hand until the 10th inst. I find myself under some concern, in reading that part wherein I am considered a member of the new State. I beg leave to assure your Excellency that I have no part with them, but consider myself under your immediate direction, as agent for the State of North Carolina, until the Assembly shall direct otherwise. I am now on the duties of that office, and have had more trouble with the Indians, in the course of the summer, than I ever had, owing to the rapid encroachments of the people from the new State, together with the 'talks' from the Spaniards and the western Indians."

Whatever his predecessor had done, Governor Caswell was not disposed to usurp any of the prerogatives of the General Government. Accordingly, he submitted the "talk" of Old Tassel to Congress, recommending that a treaty should be at once made with the Cherokees, and naming Joseph Martin as peculiarly fitted, by his familiarity with those Indians, and his knowledge of the questions in dispute between them and the settlers, to act as one of the commissioners. Congress had for some time contemplated some action in reference to affairs with the Southern Indians, and it now promptly appointed Joseph Martin, of North Carolina; Andrew Pickens, of South Carolina; and Lachlan McIntosh and Benjamin Hawkins, of Georgia, commissioners to conclude a treaty with the Cherokees. The three last named were men of the highest character, and Hawkins was familiar with the Creeks and more southern Indians; but none of the four, except Martin, had any special acquaintance with the Cherokees, or any knowledge of their relations to the Watauga settlers. Consequently, the others deferred to Martin's views, and the result was what is known as the treaty of Hopewell, by which all recent treaties were ignored, and the Indian lines were extended so as to cover a large extent of territory which had been ceded by the Cherokees to Henderson in 1776, and even portions of country which that tribe never claimed, and which had been conveyed to the whites by the Six Nations at Fort Stanwix in 1768. A considerable part of the lands recently granted by North Carolina, in payment of the arrears due to her soldiers, was declared to be within Cherokee territory, and it was agreed that they should not be settled upon by the whites. Intending settlers should be warned off, and, if they persisted in settling, "for any such obstinate intrusion, they should be liable to be punished by the Indians as they might think proper." Moreover, the treaty clothed the Cherokees with judicial and executive powers of a most extraordinary character. They might arrest any persons they believed to be guilty of a capital offense, and "punish them in the presence of some of the Cherokees, in the same manner as they would be punished for like offenses committed on citizens of the United States." The treaty, in short, placed the Cherokees upon a par with the most civilized nations, and made Congress the unwitting instrument of the most flagrant injustice to its own law-abiding citizens.

By this extravagant and needless concession to the Cherokees, some thousands of the loyal supporters of the Government were denied both State and national protection, and left exposed to the savage mercy of a nation of cut-throats, who, despite repeated cessions, could now claim this territory as their hunting-ground. The alternatives before the settlers south of the Holston and

French Broad were now either the abandonment of their homes or a conflict for their possession with the whole Cherokee nation. The last they could not meet without the aid of Sevier, and this he could not give without arraying against himself not only North Carolina and the Cherokees, but the General Government of the country. It was probable that the settlers would not abandon their homes; they were men who had never yet turned their backs upon an Indian; and it was certain that Sevier would not stand by and see them slaughtered by the savages. What human power, then, could hinder a collision between him and the United States, and his consequent defeat, outlawry, and final ruin? This was, no doubt, the thought of Martin, and with this thought he must have put his hand to the treaty of Hopewell.

It was in these circumstances—opposed by established law, betrayed by pretended friends, and on every side surrounded by apparently insurmountable difficulties—that Sevier met the convention which, in November, 1785, assembled in the little log court-house at Greeneville to form a permanent Constitution for the State of Franklin.

CHAPTER IV.

THE BEGINNING OF TROUBLES.

To this convention came John Tipton—Sheba, the son of Bichri—who had somehow procured himself elected a deputy, and also the Rev. Samuel Houston, progenitor, or near kinsman, to that other Sam Houston, who did many brave things, but none braver than riding by the side of Lincoln when he deemed that good man's life in danger on the eve of his inauguration. In the pocket of the reverend gentleman was a ready-made constitution, the handiwork of himself and his friends during the long months which had elapsed since the session of the organizing convention. This Constitution, when Sevier had taken the chair, and a blessing had been asked upon the deliberations of the delegates, the worthy clergyman proceeded to unroll, asking permission that it might be read and submitted to the vote of the convention. Permission was readily accorded, for Houston was a man much esteemed—a cast-iron man, of rigid principles and fixed opinions, run in the Scotch Presbyterian mold, but nevertheless holding in solution that kind of salt which keeps this world "sweet and wholesome." How much time was consumed in the reading is not stated ; but it must have been the better part of a day, for the document was longer than the '· Westminster Catechism'.' and the " Thirty-nine Articles " put together, and it was of much the same character. It proposed to run the new government on theological principles ; and, to secure the purity of its legislative and administrative branches, it provided that no person should be eligible as a representative, or competent to hold any civil office under the new State, who was of "immoral character, or guilty of such flagrant enormities as drunkenness, gaming, profane swearing, lewdness, Sabbath-breaking, and such like ; or who will, either in word or writing, deny any of the following propositions, viz.:

" 1. That there is one living and true God, the Creator and Governor of the universe.

" 2. That there is a future state of rewards and punishments.

" 3. That the Scriptures of the Old and New Testaments are given by Divine inspiration.

" 4. That there are three divine persons in the Godhead, co-equal and co-essential."

To other sections of a like orthodox character were added many admirable provisions for the promotion of education, the preservation of good order, and the strict enforcement of law and impartial administration of justice ; but the whole was quite as well adapted to the inhabitants of the planet Saturn as to the heterogeneous population which then tenanted the trans-Alleghany region.

An animated discussion followed the reading of this document, in which its advocates exhibited an acrimony altogether unorthodox. They speedily developed the fact that here, in these far-western backwoods, near the close of the eighteenth century, there existed as much intolerant bigotry and ill-directed religious zeal as was to be found in New England at the much earlier period (1674) when the zealots of that region made themselves so obnoxious to their neighbors that the stolid Dutchmen of New York passed a law forbidding all intercourse with the Yankees. The large minority which voted for this Utopian Constitution showed that this intolerant spirit prevailed among a considerable portion of the community. While the discussion was in progress, the loquacious John Tipton sat in his place as dumb as an oyster; but, when the decision came to be made, he gave his vote in the affirmative! Strange that this man, whose daily life was a flagrant violation of some of its prohibitions, should sustain an instrument which would shut him out forever from what he most coveted—official position! Perhaps, however, he counted on a much-needed amendment of life, or saw in this strong religious phalanx the nucleus of a party which might be arrayed for the overthrow of Sevier, and his own political elevation. Whatever the cause, it is capable of demonstration that, at some moment during this day's session, Tipton was suddenly converted from a boisterous upholder of secession to a zealous advocate of North Carolina and the old order of things.

When the voting was over, Sevier arose, and, in a temperate and conciliatory address, alluded to the good order and general prosperity which had prevailed during the past year, while the people had lived under the old Constitution. The world, he said, was governed too much. Good order, social progress, political prosperity, depended not so much upon a multiplicity of laws as on the proper enforcement of a few good ones. The old laws were good enough ; the trouble had been in their lax administration. He was glad to see so large a number zealous for social order and a strict observance of religious duty. Such men were the salt of the earth, shining lights set to show the world the beauty of a spiritual life, and to lead men up and out of a mere natural and animal condition. Without them and their principles modern civilization could not exist ; but he questioned the expediency of bringing religious tenets into a civil constitution. The union of church and state existed in some of the older countries, but it was clearly contrary to the teachings of the Bible and the example of Christ, who had said, " Who made me a judge or a divider over you ?" and "Render unto Cæsar the things which are Cæsar's, to God the things which are God's." Such things should be left to spiritual teachers; and more zealous, intelligent, and self-devoted men of this class could not anywhere be found than now ministered to the little flock gathered there beyond the mountains. In conclusion, he proposed the adoption of the Constitution of North Carolina, with such modifications as would more perfectly adapt it to the condition of the over-mountain people.

This was done, after considerable discussion, and against the written protest of nineteen of the members, among whom were Samuel Houston, John Tipton, John Blair, James Stuart, and George Maxwell, all of whom were soon to be arrayed in bitter hostility to the Franklin government. During the discussion it had been pertinently asked: "If we adopt the Constitution of North Carolina, why not adhere to the government of North Carolina? If we are to live under her laws, how shall we be better off when standing alone than when united to her, and secure in the protection she now so abundantly promises for the future?" This idea was the stock in trade of the party which Tipton soon attempted to organize in opposition to Sevier's government.

For North Carolina had now outdone the gracious father in the parable. He made haste to welcome the returning prodigal; she had not only gone to meet him when he was yet a great way off, but had sought him out in that far country before he had the remotest thought of returning to the old family mansion. Her Legislature had refused to receive the delegates whom Sevier had appointed to arrange the terms of separation; it had turned a deaf ear to numerously signed petitions to that end from the people of Franklin, but it soon afterward had passed an act with this preamble:

"*Whereas*, many of the inhabitants of Washington, Greene, and Sullivan Counties have withdrawn their allegiance from this State, and have been erecting a temporary separate government among themselves, in consequence of a general report and belief that the State, being inattentive to their welfare, had ceased to regard them as citizens, and had made an absolute cession, both of the soil and jurisdiction of the country in which they reside, to the United States in Congress; and *whereas*, such report was ill-founded, and it was, and continues to be, the desire of the General Assembly of this State to extend the benefits of civil government to the citizens and inhabitants of the western counties, until such time as they might be separated with advantage and convenience to themselves; and the Assembly are ready to pass over and consign to oblivion the mistakes and misconduct of such persons in the above-mentioned counties as have withdrawn themselves from the government of this State, to hear and redress their grievances, if any they have, and to afford them the protection and benefits of government, until such time as they may be in a condition, from their numbers and wealth, to be formed into a separate commonwealth, and be received by the United States as a member of the Union: Therefore, be it enacted," etc.

The above would seem to indicate that it was not the prodigal son, but the righteous father, who had come to a hopeful repentance. However, a reading of the law which follows this " Be it enacted " dispels this illusion.

It provided for a total change in the manner of holding elections in the western counties. It authorized any
"three good and honest men" to open a poll, constitute
themselves inspectors of election, and return as elected
whoever might receive a majority of the votes cast for
State offices by the persons then present. This enabled,
and it was intended to enable, any ten or a dozen voters,
in a voting population of perhaps many hundreds, to
come together and elect members of the North Carolina
Senate and House of Commons, who, though chosen by
an insignificant minority, could claim to represent the
entire community. It is not known who originated the
measure, but it was evidently conceived in a spirit of bitter hostility to Sevier and his government. Its covert
malice was worthy of the man whose adroit diplomacy
had brought about the treaty of Hopewell; and it is certain that he was then in attendance on the North Carolina Legislature. Alluding to it subsequently in a letter
to Governor Caswell, Judge Campbell said: "If it was
intended to divide us, and set us to massacring one
another, it was well concerted; but it was an ill-planned
scheme, if intended for the good of all."

Then followed a marriage whose bans are forbidden
by both reason and Scripture—a union of the God-
fearing, upright, but narrow-minded clergyman with
the unprincipled demagogue, whom we now style the
"pot-house politician"—for the race has not altogether
died out in this country. The clergyman had his Constitution put in type—sending the precious manuscript

all the way to Philadelphia for the purpose—and in pamphlet form it was now circulated everywhere among the godly, with the appended query, "What better are we off than if under North Carolina?" And, of a truth, they were no better off so far as any Constitution could make them; for among the laws of North Carolina were statutes, as old as 1741, which prohibited drunkenness, Sabbath-breaking, and profane swearing, under a penalty, for each offense, of ten shillings. But, alas! the major part of the population sinned against these laws daily, and hence they had fallen into desuetude, for a general tax of a dollar and a quarter per diem would impoverish any rural people in a twelvemonth.

It is not to be supposed that Tipton circulated many copies of the evangelical Constitution among his barroom associates; nevertheless, he used much the same arguments as his clerical coadjutor. Neither found at first many adherents, and they never had any among the more westerly settlers, who were exposed to daily incursions from the Indians, and knew no other salvation from border perils than Nolichucky Jack and his riflemen. But in Washington County, among the settlers along the base of the mountains, who dreaded a collision with North Carolina, and now seldom saw the face of a Cherokee, they gained a few converts during this winter and the following spring and summer—how many is not known, but enough to secure, under the recent law, a seat in the North Carolina Senate to John Tipton.

One of Tipton's boon companions was now the Sheriff of Washington County, and he issued, and caused to be posted in several inconspicuous places, a notice for an election of members to the North Carolina Assembly. The paper, which has been preserved in Ramsey's "Annals of Tennessee," was as follows :

"July, 19th day, 1786.

"ADVERTISEMENT.—I hereby give Publick Notice, that there will be an election held the third Friday in August next, at John Rennoe's, near the Sickamore Sholes, where Charles Robertson formerly lived, to choose members to represent Washington County in the General Assembly of North Carolina, agreeable to an Act of Assembly, in that case made and provided, where due attendance will be given pr me.

"GEO. MITCHELL, *Shff.*"

In accordance with this notice an election was held at the Sycamore Shoals, where Sevier and his men had gathered, six years before, for their weary march to King's Mountain. How many came together, or what number cast their votes, can not now be ascertained ; but ten ballots were as effectual as ten hundred, and consequently John Tipton was elected to the Senate, and James Stuart and Richard White were duly declared members of the House of Commons of North Carolina. Henceforth, therefore, this "man of Belial" was to be in a position to do essential damage to the new government.

The fame of Sevier and Shelby had spread throughout the State, but the name of John Tipton had never yet traveled across the mountains. The North Carolina legislators, who knew next to nothing about the western counties, knew absolutely nothing about the new Senator, except, perhaps, that he was a member of a most honorable family. He was plausible of address, and glib of tongue ; they would therefore listen to his opinions, accept for gospel his statement of facts, and thus let their legislation be molded by a man who, caring not a Continental dollar for the good of the people, sought only the overthrow of Sevier and his own advancement. Even Governor Caswell would be influenced by him. That he was is apparent from his letters to Sevier, which are still preserved in the archives of North Carolina. Difficulties, therefore, were to thicken around Sevier ; and, beleaguered as he would be by open enmity and secret conspiracy, by internal discord and external hostility, it would be a miracle if he should sustain himself and his new government. But, whether in success or in defeat, he would walk erect, for he was crippled by no unworthy motive, and was sustained by a single desire to be of service to his country. Moreover, and more than all, he had that to lean upon which makes the strong man still stronger—the steadfast devotion of the large-minded and large-hearted woman who for thirty-five years walked loyally by his side.

It is probable that Sevier attached at first very little importance to the opposition of Tipton and his associates.

He was not accustomed to lightly esteem an adversary ;
but this man, he must have thought, could have no
influence in any right-thinking community.   But, whatever he may have thought of these movements, a more
pressing danger now demanded his attention.   The
Cherokees had gone upon the war-path, and were now
making their long-expected raid upon the border settlements along the French Broad and Holston.

By the treaty of Hopewell, as has been stated, the settlers south of the Holston and French Broad were admitted to be intruders upon Cherokee territory.   They
had not yet removed from these lands, and the Creeks,
who were now in alliance with Spain for the extermination
or driving off of the American settlers, were constantly
pressing Old Tassel to make war upon them ; but the old
king and his chieftains still held back, from a wholesome
dread of Nolichucky Jack and his riflemen.   But, in the
early days of 1786, the treacherous Indian agent, Joseph
Martin, could apprise Old Tassel that the sun of Sevier
was about to suffer a sudden eclipse—that North Carolina was fixed in the determination not to recognize his
government, and that she was about to appoint other
officers to command the western militia, which step
would render Sevier powerless, and leave the intruding
settlers altogether at the mercy of the Cherokees.   That
Martin did this is not positively known, and I would not
picture him any worse than he was.   The incontestable
truth about this man is bad enough, and sad enough,
and calls for no exaggeration.   However, this much is

fact—that Martin was then among the Cherokees, and the duties of his office brought him into intimate relations with their king; and that Old Tassel was, about that time, informed of an intended reorganization of the western militia, which did not, and could not, occur till the North Carolina Legislature came together, some months later. Martin was fully informed as to the views and intentions of the leaders of that body, and only some person having that knowledge could have given Old Tassel that information.

The old king loved peace, but his warriors were impatient of the near neighborhood of the whites, and were smarting under the repeated taunts of the Creek chief McGillivray, who charged them with cowardice because they tamely submitted to the encroachments of the pale-faces. The power of an Indian king in time of war is supposed to be absolute; but, like such civilized monarchs as are nominally absolute, he is controlled, more or less, by the will of his people. So it was that Old Tassel, averse as he was to hostilities, had to see early in July a strong body of his warriors go upon the war-path. For some unknown reason, they did not descend at once upon the encroaching settlers, in defending whom Sevier would have come in conflict with the United States and the Hopewell treaty; but they fell upon those north of the Holston, in what is now Knox County, who were clearly within treaty lines, and therefore entitled to both State and national protection. They first attacked the house of a Mr. Biram, on Beaver Creek, and killed two young men in the neighborhood; and then they scattered, to spread havoc throughout the settlements. Many of the settlers fell back at once to stations higher up the Holston; others collected behind hastily constructed defenses, in hopes to hold their ground till Sevier could come to their rescue.

Their messengers found Sevier eighty miles away, at his home on the Nolichucky. He heard the tidings without surprise, for hostile action was daily looked for from the Indians. This might be a mere raid to drive off the intruding settlers, or it might be the signal for an expected general savage uprising along the entire border. Whichever it was, Sevier did not pause to reflect upon it, or to question if he should come in conflict with United States authority. His old comrades were in danger, and that was enough to bring Nolichucky Jack to the rescue. Without stopping to call in his militia, he sprang at once into the saddle, and, with only the half-dozen men who were about him, was in a few hours on his way to the border as fast as his fleet bay mare—the nimblest-footed animal in the territory—could carry him.

The attack had been made on the 20th of July; and on the 23d, gathering his force as he rode along, Sevier, with one hundred and sixty of his men, was at Houston's Station, midway between Little River and the Little Tennessee, and only twelve miles from the Indian towns on the Tellico. The messengers had ridden eighty miles, Sevier one hundred and ten, mustering meanwhile this body of riflemen, within the space of three days! It was by such celerity of movement that he utterly disconcerted his savage enemies. While they looked for him in one quarter, he was miles away in another—in the Indian rear, or in the very heart of their country. But he never moved without a well-considered plan; and now as he rode along he heard that the Cherokees were being held at bay by the Holston settlers, posted behind their hastily constructed defenses. He knew the men, and, knowing them, felt sure they could hold out till his regular militia had time to come to their rescue. One of his brigadiers, General Cocke, could be thoroughly depended upon. He was the same who had been, in 1776, when a captain of militia, the first to suggest that the one hundred and seventy men who held Fort Patrick Henry, should march from behind their log walls to win, in the open field, the battle of Long Island Flats. On his rapid way Sevier sent back word to Cocke to muster a force as quickly as he could, and hasten to the rescue of the settlers. Then he pushed on to Houston's, thirty miles in the rear of the raiding Cherokees.

Arrived at Houston's, Sevier gave his men a night's rest, and then he plunged at once with his slender force into the very heart of the Indian country. The war they were visiting upon the homes of the whites he would carry to the wigwams of the Cherokees, and it would go hard if they did not pay for this raid,

with interest trebly compounded. To appreciate the
boldness of this movement, it needs to be understood
that the body of raiders now in Sevier's rear numbered
not less than five hundred, and that he was advancing
in the face of twenty-five hundred active warriors, who
would soon surround him, and might ambush every
pass by which he could return to the settlements; for
he was entering a mountain-region, covered with forest, and broken into narrow defiles, where a handful
could dispute the passage of a thousand—which defiles
were often the only passable route for a body of horsemen. The movement was extremely perilous, and, for
any other man to attempt it, would have been the
height of temerity. But there seems to have been
some magic about Sevier which gave success to the
most desperate enterprises; and he had himself come
to believe in his own invincibility. This and other
exploits of his would be incredible were they not fully
verified as authentic history.

Leaving the Cherokee villages along the Tellico upon
his flank, Sevier forded the Little Tennessee at Island
Town, crossed the Tellico Plains, and then, scaling the
Smoky Mountains, fell upon what were known as the
valley towns, along the Hiwassee. Three of these he at
once destroyed, killing fifteen warriors. The rest of the
Indians fled panic-stricken into the forest and the neighboring highlands, leaving their homes, as they supposed,
to certain destruction. But Sevier now held his hand.
He had done enough to requite ten to one the raid of

the savages, and to deter them from further aggression ;
and he never wantonly destroyed lives or property.
Besides, prudence demanded that he should make his
way out from the savage cordon by which he was encircled before the warriors could concentrate and effectually obstruct his progress.

To give his troops a night's rest, he went into camp,
in one of the abandoned Indian villages, sending out
trusty scouts to scour the country, and see that it was
clear of any body of the enemy. The scouts soon returned, reporting that they had struck the trail of a
large number of the enemy. Instantly every horse was
bridled and every rifleman was in his saddle. Following the lead of the scouts, they soon struck the Indian
trail, which Sevier's experienced eye at once saw was that
of fully a thousand men, commanded, as he surmised, by
John Watts, the most cunning and daring of all the
Cherokee leaders. Sevier knew him well, Watts having
once guided him to the destruction of the Chickamauga
towns ; and he did not court a conflict with this redoubtable Indian chief, backed by a force six to his one, and
with rugged defiles and mountains a mile high between
him and the settlements. The route taken by Watts was
the one Sevier would naturally have followed. It led
through a narrow ravine where, doubtless, the wily half-
breed now lay in wait for the whites, concealed in the
forest undergrowth. Sevier divined this, and, turning
his horse's head, he led his men back to the encampment. There, setting a strong picket to guard against

surprise, he gave his weary troop a few hours' rest, and then in utter silence, before the break of day, he led his men, by an unfrequented route, up and over the tall and rugged Unakas, and turned his back upon his enemies.

This intrepid raid of Sevier into the heart of their country struck terror among the Cherokees, and led the marauders along the Holston to retreat hastily to their homes upon the Tellico. His end thus accomplished, Sevier led his little force, without the loss of a single man or a single horse, back to the settlements.

Meanwhile, General Cocke had not been inactive. The messengers of Sevier reached him on the 23d, the day of his own arrival at Houston's Station. Mustering at once two hundred and fifty men, Cocke set out without delay to the relief of the Holston settlers; but hearing of his approach, and of the advance of Sevier into their country, the Indians hastily fled, leaving the settlement to its wonted quiet. Having certain information that the savages who had killed the two men were mostly from along the Little Tennessee and Tellico, Cocke followed at once upon their trail, determined to demand them from Old Tassel for summary punishment. It was a bold movement, but Cocke was a brave man; besides, he counted on the dread the Cherokees had of Sevier, and the panic his advance had already spread among the warriors.

Arriving unmolested at what is still known as 'Chota Ford, six miles from Echota, Cocke sent forward a prisoner, inviting the chieftains to a conference. This ford is a beautiful spot, fringed with low hills, that are still crowned with gigantic oaks and poplars, some of which have looked down on stirring scenes, for they stood there when 'Chota Ford was the gateway into the Indian country; when innumerable red warriors waded its broad but shallow stream; when mounted white men galloped across it to hunt those warriors in their mountain lairs; and when, at a later time, "Old Hickory" led over it his three thousand Tennesseeans, cutting for them a swath through the forest, still called Jackson's road, straight as an arrow, and broad as any boulevard on the continent. But all these things have passed away, and now 'Chota Ford is as still as a churchyard, except at seasons of high water, when an old negro, crooning a low hymn, ferries travelers over the river at a dime a trip.

To this quiet spot came the Cherokee chieftains on the 31st of July, 1786, to hold a "talk" with the pale-faces after the Indian fashion. Among them were Old Tassel, Hanging Maw, and other noted warriors, all bedecked in leather breeches fringed with wampum, and their heads crowned with eagle-plumes or the tail of the rooster. Conspicuous by his absence was John Watts, the renowned half-breed, who might still have been lying in wait in that narrow defile beyond the Unakas—waiting for Sevier, who was now quietly at home with his "bonnie Kate," in his shady Mount Pleasant, far away on the Nolichucky.

The Indians were grave, dignified, and taciturn, and their manner indicated that they were not entirely sure

9

that John Watts had not at last entrapped the great
eagle of the pale-faces. But their bearing made no impression on Cocke, who abruptly opened the conference
by upbraiding them for their murders and robberies, and
their flagrant violation of the treaty with the people of
Franklin ; and he added : " We, in plain words, demand
from you the murderers who have killed our people ; and
all the horses you have stolen from us, and from the
people on the Kentucky road and the Cumberland.
On these terms we will be brothers with you, and continue so until you do more murder on our frontiers,
when we will come down and destroy the town that does
the mischief. On these terms we will make peace with
you, and be friends. If not, we are warriors. It is what
you will."

To this, straightening up his bent form, with all the
air of an Indian king, Old Tassel answered as follows :
"Now I am going to speak to you, brothers. We have
smoked. The Great Man above sent the tobacco. It
will make your hearts straight. I come from 'Chota. I
see you. You are my brothers. I am glad to see my
brothers, and hold them fast by the hand. The Great
Man above made us both, and he hears the talk. They
are not my people who spilt the blood, and spoiled the
good talk a little. The men that did the murder are
bad men, and no warriors. They are gone, and I can't
tell where they are gone. They lived in Coytoy, at the
mouth of Holston. This is all I have to say. The Great
Man above has sent you this white talk to straight your

hearts through. I give you this pipe, in token of a straight talk. I am very sorry my people has done wrong, to occasion you to turn your backs. A little talk is as good as much talk; too much is not good."

To this Cocke very briefly replied that, as Old Tassel was not disposed to give up the murderers, as required by the treaty, he should take and deal with them himself. He should go at once to Coytoy, and there, if they desired any further talk, the chieftains might come to him. This ended the conference, and Cocke set out at once for Coytoy, a small Indian village near Southwest Point, where the Clinch and Holston unite to form the broad Tennessee. He had scarcely entered the place, before some of the Holston settlers who were with him recognized two of the savages as being with the party that did the murders. They were at once sent, by well-directed rifle-shots, to the happy hunting-grounds, and then their cabins and other properties were destroyed, and the village council-house, in which the raid had been planned, was sent skyward in smoke and cinders. But no damage was done to other portions of the village, the intention being to impress the Indians that none but the guilty would be punished.

The ruins were still smoldering when, on the 3d of August, Old Tassel and his principal chiefs entered the village. Among them now was John Watts, who had brought to them tidings of the havoc done by Sevier, and of his escape from the trap which he had laid for him. He and the rest were entirely subdued and crest-fallen. It was of no avail to fight the pale-face chief, who moved like the wind and smote like the whirlwind. This they said, and much more that I will not repeat, for before me are the words of Old Tassel: "A little talk is as good as much talk; too much is not good." Suffice it to say that the Indians agreed to give up the other murderers as soon as they could be secured, and promised to live in perpetual amity with their white brothers. One of Cocke's officers, visiting them not long afterward, reported: "They seem very friendly, and well satisfied we should settle the country; and they say they will sell us the country to the south of the [Little] Tennessee, if we will keep the Creeks from killing them; or they will leave the country entirely, if we will give them goods for it; and I am convinced, from their late conduct, and accounts I have had from them, that the whole country to the Georgia line, on this side of Cumberland Mountain, may be had from them for a very trifling sum." All which might have come to pass, but for the continued and obstinate resistance of North Carolina to Sevier's government.

Thus the well-directed energy of Sevier and Cocke speedily dispelled the war-cloud which had gathered over the Cherokee nation; but there still remained the more portentous cloud which overhung the whole frontier, and whose scattered forces McGillivray, at the behest of Spain, was striving to gather into his hand, that he might hurl them, in twenty thousand lightning-bolts, upon all the border settlements.

CHAPTER V.

HAVING now, for a time at least, reduced the Cherokees to peaceable behavior, Sevier could turn his attention to affairs at home. They were not in an entirely satisfactory condition. The unnatural marriage between roistering ambition and well-meaning bigotry was already producing a progeny of evils, young yet, and incapable of much mischief, but bound to grow—as all evils do— unless strangled in their infancy. How to strangle them was now the question. How could Sevier do this except by conciliating their source of life and strength, the sapient Legislature of North Carolina ?

He had made overtures to that body for a friendly adjustment of affairs at its previous session ; but his messengers had been repulsed, and denied even a hearing. But in the threatening attitude of Indian affairs it was now important that all pending difficulties should be arranged with North Carolina, and hence he determined to send to its Legislature again other messengers — men gifted with both logic and the art of persuasion—in the hope of bringing about an honorable adjustment. For the man of logic he chose David Campbell, then holding the appointment of Chief-Justice from both Franklin and North Carolina; and, for the man of rhetoric, William Cocke, the same who had recently "persuaded" Old Tassel—for General Cocke could talk as well as fight, and, though somewhat blunt and plain-spoken, could so sugar-coat his words as to make them palatable to any mind not blunted by prejudice or obstinate ignorance. To secure these commissioners greater consideration, Sevier himself addressed Governor Caswell a letter in advance of their departure, the principal portions of which were as follows:

"MOUNT PLEASANT, FRANKLIN, 28th October, 1786.

"SIR: Our Assembly has again appointed commissioners to wait on the parent State, which I hope will cheerfully consent to the separation as it once before did.

"It gives us inexpressible concern to think that any disputes should arise between us, more especially when we did not in the first instance pray the separation, but adopted our course after what was done by act of your Assembly. We humbly conceived we should do no wrong by endeavoring to provide for ourselves; neither had we the most distant idea that the cession act would be repealed, otherwise matters might not have been carried to the length they are. The propriety of the repeal we do not attempt to scrutinize, but permit us to say we discover many embarrassments both parties are likely to labor under in consequence of it. . . .

"I hope your Assembly will take under their serious consideration our present condition, and we flatter ourselves that august body will not submerge in ruin so many of their late citizens, who have fought and bled in behalf of the parent State, and are still ready to do so again should there be occasion. Our local and remote situation is the only reason that induces us to wish for a separation. Your Constitution and laws we revere, and we consider ourselves happy that we have had it in our power to get the same established in the State of Franklin, although it has occasioned some confusion among ourselves. We do, in the most candid and solemn manner, assure you that we do not wish to separate from you on any other terms, but on those that may be perfectly consistent with the honor and interest of each party; neither do we believe there are any among us who would wish for a separation, did they believe the parent State would suffer any real inconveniency in consequence thereof. We would be willing to stand or fall together, under any dangerous crisis whatever. . . .

"We can not be of opinion that any real advantages can be obtained by a longer connection. Our trade and commerce are altogether carried on with other States, therefore neither party is benefited on that head; and whether it can be suggested that the business of government can be extended from five to eight hundred miles distance, is a matter I leave to your own good sense to judge of ; and, further, it can not be supposed that the inhabitants who reside at that distance are not equally entitled to the blessings of civil government with their neighbors who live east, south, or at any other point, and not one fourth of the distance from the seat of government, and who enjoy the incomparable advantages of the roads and other easy communications you have on the east of the Appalachians."

This much Sevier had written, when it evidently occurred to him that Tipton, in his seat in the North Carolina Senate, would be in a position to throw serious obstacles in the way of any negotiation, and he added : " I heartily wish your Legislature had either not repealed or never passed the cession act, for probably it may occasion much confusion, especially should your Assembly listen too much to prejudiced persons, though this I have no right to suggest. I fear we may have a sufficient quarrel on our hands without any among ourselves.

" I am authorized to say that no people can think more highly of your government than those who want the separation, and they only wish it to answer their better conveniency ; but, though wanting to be separated in government, they wish to be united in friendship, and hope that mutual good offices may ever pass between the parent and infant State, which also is my wish and desire."

The Legislature of North Carolina began its session early in November, but it was not till the 30th of that month that General Cocke could set out on the embassy, and then Judge Campbell was confined to his home by sickness. He could not, therefore, accompany Cocke, but, instead, he sent by him to Governor Caswell a letter to be laid before the Assembly. This letter throws so much light upon the condition of things in Franklin, that a portion of it is here quoted. He said: "If we set out wrong, or were too hasty in our separation, this country is not altogether to blame; your State pointed out the line of conduct which we adopted; we really thought you in earnest when you ceded us to Congress. If you then thought we ought to be separate, or if you now think we ever ought to be, permit us to complete the work that is more than half done; suffer us to give energy to our laws and force to our councils, by saying we are a separate and independent people, and we will yet be happy. I suppose it will astonish your Excellency to hear that there are many families settled within nine miles of the Cherokee nation. What will be the consequence of those emigrations? Our laws and government must include those people, or they will become dangerous; it is vain to say they must be restrained. Have not all America extended their back settlements in opposition to laws and proclamations? The Indians are now become pusillanimous, and consequently will be more and more encroached upon; they must, they will be, circumscribed.

"It was not from a love of novelty or the desire of title, I believe, that our leaders were induced to engage in

the present revolution, but from pure necessity. We
were getting into confusion, and you know any government is better than anarchy.   Matters will be differently represented to you, but, you may rely on it, a great
majority of the people are anxious for separation. Nature has separated us; do not oppose her in her work. By
acquiescing you will bless us, and do yourself no injury :
you will bless us by uniting the disaffected ; and do yourself no injury, because you lose nothing but people who
are a clog on your government, and to whom you can
not do equal justice by reason of their detached situation."

The foregoing letters of Sevier and Campbell were
duly laid before the Legislature by Governor Caswell,
and at the bar of that body—whom, by a great stretch of
courtesy, Sevier termed "august"—General Cocke appeared early in December. He was given a hearing, and
the address he made on the occasion is fully reported in
Judge Haywood's "History of Tennessee." It is too
lengthy for reproduction here, but a brief synopsis of it
can scarcely be omitted, inasmuch as it gives a clear view
of the situation of the settlers, as seen by one of themselves ; and expresses the sentiments of Sevier and of all
the best men beyond the Alleghanies.

General Cocke began by pathetically depicting the
situation of his distressed countrymen. He ascribed the
separation, as had Sevier and Campbell, to the difficult
and perilous condition in which the western settlers had
been placed by the act of cession of June, 1784. They

were surrounded by hostile savages, who often committed upon them the most shocking barbarities ; and by
the passage of that act they suddenly found themselves
without the ability to raise or subsist troops for their
protection, " without authority to levy men, without
power to levy taxes for the support of internal government, and without the hope that any of their necessary
expenditures would be defrayed by the State of North
Carolina, which had then become no more interested in
their safety than any other of the United States. . . .
These considerations full in view, what were the people
of the ceded territory to do to avoid the blow of the up-
lifted tomahawk ? How were the women and children
to be rescued from the impending destruction ? Would
Congress come to their aid ? Alas ! Congress had not
yet accepted them, and possibly never would." And, if
it did accept of them, it would take time to deliberate
upon their situation, and in that time all might be lost.
" The powers of Congress were too feeble to enforce contributions." Action on the part of the several States
would have to be voluntary ; and would they be willing
to burden themselves for the defense of a people not connected with them by any ties of near kindred ? And, if
they gave willing aid, might it not be too limited to do
any good ; too tardy to be of any practical service ?
What were the settlers to do in such circumstances ?
Would common prudence justify a reliance upon such
prospects ? Could their lives, and the lives of their
families, be staked upon them ? Immediate and press-

ing necessity called for the power to concentrate the scanty means they possessed to save themselves from destruction. "A cruel and insidious foe was at their doors. Delay was but another name for death!" They might supinely wait for events, but the first event would be the yell of the savage through all the settlements. Their unpreparedness would be sure to invite attack, for it was the nature of the savage to take sudden advantage of the weakness of an enemy.

And, he continued : "The hearts of the people of North Carolina should not be hardened against their brethren, who have stood by their side in perilous times, and never heard their cry of distress without instantly marching to their aid. They have bled in profusion to save you from bondage, and from the sanguinary hands of a relentless enemy, whose mildest laws for the punishment of rebellion are beheading and quartering. When, in the late war, driven from your homes by the presence of that enemy, we gave to many of you a sanctified asylum, and gladly performed the duties of hospitality to a people we loved so dearly ; and every hand was ready to be raised for your protection. . . .

"The act for our dismissal was, indeed, recalled in the winter of 1784. What, then, was our condition ? More penniless, defenseless, and unprepared, if possible, than before, and under the same necessity to meet and consult together for our common safety. The resources of the country were all locked up, and where is the record that shows any money or supplies sent to us ?—a single soldier ordered to be stationed on the frontier, or any plan formed for mitigating the horrors of our exposed situation? On the contrary, the savages are irritated by the stoppage of those goods which were promised as compensation for the lands taken from them. If North Carolina must yet hold us in subjection, it should at least understand to what a state of distraction, suffering, and poverty her vacillating conduct has reduced us; and the liberal hand of generosity should be widely opened for our relief from the pressure of our present circumstances; all animosity should be laid aside and buried in deep oblivion, and our errors be considered as the offspring of greater errors committed by yourselves. Far from your hearts should be the unnatural purpose of adding to the affliction from which we have suffered too much already. It belongs to a magnanimous people to give attentive consideration to circumstances in order to form a just judgment upon a subject so much deserving of their serious meditation; and, having formed such a judgment, to pursue with sedulous anxiety a course suitable to the dignity of their own character, consistent with their own honor, and best calculated to allay that storm of distraction in which their hapless children have been so unexpectedly involved. If the mother State shall judge the expense of our adhesion too heavy to be borne, let us remain as we are, to support ourselves by our own exertions; if otherwise, let the means for the continuance of our connection be supplied with a degree of liberality that will demonstrate

10

sincerity on the one hand and secure affection on the other."

With these legislators the words of Cocke could find no "fit audience." He had urged that the "liberal hand of generosity" should be opened for the relief of the western settlers, who, let it be remembered, had, with their own blood and treasure, acquired every rood of land then possessed by North Carolina beyond the mountains. With grants of some of this land that State had paid the men who had fought for her in the Revolution, and from sales of the remainder she was daily in receipt of a large revenue. But all this these legislators forgot, or did not care to remember. Before their narrow minds, besotted by ignorance, there doubtless arose the vision of a standing army, perhaps a thousand strong, supported by North Carolina for the protection of the border. Their sole political maxim was, "Escape your taxes, and keep down taxation," and now they saw that a half-dollar, perhaps a whole one, was likely to be extracted from every one of their pockets.

But all men, however degraded, have some sense of justice. No human being ever yet committed a deliberate wrong without inventing for himself, or having invented for him, some sophistical excuse to conceal its enormity from his conscience. These legislators had at hand embodied sophistry and downright falsehood in the "man of Belial," who now assured them that these tales of Indian atrocity were told merely to frighten money out of the State treasury; that the settlers, though too feeble to stand alone, were well enough off under the sheltering wing of North Carolina ; that the Cherokees were copper-complexioned Christians—wise as serpents, but gentle as doves—and altogether harmless if their rights were not encroached upon ; and that all that was needed to restore peace, good order, and a delightful state of things among the over-mountain people, was to depose their factious leaders, and put new and loyal men into every civil and military office in the Territory. Some men fit for such positions could be found over there—among whom he may have mentioned himself, Martin, and other of his boon companions—but the larger number might be drawn from among the friends of the legislators in North Carolina.

A lie may prosper if there is no one by to contradict it, and it accords with the views and inclinations of its auditory. There was no one present to expose these falsehoods, and they were exactly adapted to the sordid views of these legislators. They offered also an agree-able salve to their feebly aroused consciences, and con-sequently these Solons proceeded to trample the truth under foot, and to turn and rend the men who had uttered it. But what they did will best be told by quoting from a letter that Governor Caswell wrote to Sevier. It was as follows :

"Kinston, 23*d February*, 1787.

"Sir : I was favored with your letter of the 28th of October, on the subject of a separate and independent government on your side of the Appalachians, which I did myself the honor of laying before the General Assembly. Their resolutions and determinations on that subject, I had flattered myself it would have been in my power to have forwarded you copies of by this time. It must, therefore, suffice that I acquaint you for the present that the Assembly, *from the representations of persons from among yourselves,* was induced to believe it was proper for the people to return to subjection to the laws and government of North Carolina; that they are not yet of strength and opulence sufficient to support an independent State; that they, the Assembly, wish to continue the benefits and protection of the State toward them until such time as their numbers and wealth will enable them to do for themselves. . . .

"Thus, sir, you have in substance, as far as I recollect, the amount of the proceedings of the Assembly, save the appointment of civil and military officers for the three old and a new county; the brigade to be commanded by Evan Shelby, Esq. In the civil department Judge Campbell is reappointed; and the representatives have carried out commissions for the county officers, civil and military. I have not a doubt but a new government may be shortly established, if the people would unite, submit to the former government, and petition for a separation. This, I think, is the only constitutional mode, and I firmly believe, if pursued, will be a means of effecting a separation on friendly terms, which I much wish."

More distinctly than the Governor states it, the Legislature had declared that all offices, both civil and military, whose incumbents had exercised authority under the new State, should be considered vacant, and proper persons should be appointed to fill them by the Assembly, and they be at once commissioned by the Governor as the law directed. This removed from office every justice of the peace and every commissioned officer in every regiment in the western counties, thus at one blow decapitating Sevier's government and depriving the country of experienced civil officers whom it trusted, and of military leaders under whom it had served for years, and without whom it could not hope to be safe from the murderous incursions of the Cherokees.

Having done this, the Assembly proceeded to fill these offices with inexperienced men, the most of whom were non-residents, unknown to the people of Franklin, and not a few were worthless characters, appointed through the favoritism of some functionary of North Carolina. Colonels for Washington and Sullivan Counties they made of John Tipton and his creature, George Maxwell; and for a new county—which had been erected and named Hawkins—of one Hutchings, a hair-brained North Carolinian, without the coolness of judgment which might be required by circumstances.

Thus did North Carolina do her utmost to alienate the affections of the western settlers, and introduce among them such elements of discord as might incite to actual war, which, in the discordant relations then

existing between the various States, would probably
have been attended by wide-spread and disastrous consequences. For the evil would not have been confined
to that narrow arena. A small fire, carelessly lighted by
some idle camper-out, has been known to overspread and
overwhelm a mighty forest.

CHAPTER VI.

THE CHOSEN ALTERNATIVE.

THE "sufficient quarrel," to which Sevier referred in his letter to Governor Caswell, was a vast combination which the Creek chief, McGillivray, at the instance of Spain, had been, since June, 1784, striving to form among the Southwestern Indians for the extermination of the Western settlers. Of his hostile designs Sevier had early intelligence, and in May, 1786, he wrote to Governor Telfair, of Georgia, apprising him of the danger. The Governor replied that the Creeks were constantly harassing the Georgia frontier; that he was attempting to negotiate a peace with them, but was fearful a war was inevitable; and he suggested that in case of hostilities there should be co-operation between the forces of Franklin and Georgia. To this Sevier cordially assented, and on August 27, 1786, Governor Telfair dispatched to him commissioners, with his appointment as brigadier-general in the army of Georgia, and a letter in which he represented that it would "be greatly to the success of both armies to begin their movements at one and the same time," and

154734

suggesting the 1st of November as the date for marching.

The reception which Sevier gave the Georgia commissioners may be gathered from a letter addressed to
Governor Telfair by Major Elholm, a distinguished
Polish officer of Pulaski's Legion, who happened to be
then in Franklin. Murray's Grammar was not at that
time in existence, and English was not the major's
vernacular language ; nevertheless, he expresses himself
with sufficient force and clearness. His letter was as
follows :

"GOVERNOR SEVIER'S, FRANKLIN, *September* 30, 1786.

"SIR : I does myself the honour to inform your
Excellency that your commissioners set out from this
the 28th inst., by the way of Kentucky and Cumberland. They were received very politely by his Excellency the Governor, from whose zeal for to assist you,
aided by the inclination of the Franks, I am fully
convinced your embassy will meet all wished success
by the Assembly of this State, which is ordered to
assemble 12th next, by his Excellency's command, in
consequence thereof. Several of the inhabitants have
waited on the Governor, for to be informed of the
contents of the embassy from Georgia. And when
being acquainted therewith, it gave me great pleasure
to find no other apprehension appeared, but that of
making peace with the Creeks without fighting, by
which occasion, they said, so favourable a chance for

humbling that nation would fall dormant. The Governor, in order that the Americans may reap a benefit from the dread the Cherokees and Chickasaws feels for the displeasure and power of the Franks, he has dispatched letters to them, offering them protection against the Creek nation, with condition that they join him.

"Cumberland (Robertson's colony), it seems, has at this time in contemplation to join in government with the Franks. If so, so much the better, and it would surely be their interest so to do, as they are yet few in numbers, and often harassed by the Indians.

"Judging from apparent circumstances, you may promise yourself one thousand riflemen and two hundred cavalry, excellently mounted and accoutred, from this State, to act in conjunction with Georgia.

"Governor Sevier has received letters from the principal men in Cumberland, which inform him of a convention held lately at that place, when commissioners were chosen by the people with power for to join with the Franks in their government.

"Mr. John Tipton's party, which is against the party of the new government, seems deep in decline at present, which proves very favourable to the embassy from Georgia."

The Franklin Legislature came together on the call of Sevier, on the 12th of October, and at once passed an act authorizing the Governor to call out, for immediate service, one fourth of the militia, and to hold the entire force in readiness to repel any attack from the Indians.

The troops thus called for were at once enrolled, and held in readiness to march on the demand of Georgia; but they were not dispatched immediately to the frontier, because McGillivray promptly disavowed the acts of his marauding followers, and expressed a desire for peace with the Georgians. This proposal was merely a subterfuge to gain time for more efficient preparation, and to make certain of the co-operation of the Cherokees. It was so understood by Sevier, who now made ready his entire militia for what was generally believed to be a more formidable war than any that had yet threatened the western settlements. Thus the country remained—in daily expectation of attack from twelve thousand combined Creeks, Seminoles, and Cherokees—until the ensuing March (1787), and then came to Sevier the already quoted letter from Governor Caswell, which informed him that the Legislature of North Carolina had decapitated every officer of his government, from himself, the highest, down to the lowest civil and military official. This action could not be mistaken. It meant "rule or ruin" to North Carolina or to Franklin, and perhaps to both. Another forward step on the part of Sevier would be downright, defiant rebellion. This he fully understood, and when he took it he was prepared to meet all the consequences of his action.

It was a momentous crisis in Sevier's career, and in that also of the nearly thirty thousand people whose well-being and safety depended upon his continuing to be their leader. Only two courses were open to him—either submission or open rebellion; and that he fully appreciated the gravity of his position is shown by the fact that he took no less than thirty days to decide upon his action. He decided upon rebellion; but, in doing so, I think it will be seen that he was actuated by the same disinterested patriotism which had so often before led him to hazard his all for the good of his country.

To judge correctly of his subsequent course, it is necessary to take a brief view of the circumstances by which he was now surrounded. The country was feeling the effects of the Spanish imbroglio which, from 1784 to 1796, harassed the Western settlers and endangered the continuance of the Union. A full account of this perilous complication falls more appropriately into a life of Robertson than into one of Sevier, but a brief view of it must here be taken, because it rested with Sevier, more than with any other man, to decide whether the Spanish proposals should be accepted or rejected by the Western settlers.

For a brief period Spain had shaken off the lethargy in which she had been sunk for more than a century. Recalling her former greatness, her able and far-sighted king, Charles III, had asserted for her again a voice among European nations, and he had resolved to

infuse new life into her vast possessions beyond the
Atlantic.   To exalt Spain, and cripple the world-power
of Great Britain, he had joined with France in aiding
the revolted colonies to achieve their independence;
and he had planned the erection of a great empire in
America, a new Spain, to extend from the Alleghanies
to the Pacific, with New Orleans as its capital and
chief port of entry.   All the vast region beyond the
Mississippi was then Spanish property.   Spain also
held Florida, and the mouths of the great river, and
claimed so much of the territory east of it as is west
of the eastern angle of the Gulf of Mexico, and the
Hiwassee, Clinch, and Tennessee Rivers—that is to say,
nearly all of the present States of Alabama and Mississippi, so much of Tennessee as lies west of those rivers,
and a considerable portion of Kentucky to its northern
boundary on the Ohio.   This vast region Charles III
designed should be a great mediæval empire, free from
the intrusion of Anglo-Saxon ideas, and a strong bulwark to Catholic Christianity.   He had overlooked
the insignificant settlements on the Watauga and in
Kentucky; but the war which crippled Great Britain
was no sooner over than he awoke to the fact that,
while he had been intent upon crushing one enemy,
another had sprung into life—an enemy fewer in numbers but far more dangerous, because nearer home, and
already proclaiming civil and religious liberty at the
very doorway of his dominions.

Instantly the Spanish king prepared to crush this

new enemy. To extirpate and drive back the western settlers, he instructed his Governor of Louisiana and West Florida, Don Estephan Miro, to arm the Indians, and incite them to a war of extermination against the colonists ; and, to discourage further settlements beyond the mountains, he announced to the United States Government that under no circumstances would he consent to the navigation of the Mississippi by the Americans. Thus shut out from the markets of the world, no sane Virginian or New-Englander would think of erecting his domicile beyond the Alleghanies. So Charles III thought, and he was sanguine that twenty thousand native warriors, armed and backed by Spain, would make short work with the handful of heretics who had already ventured beyond the mountains.

But Charles III had overestimated the strength of his allies, and underestimated that of his enemies. Of these twenty thousand warriors, seven thousand were Choctaws and Chickasaws, who had been won over to the Americans through the friendship for Robertson of Piomingo, the Chickasaw king ; and nearly three thousand were Cherokees, who were paralyzed by the pacific disposition of Old Tassel, and a dread of John Sevier's rifles. The remainder of this savage force, namely, six thousand Creeks, two thousand Seminoles, and two thousand Chickamaugas, were, indeed, pledged to the Spanish king by a treaty between Alexander McGillivray, the Creek chief, and Governor Miro, made at Pensacola, on June 1, 1784; but the Creek chief had

11

ever since feared to meet, without the aid of the other tribes, the combined forces of the settlers. This aid, however, he had hoped, and still did hope, to get; and meanwhile he was showing his zeal for Spain, and keeping alive the spirit of his warriors, by constant raids upon Robertson, who, at one time, with but seventy men, and with never more than a thousand, had for seven years held at bay, or beaten off, these nations of savages.

And the Kentucky settlements, which in 1779 had numbered only one hundred and seventy-six white men, now (1787) contained a population of not less than thirty thousand souls, and a like number were on the Holston and Watauga under Sevier, and fully seven thousand on the Cumberland under Robertson. Allowing for the usual excess of men over women in all new settlements, this population of nearly seventy thousand would have furnished at least eighteen thousand riflemen, not a man of whom would passively submit to be exterminated. They were more than a match for double their number of Indians, and consequently the design of the Spanish king was impossible of execution.

These facts came at last to the knowledge of Charles III, and then his policy underwent a sudden change from one of hostility to one of conciliation and brotherly kindness. He sought no longer to exterminate the settlers, but to get them under his control, by inducing them—if he could not otherwise do it—to establish an independent republic between the Alleghanies and the

Mississippi, under his protection. This would dismember and weaken the Union, and prevent it ever becoming a power great enough to endanger the safety of his North American possessions. It would also close forever the western half of this continent to the entrance of Anglo-Saxon civilization.

This separation the Spanish king proposed to bring about by showing the colonists the vast advantages they would derive from a Spanish alliance, and by fostering the dissatisfaction which was fast growing up among them toward the seaboard States. To this end he relaxed the rigor of his embargo upon the Mississippi, though he exacted such duties on passing and landed produce as would leave all profits in the hands of his underlings. Many of the settlers availed themselves of this commercial opening, and tested the fact that tobacco, worth at home but two dollars per hundred, found a ready market in New Orleans at nine dollars and fifty cents; and they saw that with such returns their smiling Kentucky and Cumberland valleys, where the "fragrant weed" lay rotting on the ground, would speedily be transformed into a vast El Dorado—a land of the "golden leaf"—if only the onerous duty were once removed.

Upon this the Western people demanded of Congress that it should effect such a treaty with Spain as would give them free trade upon the Mississippi. In answer to this, Congress replied: "We have negotiated to that end since 1784; but the Spaniards refuse to listen to any proposals for the opening of that river. Its free navigation was ceded to us by Great Britain, and you have a natural right to it; but it can not be had without a war with Spain, and for that the country is not now prepared. That point ignored, we can form an advantageous treaty with that nation—one that will revive trade, bring in gold and silver, and thus relieve our national embarrassments. Therefore, the navigation had better be waived for the moment. It is not needed by you at present. You are too few in numbers to require a foreign commerce; and you have no more surplus coin and tobacco than can be consumed by incoming settlers. When you and the country are stronger, we shall be able to demand and enforce the free navigation of that river."

The above is, in effect, what the settlers gathered as to the acts and intentions of Congress, and on the heels of it came the report that John Jay, the U. S. Secretary of State, had recommended to that body, in secret session, the making of a treaty with Spain, which would concede her right to control the Mississippi, and close it for twenty years to American commerce; and that seven of the States—only nine being required to ratify a treaty—had voted in favor of this concession.

The tidings excited intense indignation throughout the Western country. Never before had such excitement been known there, not even when the savages were pouring in resistless numbers upon the well-nigh defenseless settlements. The settlers saw themselves shut out from the civilized world, and left at the mercy of a foreign nation. With their barns and warehouses filled to overflowing, they had no outlet for their produce. They had a natural right to a route to the sea, and they were now to be denied that right, simply to fill the already plethoric pockets of the Eastern traders. The wrongs which had brought about the revolt from Great Britain were not near so great nor half so galling as these. Was it for this they had fought the Indians, and made in the wilderness a highway for freedom—to be themselves bound hand and foot, at the will of the ruffled-shirted gentry on the seaboard? Such injustice could not and would not be borne. They would throw off their allegiance to the Central Government, set up a government of their own, and, if need were, with their eighteen or twenty thousand riflemen, they would force a passage to the sea. This was the language now heard in every hut and every hamlet from the Watauga to the most remote district in Kentucky.

And this language was pleasant to the ears of the Spanish king. It was to arouse just this feeling that he had instructed his envoy, Gardoqui, to decline to open to the United States the navigation of the Mississippi; and quickly he seized upon this opportunity to sever the Western people from the Union. Through Miro he now said to Robertson and other of the Western leaders: "We will freely grant to you what we have refused to the trading aristocracy on the Atlantic. We will admit your produce to our ports free from all duty, and give you in perpetuity unobstructed navigation of the Mississippi. We will call off, and, if need be, drive off, the Indians from harassing you. We will release to you all claim that we have to the territory which you occupy; and we will stand by you like loving brothers, with sword and bayonet and heavy artillery, if you will but cut loose from the Eastern shopkeepers, and set up for yourselves a free and independent republic in this glorious valley of the Mississippi."

The above is the purport of the declaration of the Spanish king, and we may easily imagine how it was generally received among a people bleeding from the wounds of an interminable savage warfare, and smarting under what seemed to them the unmerited neglect and indifference of the General Government. Robertson had been in frequent correspondence with Miro since 1782. He had reason to consider him a high-toned, kind-hearted Castilian gentleman, who resorted to the employment of savages, not from cruelty, but from state policy; and he had sought to conciliate his good-will, and mitigate the savage warfare upon his settlement, by giving the name of "Miro District" to the Cumberland region when, in 1783, it was set off from Watauga by North Carolina. The compliment had won for Robertson the decided friendship of the Spanish governor, though it did not induce him to obstruct the policy of his sovereign; and now, when that policy had undergone a radical change, Robertson was the first to whom it was communicated. By Robertson these proposals were at once forwarded to Sevier, and they came to Sevier just at the time when Governor Caswell apprised him that the North Carolina Legislature had swept both himself and his government from political existence.

I have not been able to discover Sevier's answer to these Spanish overtures. His subsequent course shows that it must have been a decided refusal; but the following extract from a letter to him from the heroic Elijah Clarke, of Georgia, makes it evident that he was deeply interested in the project of opening the Mississippi to Western commerce. Clarke had been Sevier's devoted friend ever since the time when, in 1780, he had found a refuge at his house on the Nolichucky, and now under date of Augusta, February 11, 1787, he wrote to him as follows:

"DEAR SIR : I received your favor by Major Elholm, who informed me of your health. Assure yourself of my ardent friendship, and that you have the approbation of all our citizens, and their well wishes for your prosperity. We are sensible of what benefit the friendship of yourself and the people of your State will be to Georgia; and we hope you will never join North Carolina more. Open a land-office as speedily as possible, and it can not fail but you will prosper as a people : this is the opinion current among us.

"I have considered greatly on that part of your letter which alludes to politics in the Western country. It made me serious ; and, as seven States have agreed to give up the navigation, it is my friendly advice that you do watch with every possible attention, for fear that two more States should agree. I only observe to you that the Southern States will ever be your friends. I know that you must have the navigation of the Mississippi. You have spirit and right : it is almost every man's opinion that a rumor" (an outbreak) "will rise in that country. I hope to see that part myself yet. Adieu. Heaven attend you and every friend !"

This letter of General Clarke expresses the nearly unanimous sentiment of the people of Franklin at this period in regard to a reversion to North Carolina. They were prepared·to resist it, "even unto blood." This is shown by the following extract from a letter of Judge Campbell, the recently appointed Chief-Justice of the North Carolina Superior Court, to Governor Caswell, dated March 18, 1787. He said : "The sword of justice and vengeance will, I believe, be shortly drawn against those of this country who attempt to overturn and violate the laws and government of Franklin, and God only knows what will be the event ! If any blood is spilt on this occasion, the act for partial elections from your country" (which had placed Tipton in the North Carolina Senate) "will be the cause of it ; and, I am bold to say, the author of that act was the author of much evil.

That your Excellency may not be in the dark about the spirit and determination of a great majority of these people, in supporting, maintaining, and defending their beloved Franklin, I shall give you a brief and concise detail of what has transpired here since the fate of our memorial and personal application to the Legislature of North Carolina has been announced to us. Pains have been taken to collect the wishes of the people respecting a reversion; many who were formerly lukewarm are now flaming patriots for Franklin. Those who were real Franklinites are now burning with enthusiastic zeal. They say that North Carolina has not treated us like a parent, but like a step-dame. She means to sacrifice us to the Indian savages; she has broken our old officers, under whom we fought and bled, and placed over us many men unskilled in military achievements, and who were none of our choice. . . . You must not conclude we are altogether unanimous; but I do assure you that a very great majority, perhaps nineteen twentieths, seem determined to persevere at all hazards."

A letter from Hutchings, the newly appointed North Carolina colonel of Hawkins County, to Governor Caswell, at about the same date, was to the same purport; and he added: "There are many plans and matters agitated by them which seem to have a tendency to dissolve the Federal bands. Several letters I have in my possession can be spoken of in no other way."

From the above it would seem to be clear that the people of Franklin had now resolved on armed resistance

to North Carolina; and that among them was heard a
subdued talk of throwing off allegiance to the Federal
Union.   It is not to be supposed that the Spanish proposals were as yet generally known ; but they were
known to Sevier, and therefore he had before his view
the entire situation—the whole people west of the Alleghanies ripe for revolt, and Spain pledged to assist them
in asserting and maintaining their independence of the
General Government.   Once before Sevier had gone with
the current, and for doing so he has been styled—by
those not attentive to his entire career—a demagogue,
and accused of personal ambition.   What will they say
of him if he shall now resist the tide, refuse to lift a
hand against North Carolina or the Federal authority,
and, with the loss of all he has, and at the hazard of his
life and liberty, not only save his own people from savage assault, but hold the entire West to its moorings in
the Union ?   To appreciate what he did, it is necessary
to consider what he might have done, had he not been
as true a man and as pure a patriot as can be found in
American history.

The whole West, as has been shown, was ripe for
rebellion.   Under Isaac Shelby, Benjamin Logan, and
George Rogers Clark, five thousand men could have been
raised in Kentucky ; three thousand more could have
been recruited by Arthur Campbell in Southwest Virginia ; at least one thousand by Robertson on the Cumberland ; and Elijah Clarke, who had said, "I hope to
see that part myself yet," could have been counted on to

lead five thousand over the mountains from Northern Georgia. All of these men, except George Rogers Clark, had served under or with Sevier; all were devotedly attached to him; and all, knowing his military genius, would gladly have accepted his leadership. Campbell and Robertson had already proposed to join their fortunes with those of Franklin, and Sevier had only to speak the word to rally the others to his side, and then, counting his own troops, he would have been at the head of not less than twenty thousand of the best fighting men in the country. Opposed to him would have been the wretched "sand-hillers" of North Carolina, with not one competent leader, and perhaps the General Government—I say "perhaps," because the old Confederation had then neither strength nor vitality. It was at the point of dissolution, and its representatives in Congress were at that very moment debating the new Constitution, which was not adopted by all the States till more than two years afterward. Moreover, a majority of that body were from the Eastern and Northern States, where the general opinion was that the Union already covered too much territory. They would have been content with the Alleghanies as its western boundary, and it is not probable that they would have submitted to the expense of maintaining a large armed force for the subjugation of the West.

This was the outlook to Sevier if the Spanish proposals were not accepted. But, if even a temporary alliance had been formed with Spain, this army of

twenty thousand men would have been augmented by
twenty thousand Indian warriors, who had for "'Chucky
Jack" a superstitious veneration, and every one of whom
would have followed him, believing that in doing so he
was under supernatural protection. With this alliance
the Mississippi would have been opened, a trade established upon it that would soon have flooded the West
with gold and silver, and the murderous tomahawk
would have been so deeply buried that it might never
again be brandished above the white man's dwelling.
And, in alliance with Spain, Sevier could have counted
with absolute certainty upon no interference from the
Central Government; for had it not already for three
years borne with wrong, indignity, and savage outrage
upon its Western citizens, rather than provoke a war
with the Spaniards; and did it not pursue the same
policy for seven years longer?

Each of these courses was now open to Sevier, and
either of them would unquestionably have resulted in the
independence of the West. Is it not within bounds to
say that such another opportunity for what is termed
"great achievement" has seldom been presented to any
ambitious leader in this country?

On the other hand, what would have been the result
had Sevier given up his command, and submitted to the
government of North Carolina? Three thousand well-
deserving people, who, relying on the faith of North
Carolina, had settled on the Indian lands, would have
been at once driven from their homes, or else outlawed

and delivered over, in express terms, by the treaty of Hopewell, to the relentless fury of untamed savages; and more than this, the whole Watauga country would have been stripped of its tried military leaders, and exposed, without so much as a competent captain of militia, to the impending attack from McGillivray and his twelve thousand warriors. This is not too much to say, for Evan Shelby, though an old and tried soldier, was now feeble with age, and incompetent to lead in such an emergency; and Tipton and Martin, the only colonels worthy of mention, had not the confidence of the people. They were willing enough to lead, but, as very soon appeared, the "tall Watauga boys" were not willing to follow them. Thus the salvation of Watauga, and the safety of every man, woman, and child in its scattered settlements, rested upon Sevier, and demanded that he should, at least for a time, retain control of its military organization.

These were the facts which of necessity Sevier had before him for the thirty days during which he had his future course under consideration. There is no word from him to indicate his decision; but the scanty records which exist, and his subsequent action, clearly show it to have been as follows:

He would form no alliance with Spain. Light has no affinity with darkness, and American freedom would not ally itself with Spanish tyranny.

He would not aid or countenance any effort to dismember the Union. He had fought to establish it,

12

and he would again risk his life for its preservation.

He would not lift his hand against one of his countrymen, nor would he resist by force the arbitrary acts of
North Carolina. He would conciliate that State, if possible, by moderate measures, and a right presentation of
facts, and in all honorable ways would endeavor to preserve peace between the two peoples.

But he would, at all hazards, defend against Indian
attack the Watauga settlers and the people who were
outlawed by the treaty of Hopewell. The better to do
this, he would retain in force the civil and military
organization of Franklin for the single year that remained of his term as Governor. That period having
expired, he would no longer be eligible to that office ;
but then, if danger from the Indians continued, he
would head the militia as their volunteer leader. By
this course he might come into collision with North
Carolina, and be subjected to a charge of high treason ;
but this was a personal risk, involving only his own life
and liberty, and he would assume it to protect the
Watauga people.

Having resolved upon this course, Sevier, on the 6th
of April, 1787, addressed the following letter to Governor Caswell :

"Sir : I was favored with yours of 23d February, in
which your Excellency was pleased to favor me with a
detail of the proceedings of your Assembly. I must own

I had the fullest hopes and confidence that that body, before their rising, would have either agreed to the separation, on honorable principles and stipulations, or otherwise endeavored to have reunited us upon such terms as might have been lasting and friendly ; but I find myself and country entirely deceived ; and, if your Assembly have thought their measures would answer such an end, they are equally disappointed. But I firmly believe, had proper measures been adopted, an union, in some measure, or perhaps fully, would have taken place.

"We shall continue to act as independent, and would rather suffer death in all its various and frightful shapes than conform to anything that is disgraceful."

To this letter Caswell replied promptly, and in a most kindly spirit, urging upon Sevier patience and moderation. In an indirect way he censured the course of the Legislature by saying : "I can not account for the conduct of our Assembly in their last session. I know some of the gentlemen's sentiments did not coincide with my own. . . . My ideas are that Nature, in this formation of the hills between us, and directing the courses of waters so differently, had not in view the inhabitants on either side being long subject to the same laws and government. I conclude by recommending unanimity among you, as the only means by which your government ever can obtain energy, even when the separation is effected by consent of North Carolina."

Six months prior to the date we are considering, Major Elholm had written to the Governor of Georgia, "Mr. John Tipton's party seems deep in decline at present." It was so, and so would have continued—a mere corporal's guard, and not a party—and it would speedily have died a natural death, but for the passage of the law beheading the Franklin government. That act was no sooner passed than Tipton himself received new life, and, waiting only for the commissions for the new officials, hurried over the mountains into Franklin, proclaiming everywhere the overthrow of Sevier and his government. He arrived some weeks before the official dispatches, and at first the people listened with incredulous ears to his tidings, but when they saw courts being organized under the new justices, and placards posted at every cross-roads calling upon the militia to muster under the new officers, they believed his report, and the general rage and consternation became unbounded. "Does North Carolina," they asked, "intend to deliver us, bound hand and foot, to our enemies? In the face of a great Indian war, will she depose our tried leaders, and set over us officers who know nothing of savage warfare? And what kind of law or equity can we get from these irresponsible men whom she has made our civil justices?" Only in the two older counties could men be found who would accept the new appointments, and even there the feeling ran so high that, had it not been for the pacific counsels of Sevier, violence might have been done to the new officials.

But this storm of indignation did not intimidate
Tipton. Turmoil was his natural element, and he was
of so reckless a courage that, right or wrong, with five
men at his back, he would anywhere have met a thousand. He went on delivering the commissions, organizing justices' courts in log-cabins and cross-road school-
houses, and forming such skeletons of military companies
as could be got together from among his own and Houston's adherents, who now, according to Judge Campbell,
numbered not more than five men in a hundred. This
slender battalion, it would seem, could not be dangerous,
and need not be feared by a majority, large, compact,
and powerful ; and yet there was danger in it, for behind
this ribald, disorderly crew, so out at the elbows and
out of character, was that silent, omnipotent force,
which we call Law, and which, whoever resists, is himself at once an outlaw and a criminal.

Though he could not at the time muster a hundred
men, Tipton knew his legal strength, and he determined
upon such aggressive measures as would overturn Sevier's
pacific policy, and bring on such a collision with North
Carolina as, he thought, would be fatal to the new government. He had organized a court for the county of
Washington at a log-house on Buffalo Creek, about ten
miles from Jonesboro, and, procuring a warrant from
this court, he collected a body of some fifty armed men,
and descended one day in early March upon the regular
tribunal, then in session at the county-seat. The records of the court being refused him, he proceeded to

drive the judge, jury, lawyers, and spectators out-of-doors, and then bore away the records in triumph to his own court on Buffalo Creek. James Sevier, who when a boy not yet sixteen had fought by his father's side at King's Mountain, was the clerk of the regular court, and, now promptly gathering a number of men, he descended in turn upon Tipton's court, regained the captured papers, and bore them away to his own dwelling. Here, a few nights later, he was surrounded by a still stronger party, the papers forced from him, and again borne away by Tipton. But young Sevier was not to be thus overcome by what he deemed a party of lawless ragamuffins. He collected another body of men, again recaptured the papers, and on this occasion hid them in a cave, where they might be as secure as the old charter in the famous oak of Hartford. "However," says Haywood, "in these removals many valuable papers were lost, and at later periods, for want of them, some estates of great value have also been lost." Some of these papers came subsequently into the possession of Dr. Ramsey, and he reports that they bore evidence of having at some time been in very damp quarters. No blood was shed in these various collisions, for on each occasion only the attacking party was armed.

These disorderly proceedings increased the public excitement, and the Franklin Legislature, then in session, sought to put a stop to them by passing an act to punish by imprisonment every person who should attempt to exercise the authority of a justice of the peace, or perform the duties of any other civil office, by commission from the State of North Carolina. Sevier refused to sanction this law, and it consequently was inoperative; but it required all his remarkable powers of conciliation to prevent the people resorting to summary and illegal measures, that would inevitably have resulted in bloodshed.

This first crop of dragon's teeth, which sprang from the hostile legislation of North Carolina, warned Sevier that something must at once be done to stop the evil, and secure against further profanation the recognized courts of justice. Evan Shelby had been appointed by the old State brigadier-general of the entire western militia, and this, though as yet he was in command of only skeleton regiments, made him the highest representative of North Carolina in the Territory. In anticipation of the hostile feeling which the obnoxious act of his Legislature would arouse in Franklin, Governor Caswell had written Shelby to exert every influence to pacify the people, and now Sevier applied to him for his co-operation in some feasible measure calculated to restore the public tranquillity. The result was an agreement which in effect established two governments in Franklin; and this shows that Sevier never intended to sustain his authority by force, and only sought to retain power until the present danger from the Indians should be over. The agreement, as reported by Evan Shelby to Governor Caswell, was as follows:

"At a conference held at the house of Samuel Smith, Esquire, on the 20th day of March, 1787, between the Honorable Evan Shelby, Esquire, and sundry officers, of the one part, and the Honorable John Sevier, and sundry officers, of the other part : *Whereas*, disputes have arisen concerning the propriety and legality of the State of Franklin, and the sovereignty and jurisdiction of the State of North Carolina over the said State, and the people residing therein : the contending parties, from the regard they have to peace, tranquillity, and good decorum in the western country, do agree and recommend as follows :

"*First*. That the courts of justice do not proceed to transact any business in their judicial departments, except the trial of criminals, the proving of wills, deeds, bills of sale, and such like conveyances; the issuing of attachments, writs, and any legal process, so as to procure bail, but not to enter into any final determination of the suits, except the parties are mutually agreed thereto.

"*Secondly*. That the inhabitants residing within the limits of the disputed territory are at full liberty and discretion to pay their public taxes to either the State of North Carolina or the State of Franklin.

"*Thirdly*. That this agreement and recommendation continue until the next annual sitting of the General Assembly of North Carolina, to be held in November next, and not longer. It is further agreed, that if any person guilty of felony be committed by any North Carolina justice of the peace, that such person or persons may and shall be received by the Franklin sheriff or gaoler of Washington, and proceeded against in the same manner as if the same had been committed by and from any such authority from under the State of Franklin. It is also recommended that the aforesaid people do take such modes and regulations, and set forth their grievances, if any they have, and solicit North Carolina, at their next annual meeting of the General Assembly, to complete the separation, if thought necessary by the people of the western country, as to them may appear most expedient, and give their members and representatives such instructions as may be thought most conducive to the interest of our western world, by a majority of the same, either to be a separate State from that of North Carolina, or to be citizens of the State of North Carolina.

"Signed and agreed, on behalf of each party, this day and year above written.

"EVAN SHELBY,
"JOHN SEVIER."

Sevier had now chained the winds, and all would be well if they did not slip from his grasp, rush violently together, and he be caught in the whirlwind.

CHAPTER VII.

Two years had now passed since Sevier assumed the reins of the Franklin government, and during the whole of that period the country under his control had experienced unbroken prosperity. Education had been fostered, law had been duly administered, and crime had been a thing almost unknown. Tradition and the records of Washington County—so far as they have been preserved—report not a single capital crime to have been committed in the district. Money had not been abundant, but the thirty thousand dollars of silver coined by Charles Robertson had been enough for ordinary exchanges, and, peltry being still receivable by the collectors, every man had a ready means of paying his taxes. These had been light—"one shilling the poll, and sixpence per hundred acres"—and the best of agricultural land was obtainable at "forty shillings per hundred; the first ten shillings in hand, and two years' credit for the other thirty shillings." Thus every man had within his reach a home and a competence; and, though a heavy war-cloud hung continually over the border, he could sit "under his own vine and fig-tree" without fear, seeing that Nolichucky Jack and his four thousand riflemen stood guard over his dwelling. So strong was this feeling of security that settlements had been extended on the lands south of the French Broad—acquired by the treaty between Sevier and the Cherokees—to within nine miles of the Indian towns on the Tellico. It was a singular spectacle, this, of a whole people living in scattered settlements, and beleaguered on three sides by savage foes, yet resting without a thought of danger, because of the moral power of one man, whose single name held harmless a swarm of warlike enemies. But this reign of peace and law and fraternal feeling was now to be for a time interrupted by the machinations of a few reckless and ambitious men, who, with no power or influence of their own, were rendered potent for evil by the "mother-State," which had never expended a dollar nor provided a soldier for the aid or protection of its western citizens.

For a time the two co-ordinate governments moved along, side by side, without jar or collision. The North Carolina sheriff lodged his prisoners in the Franklin jail on free straw and at free rations; the rival justices held court simultaneously at opposite ends of the little log school-houses, and officiated conjointly at the weddings of such young men and women as desired to hold together, whichsoever administration should fall to pieces; and thus it happened that many a man might be met in after-years who, with never but one wife, had yet been twice married. The lion and the lamb had, in truth, come to lie down together, though, unfortunately for the lamb, the little child whose office it is to muzzle the larger beast was absent on this occasion.

This state of things could not have continued for a day had not these people cherished a high respect for law and order, and a genuine regard for one another. As it was, it lasted fully forty days, and until the partisans of North Carolina saw that only through "much tribulation" could the old State recover her lost dominion, and—what was of more consequence to them—they achieve the power they so much coveted. The desire among the people for separation was well-nigh unanimous; if the present good feeling continued, it would become altogether so, and the Governor of North Carolina had distinctly said that unanimity would secure the wished-for independence of Franklin. Therefore, this harmony must be broken, the dregs of society stirred up to the surface, and discord introduced into a peaceful community, if Tipton and his boon companions did not wish to be reduced to political nonentity. A small stone cast into a placid pool will ruffle the waters to its farthermost extremity; so now a few spoken words set in commotion the entire country around Watauga. These words were: "By what authority did John Sevier and General Shelby make that anomalous compact? Can a man serve two masters? If not, then choose ye: 'If the Lord be God, follow him; if Baal, then follow him.'"

· The words spread, and thus was that modern invention, party politics, introduced among this primitive people. Soon at every cross-road gathering was heard discussion, and then wrangling, and then shouts for North Carolina and for Franklin. The partisans of the new State continued very largely in the majority, but their leader had enjoined upon them peace, forbearance, and brotherly kindness ; and, his Quaker policy being well understood, the factious minority were emboldened to acts of violence. Court-houses were again rifled, and peaceable meetings broken up by the disorderly adherents of Tipton, who in some cases resorted to "knock-down arguments." This was too much for the unregenerate manhood of such of Sevier's friends as had not pondered upon the thirty-ninth verse of the fifth chapter of St. Matthew's gospel. They returned blow for blow, and thus an animosity was engendered which, in some families, lasted till far into another century. No blood was shed in these encounters, because, as if by tacit consent, no deadly weapons were employed ; but a reign of violence was inaugurated which could not safely continue unchecked in any community.

Meanwhile, Evan Shelby was resting in patriarchal ease at his cattle-farm of King's Meadows, utterly ignorant of the unbrotherly dissension which was going on only forty or fifty miles to the south of him. At last word was brought him of this deplorable state of things by the North Carolina colonels—Tipton, Maxwell, and Hutchings—who had been the active agents in raising

13

this storm of disorder. The story lost nothing in their telling, and the old veteran listened aghast to the tale of riot and confusion. He was a cast-iron man, trained in a school of rigid discipline, and for forty years had been accustomed to the exercise of military authority. He saw that this disorder must be put down, or there was an end to all government. But how could it be put down, the discontent so general, and he with only a corporal's guard for an army? To this answered Tipton and the other colonels: "Call upon North Carolina for a thousand men. That force, backed by the moral power of law, will overawe all opposition to the old State. Besides, Sevier has announced that he will not resist North Carolina by force, and his followers will not fight if he refuses to lead them."

In accord with this suggestion, General Shelby wrote to Governor Caswell, saying, among other things: "The matter is truly alarming, and it is beyond a doubt with me that hostilities will in a short time commence. I therefore think it highly necessary that one thousand troops, at least, be sent, as that number might have a good effect; for, should we have that number under the sanction of government, there is no doubt with me they" (the disaffected) "would immediately give way."

With General Shelby at this time was Anthony Bledsoe, the right-hand man of Robertson, and one of the most influential men in the western country. He had been one of the one hundred who rushed to the rescue when, eleven years before, Sevier, with but forty men, had withstood the assault of the Cherokee king on the fort at Watauga; and he was now in Franklin to solicit Sevier's aid against an expected raid of the same Cherokees upon the settlements along the Cumberland. Sevier had promised him that, if the raid should be attempted, he would at once march a strong body of men into the Cherokee country, and chastise the savages into reason; and Bledsoe was naturally unwilling to see North Carolina array an armed force against so loyal a friend and true a patriot. By Shelby's permission he wrote the Governor, sending the letter by his messenger. He said: "Might I be permitted to request your Excellency's addressing these people, and advising them of the necessity and advantage of returning to their duty once more, and the danger and evil consequences of their persisting in the attempt of supporting an independence? I do assure your Excellency that it is my opinion your address on that occasion would have a very good effect on the principal people in the revolted party."

The Governor received these letters on May 19, 1787, at once laid them before his Council, and on the 21st he replied to General Shelby as follows: "I have stated the situation of your country to the Council, and laid your letter before them. . . . They think it would be very imprudent to add to the dissatisfaction of the people there by showing a wish to encourage the shedding of blood, as thereby a civil war would eventually be brought on, which ought at all times to be avoided, if possible; but more especially at the present, as we have great reason to apprehend a general Indian war. If the Northern and Southern tribes should unite with your Cherokee neighbors, you will stand in need, they think, of all your force, and therefore recommend unanimity among you, if it can by any means be effected, as you thereby will be much more able to defend yourselves than you possibly can be when divided, let alone the circumstance of cutting each other's throats. Besides these [considerations], it would be impracticable to raise an armed force here to be sent to your assistance at this time, if we were ever so much disposed thereto, for the following reasons: The people in general are now engaged in their farming business, and, if brought out, would very reluctantly march; there is no money in the treasury to defray the expenses of such as might be called out; nor, in fact, have we arms or ammunition."

This letter affords proof that, if Sevier, even single-handed, had then chosen to resist North Carolina by armed force, he would have been successful. There were those about him who well understood this weakness of North Carolina, and who urged him to put down the malcontents by a strong arm, feeling sure that the "mother-State" could offer no resistance. There were others who advised the same course, but who hoped North Carolina would resist, as in that case the entire West would rally around Sevier, with the result of securing the independence of the trans-Alleghany region and the opening of the Mississippi, not through a league with

Spain, but in defiance of that power, which they would speedily drive into the Gulf of Mexico. There can be no question that a large majority of the people of Franklin entertained at this time the one or the other of these views, and now urged Sevier to extinguish by force all resistance to his authority. The pressure upon him must have been great, but he stood firmly by his original resolution. "I will," he said in effect, "constrain no man to maintain the Franklin government. If the people support it, it will stand; if they do not support it, it will fall. Not in any case will I consent to establish it by shedding the blood of my neighbors or my countrymen."

But, though he refused to resort to force, Sevier again attempted to bring about a peaceable settlement with North Carolina. All his direct overtures had failed, and he now sought the intervention of Georgia, with whose Governor he had been in frequent correspondence in relation to the expected Indian uprising, and where he had many friends among the best citizens. Among these, the Hon. William Downs had just written him: "I have had the opinion of a number of the greatest politicians in our State respecting yours, who give it as their opinion that it will support itself without a doubt; and, from what I can understand, they would give every assistance in their power." Of this feeling Sevier now proceeded to avail himself by dispatching Major Elholm to the Governor to solicit his good offices in bringing about an adjustment of the difficulty with North Caro-

lina. He closes his letter to him with this paragraph :
"Permit us to inform you that it is not the sword that
can intimidate us. The rectitude of our cause, our local
situation, together with the spirit and enterprise of our
countrymen in such a cause, would inflame us with confidence and hopes of success. But when we call to mind
the great number of internal and external enemies to
American Independence, it makes us shudder at the very
idea of such an incurable evil, not knowing where the
disorder might lead, or what part of the body politic the
ulcer might at last infect."

Both the Governor and the Legislature of Georgia
took prompt measures to further Sevier's views ; but, before any result could be arrived at, a general revolution
occurred in the sentiment of the Franklin people, which,
considering the bitter feeling previously existing toward
North Carolina, seems altogether surprising. It was
brought about by a few kindly words from a man in
whom the Franklin people had confidence ; and it illustrates the fact that the "soft answer which turneth away
wrath" is far more potent with reasoning men than
swords and bayonets and brass artillery. These few
words were contained in a printed sheet, which, in compliance with Anthony Bledsoe's suggestion, Governor
Caswell addressed to the inhabitants of the western
counties. The document accomplished such important
results that its principal portions are here given :

The Governor addressed the people as "friends and
fellow-citizens," and then went on to say that a dis-

orderly state of affairs had been reported to him, in consequence of which "sundry good citizens have been induced to signify to Government their apprehension of being obliged to have recourse to arms. And notwithstanding the behavior of some of the refractory might justify such a measure, yet I am willing to hope that, upon reflection and due consideration of the consequences which must ensue in case of the shedding of blood among yourselves, a moment's thought must evince the necessity of mutual friendship and the ties of brotherly love being strongly cemented among you. You have, or shortly will have, if my information is well grounded, enemies to deal with which will require this cement to be more strong than ever; your whole force may become necessary to be exerted against the common enemy, as it is more than probable they may be assisted by the subjects of some foreign power—if not publicly, they will furnish arms and ammunition to the Indian tribes, to be made use of against you; and when your neighbors are so supported and assisted by the Northern and Southern Indians, if you should be so unhappy as to be divided among yourselves, what may you not then apprehend and dread? Let me entreat you to lay aside your party disputes. They have been as I conceive, and believe yet will be, if continued, of very great disadvantage to your public as well as private concerns. While these disputes last, Government will want that energy which is necessary to support her laws and civilize; in place of which, anarchy and confusion will be prevalent, and, of course, private interest will suffer.

"It certainly would be sound policy in you, for other reasons, to unite. The General Assembly has told you that, whenever your wealth and numbers so much increase as to make a separation necessary, they will be willing the same shall take place upon friendly and reciprocal terms. Is there an individual in your country who does not look forward in expectation of such a day arriving? If that is the case, must not every thinking man believe that this separation will be soonest and most effectually obtained by unanimity? Let that carry you to a quiet submission to the laws of North Carolina till your numbers will justify a general application; and then I have no doubt but the same may be obtained— nay, it is my opinion that it may be obtained at an earlier date than some imagine, if unanimity prevail among you. Although this is an official letter, you will readily see that it is dictated by a friendly and pacific mind. Don't neglect my advice on that account. . . .

"I will conclude by once more entreating you to consider the dreadful calamities and consequences of a civil war. Humanity demands this of me; your own good sense will point out the propriety of it; at least, let all animosities and disputes subside till the next Assembly; even let things remain as they are, without pursuing compulsory measures till then, and I flatter myself that honorable body will be disposed to do what is just and right, and what sound policy may dictate."

The friendly spirit seen in this manifesto was as oil poured upon troubled waters. It stilled the public excitement, and, their passions once allayed, men began to reflect coolly upon the situation. The State of North Carolina granted nothing and exacted everything, and its selfish rule had become intolerable. Many of its adherents were social nuisances, the natural enemies of law and order, and there could be no peace so long as they were in the ascendency. But was it wise to resort to one evil to suppress another, to resist law, that they might establish good order? The Governor had now distinctly said that unanimity and a little patient waiting would secure the desired separation; and was it not better to adopt this course than to incur the horrors of civil war? And, meanwhile, might they not put down the disorderly demagogues who were disturbing the peace, by going to the polls and electing to office men who would correctly represent the whole community? A large majority of the stanchest friends of the new government now came to this conclusion, and the consequence was that within sixty days the State of Franklin went quietly, and without a struggle, out of existence.

In adopting this course the western people would at first sight appear to have avoided one danger only to rush upon another, and the danger they most feared— exposure to the expected attack from the Creeks and Cherokees, with none to lead them but the incompetent officers set over them by North Carolina. But their de-

cision to loyally accept the rule of that State was made
with an important mental reservation. Their submission
was intended to extend merely to civil affairs. In military matters they should act for themselves, and choose
their own leaders. In this they deemed themselves justified by the law of self-preservation, and to this North
Carolina could certainly take no exception, if it should
be the means of defending the country against her own
and their enemies. No public announcement was made
of this; but when Evan Shelby came to enroll his brigade, to be in readiness for the expected savage onslaught, he discovered that not above five hundred men
out of a total of more than four thousand answered to
his summons. The rest would have no leader but Nolichucky Jack, for under no one else could they be assured
of victory. This appears the more striking, when it is
considered that Sevier was now merely a private citizen,
not only without legal authority, but actually proscribed,
because he had neglected to make overt submission to
North Carolina.

Nevertheless it was so, as was clearly shown late in
June of this year, when a report came that the Creeks
had made a raid into Georgia, killing no less than
twenty-five families. The attack was regarded as the
beginning of the threatened war, and Sevier called at
once for volunteers to be ready to march on the demand
of the Georgians. Every man was to arm and equip
himself, and they were to march some five hundred miles
through a trackless forest, and into the heart of the

Creek country; but at a single summons three thousand men reported themselves ready for duty to their respective brigadiers, Cocke and Kennedy.* No call came from the Georgia Governor, and the report proved to be unfounded; but the incident illustrated how completely Sevier held in hand nearly the entire military strength of the Territory. Unwilling to see another general, and he a private citizen, thus in command of his own department, Evan Shelby at once resigned—an unfortunate occurrence, inasmuch as it set over the North Carolina troops the same Joseph Martin who had concocted the treaty of Hopewell.

The country continued in hourly expectation of an outbreak of hostilities until the middle of August, when word came from Robertson that the long-meditated blow was to fall first upon the settlements along the Cumberland. It had been reported to him by the Chickasaws that at a grand council of the Creeks, held shortly before, it had been determined to fall upon and exterminate the Nashville settlers, and it was expected the Cherokee nation would join in the attack. Robertson was short of ammunition, and unprepared for an onslaught from such overpowering numbers. He had asked North Carolina for aid, but Governor Caswell had written that he was unable to give any; he had also applied to Kentucky, but feared he should get none from there

---

* Letter from General Kennedy to Governor Mathews, of Georgia, June 29, 1787.

in time. He knew that the Franklin government had been overthrown, and he was apprehensive that Sevier was in no condition to help him, nevertheless he wrote to him : "I beg of you to use your influence to relieve us. I think it might be done by fixing a station near the mouth of Elk, or by marching a body of men into the Cherokee country, or—in any manner you may judge beneficial. I candidly assure you there never was a time when I imagined we were in more danger."*

Only five days subsequent to the receipt of Robertson's letter, Sevier received one from Anthony Bledsoe, which stated that small parties of Creeks and Chickamaugas were already marauding through the Cumberland settlements, stealing horses, and killing the peaceable inhabitants, who were deserting their homes and fleeing to the forts for protection. The only way, he said, that peace could be assured to his distressed country was by distressing the Chickamaugas; and he reminded Sevier that, when he had last seen him, Sevier had proposed to send without delay an expedition against that perfidious tribe should they again attack the Cumberland settlers, of which he had requested Bledsoe to notify him.†

Sevier did not need this reminder to secure his prompt action. He at once called for six hundred vol-

---

* James Robertson to John Sevier, Nashville, August 1, 1787.
† Letter from A. Bledsoe to John Sevier, dated Sumner County, August 5, 1787.

unteers, two hundred of whom he dispatched, under
Captain Nathaniel Evans, to the immediate relief of
Robertson; the remainder, under competent officers, he
ordered to the mouth of Elk River, to build there a
fort, and intercept any parties of Chickamaugas who
might attempt to go upon the war-path. The timely
arrival of the troops under Evans, with the ammunition
they supplied, enabled Robertson to beat off the present
attack; and the sudden appearance of the other force in
the Indian country prevented any further irruptions of
the savages. The Chickamaugas regarded this force as
merely the advance of a larger one, which "'Chucky
Jack" would lead against them in case they or the
Creeks made any further hostile movement, and in fear
of this both nations suspended hostilities until a stronger
coalition should be effected.

By the compact between Sevier and Evan Shelby the
people were at liberty to pay taxes to either government
at their option. The result was that, as a general thing,
they paid them to neither, and consequently the treasury of Franklin was at this time empty. But money
was required for the fitting out of these expeditions, and
also to fully equip the force which was intended to be
marched into the Creek country; for, though every
backwoodsman had his own rifle and hunting-knife, all
were not provided with such an outfit as was required
upon protracted expeditions. Sevier had been a man
of large wealth for the times, and, ever since the first
settlement of the country, he had stood in the gap in
14

all similar emergencies, contributing liberally of his means to equip his men, and often having hundreds of them at free quarters upon his plantation. For all this he had never received any compensation from the government, and the consequence of his exceeding liberality was that he came out of the Revolution stripped of all his property, except his home, and the necessary force of negroes to work his plantation. But he had that "good name" which, even in commercial circles, is "better than great riches." He had now only to pledge this, to finish the equipment of his volunteer forces. This he did, wisely or unwisely, and the consequence was that, though he saved his friend Robertson, he put himself in the power of his inveterate enemy, John Tipton.

It was when he was thus arming troops without authority of law, and branded as a rebel by the Legislature of North Carolina, that Sevier received from the first military men of the time the highest honor which was in their power to bestow. Without solicitation on his part, he was elected a member of the Order of the Cincinnati, a society composed of the most distinguished officers of the Revolution, of which Washington was president-general to the close of his life, and to which none were admitted but men of high standing and unsullied record. Their estimate of Sevier will appear from the report of the committee which passed upon his nomination. "He had," they said, "a principal merit in the rapid and well-conducted volunteer expedition to attack Colonel Ferguson, at King's Mountain, and a great share in the honor of that day, which, it is well known, gave a favorable turn to our gloomy and distressed situation ; and an opportunity never yet appeared but what confessed him an ardent friend and real gentleman."

At this time, also, letters poured in upon him from many eminent men, advising him as to his course, and expressing the hope that he would be able to extricate himself and the western settlers from the difficulties by which they were surrounded. Among these, Benjamin Franklin wrote him frequently, but only one of his letters has escaped the ravages of our recent civil war. It is so characteristic, has so much of the "homely wisdom of Poor Richard," that such portions as bear upon the subject of this history are here copied. He said: "There are two things which humanity induces me to wish you may succeed in—the accommodating your misunderstanding with the government of North Carolina, and the avoiding an Indian war by preventing encroachments on their lands. Such encroachments are the more unjustifiable, as these people, in the fair way of purchase, usually give very good bargains ; and, in one year's war with them, you may suffer a loss of property, and be put to an expense, vastly exceeding in value what would have contented them in fairly buying the lands they can spare.

". . . If anything should occur to me that I think may be useful to you, you shall hear from me thereupon.

I conclude with repeating my wish that you may amicably settle your difference with North Carolina. The inconvenience to your people, attending so remote a seat of government, and the difficulty to that government in ruling well so remote a people, would, I think, be powerful inducements to it to accede to any fair and reasonable proposition it may receive from you if the cession act had not passed."

Dr. Franklin did not know the Cherokee Indians, nor the element then in control of the Legislature of North Carolina. Had he known them, he might have questioned the possibility of sustaining peaceable relations with the savages, or of effecting an amicable settlement with the scarcely more civilized "sand-hillers" over the mountains.

But, though submission was general in the district contiguous to North Carolina, the more westerly counties continued to hold a divided allegiance—two classes of officials acting peaceably side by side, and a majority of the people still regarding and addressing Sevier as Governor, though he appears to have no longer in any manner exercised the authority of that position. This divided allegiance did not meet the views of Mr. John Tipton, who now was the principal representative of North Carolina in the settlements. In Greene County particularly the people were obstinate in their adhesion to the new State, clinging even to its corpse after all vitality had left it, and Tipton essayed to restore the old order of things by resorting to his original expedient of capturing the records. He made the attempt in the latter part of August, and, but for the timely intervention of Sevier, the consequences would have been disastrous to himself. The incident is related in a letter to Major Elholm from General Cocke,* who was a resident of Greene County. The letter was as follows :

"Colonel Tipton appeared the other day with a party of about fifty men—of such as he could raise—under a pretense of redressing a quarrel that had arisen between our sheriff and the sheriff of North Carolina, though their principal view was to put themselves in possession of our records. This conduct produced a rapid report that they had made a prisoner of his Excellency, to carry him to North Carolina, which caused two hundred men to repair immediately to the house of Colonel Tipton before they became sensible of the mistake; and it was only through the influence of his Excellency that the opposite party did not fall a sacrifice to our Franks. During this time a body of about fifteen hundred veterans embodied themselves to rescue (as they thought) their Governor out of the hands of the North Carolinians, and bring him back to the mountains—an instance that proves our citizens to have too noble a spirit to yield to slavery, or to relish a national insult."

---

* "Columbian Magazine," for November, 1787.

This incident appears to have warned Tipton of the danger attending a continued resort to violent measures. The consequence was that he desisted from any further acts of open hostility, and resorted to secret craft to accomplish what he most desired—the overthrow of Sevier, and his own ascendency over the people, which last, he thought, could not be achieved so long as their beloved Nolichucky Jack was in the Territory. In this he reckoned without foundation, for the great majority were order-loving and law-abiding, and would, in no circumstances, have accepted Tipton as their leader. The masses—those whom Mr. Lincoln styled "the plain, common people" — are everywhere wonderfully clearsighted, and readily distinguish the unselfish patriot from the self-seeking, ambitious demagogue.

Therefore, though the war-cloud still hung black and ominous over all the border, there was peace now throughout the scattered settlements. Except in the most westerly districts, the people everywhere submitted to the rule of North Carolina, in hopes thereby to bring about the separation which Governor Caswell had proclaimed would no doubt soon result from unanimity among them. The great majority were as ardently desirous of independence as when they organized the State of Franklin; and, the North Carolina Legislature having come together in November, Sevier determined to make still another effort to effect an adjustment of the differences with the "mother-State." Heretofore he had appealed to her reason and her sense of right and expediency; now he decided to approach her on her most vulnerable side — the watchfully guarded State treasury. He commissioned Colonel Francis A. Ramsey, his late Secretary of State, to wait upon the Legislature, and propose, as an inducement to separation, the assumption by Franklin of the entire Continental debt of North Carolina, then amounting to between four and five million dollars. Colonel Ramsey was the father of the venerable historian of Tennessee, and the latter, even in extreme old age, was one of the most eloquent men I ever listened to. If eloquence be hereditary, Colonel Ramsey must have possessed remarkable powers of persuasion; but he failed to persuade these legislators. For months, however, they nibbled at the glittering bait, and there were times when the colonel thought it would be taken; but at last they told him that they had decided to stay, for the present, out of the Union, and, while they did so, they could not consent to the cession of any portion of their territory to the United States.

Meanwhile, Georgia had tired of the repeated outrages of the Creeks upon her western settlers, and its Governor had written Sevier: "The Assembly of this State are now fully persuaded that they never can have a secure and lasting peace with the Creek Indians till they are well chastised and made to feel severely the effects of war. They have passed a law for raising three thousand men for that purpose, and have em-

powered the Executive to call for fifteen hundred men
from Franklin, in addition to that number."

This letter was dated Augusta, November 12, 1787,
and was forwarded by a special messenger ; but he had a
horseback-ride of three hundred miles through the woods,
and did not reach Sevier till the 28th of that month.
Two hundred of Sevier's men were still away with
Robertson, and four hundred more were yet posted on
the Tennessee, at the mouth of Elk River, but without a
moment's delay he issued a circular calling for fifteen
hundred to go to the aid of Georgia.   In it he said : "I
think to take the field once more" ; and he offered his
men "the honor of assisting a very generous and friendly
sister State to conquer and chastise an insolent and barbarous savage nation."   He closed by saying : "I hope,
after seeing the great notice and respect shown us by the
State of Georgia, in her application for our assistance,
and the high confidence they place in our spirit and
bravery, that the people here will be animated with the
idea that, like a young officer who first enters the field,
they are competent, by their bravery and merit, to make
themselves known and respected among the nations of
the world. . . . We have not large cities and sea-ports,
which generally sink men into wealth and luxury, by
which means their offspring dwindle into effeminacy
and dissipation, yet I hope we shall always remain as
happy, free, and independent as any other people ; if
not, sure I am it will be our own fault, and we ought
never to be pitied."

The circular has a clear, metallic ring, like that of steel upon flint, and it struck fire from the hearts of the backwoods people. Within four days fifteen hundred men came together, armed and equipped, and ready for a march of four or five hundred miles into the mountains of Georgia. Such magic was there in the words of Nolichucky Jack, he merely a private citizen ; and, in fact, not so much as that, for at that very moment the Legislature of North Carolina had passed an "Act of Pardon and Oblivion" for all who had taken part in the Franklin revolt, but distinctly provided "that the benefit of this act shall not entitle John Sevier to the enjoyment of any office of profit, or honor, or trust, in the State of North Carolina, but that he be expressly debarred therefrom."

Thus did North Carolina thrust into outlawry the very man who, in the darkest hour of her history, had saved her from destruction !

Again, the men did not march on the Georgia summons, because that State decided to suspend warlike operations in consequence of the appointment of commissioners by Congress to conclude a treaty with the Creek Indians. Considerable time was consumed in the negotiation, and meanwhile Sevier's men returned to their homes, to there await his call should there be an outbreak of hostilities.

Soon tidings came from over the mountains of the outlawry of Sevier, and the failure of his final effort to bring about a separation of Franklin from North Caro-

lina. The news speedily reached the Cherokees, who now
concluded that they could make their long-intended raid
on the settlers south of the French Broad and Holston
without interference from Nolichucky Jack and his riflemen. Fear of him had held them inactive, while settlers
had been thrusting forward their cabins to the extreme
southern boundary of the lands ceded to Franklin. By
the treaty of Hopewell, the intruding settlers were
"liable to be punished by the Indians, as they might
think proper," and, having thus a legal right to rob and
murder at their discretion, the Cherokees now prepared
for an overwhelming onslaught upon these exposed settlements.

Tidings of these preparations were at once conveyed to Sevier, and without an hour's delay he mounted
his horse and set out for the frontier. He was on
the borders of Greene County, concerting measures to
repel the expected invasion, when word came to him
that his inveterate enemy, Tipton, had taken advantage of his absence to attach his property for the debt
he had contracted in fitting out the expedition for the
relief of Robertson. Either by buying up these claims,
or by inducing their holders to take summary action,
Tipton had secured a levy upon Sevier's negroes, and
removed them to his own house in waiting for their sale
under execution. Without his field-hands, Sevier would
be unable to work his plantation ; and thus, while denied
the common rights of citizenship, he was about to be deprived of the means of sustaining his family. Stung

by such implacable enmity, and indignant at so high-
handed an outrage, he listened to the fiery spirits about
him, and determined to return to his home and forcibly
recover his property.   About a hundred and fifty of his
men volunteered to accompany him, and with them he
set out at once for the house of Tipton, more than a
hundred miles distant.

Sevier always moved with great celerity, but on this
occasion the tidings of his approach preceded him.
News travels with amazing rapidity in sections destitute
of mail and telegraphic facilities ; but it is probable that
Tipton had placed spies with Sevier to give him timely
notice of his movements.   However this may have been,
he had sufficient warning of Sevier's approach to call to his
aid fifteen of his friends, and to dispatch a messenger to
Colonel Maxwell, asking him to come to his assistance
with the regiment of Sullivan County.   Tipton's house
was located on the bank of a small creek flowing into the
Watauga, about eight miles east of Jonesboro, and, like
most of the better class of backwoods dwellings of the
period, was substantially a fort, capable, when properly
manned, of resisting attack from greatly superior numbers.   A similar structure, defended by only the number of men who were now with Tipton, a few years
later, successfully resisted, in the vicinity of Nashville,
an assault from seven hundred savages.

It was a cold day, late in February, when Sevier with
his one hundred and fifty men, and a piece of small ord-
nance, arrived before this log fortification.   Seeing at a

glance that Tipton had prepared for his coming, he placed his men on some low ground out of the reach of Tipton's rifles, and sent in a summons for the surrender of his negroes, threatening to fire upon the building in case of refusal. To this Tipton returned answer, in the elegant phraseology to which he was accustomed, "Fire and be damned!" Cowardice was not one of Tipton's weaknesses. Major Elholm, who was with Sevier, now proposed to him to erect a movable battery with the small cannon, under cover of which the troops might safely advance and carry the place by assault. To this Sevier gave a prompt refusal, declaring that not a gun should be fired. But, meanwhile, some of his men, who had posted themselves upon a ledge of rocks in near vicinity to the house, observing a number of persons about to enter the place, did fire upon them, killing one and wounding another. To them Sevier at once sent orders to desist from firing, and to Elholm, who now renewed his application to storm the building, and offered to lead the assault, he gave a more emphatic refusal, saying that he had not come there to kill his countrymen.

Sevier now attempted to open negotiations with Tipton, but the latter refused all communication with him, feeling sure he could hold out until succor should come from Sullivan County, and doubtless anxious to lure Sevier on to an attack which would have placed him in the position of armed insurrection.

Thus things remained during the rest of the day, Elholm repeatedly urging the necessity of an assault before re-enforcements should arrive to Tipton, and Sevier as often refusing to imbrue his hands in the blood of his countrymen. He must have seen that only a prompt exertion of force could accomplish the object of his expedition, but he stood inactive and irresolute. On all other occasions he had been quick to resolve and rapid to execute, and his present indecision shows that he must now have been torn by conflicting emotions—his outraged feelings as a man struggling with his sense of duty as a patriot and a citizen. This struggle was seen in his demeanor, which was usually of a most winning suavity. He now for the only time in his life was reserved, austere, abstracted, and even morose, answering all who addressed him with a curt severity that was entirely contrary to his custom. Circumstances had forced him into a false position, and his loyal nature rebelled at the thought of thus appearing to be at the head of insurgents ready to engage in a fratricidal warfare. But his duty as a patriot overcame his pride as a soldier, his obligations as a citizen his outraged feelings as a man. With present outlawry and future ruin staring him in the face, he resolutely said, "Not a shot shall be fired." Dr. Ramsey truly says that in no other instance did he give "a livelier exhibition of the true moral sublime of patriotism."

The feelings of the commander seemed to infect the spirits of the men. They, too, had not come out to imbrue their hands in the blood of their friends and coun-

15

trymen. Some reckless spirits were among them, but
much the greater number had no relish for the turn
affairs had taken. The night was cold and dark, and
they gathered in silence about their camp-fires, or if they
spoke it was in suppressed voices. They had followed
Sevier on many a campaign, and always before, when the
sentries were posted for the night, they had collected in
joyous groups and passed the hours in merry laugh, and
song and jest, unrestrained by the presence of their commander, who nightly made the rounds from mess to
mess, joining in their hilarity, and addressing each one
as if he had been his intimate companion. It was thus
that Sevier made himself the comrade, friend, and idol
of his soldiery. They looked for his coming as soon as
he had seen for himself that the sentinels were in their
proper positions. But this night he did not come. He
sat by his camp-fire in moody silence, gazing abstractedly
into the blaze, and even the vivacity of his friend Elholm failed to arouse him. He gave no orders, suggested
no plan, made no preparation for either attack or defense. All through the night he sat there, absorbed in
his own reflections. What those reflections were it is not
difficult to conjecture, for we know the man and his self-
sacrificing history. Did he not think of his many years
of unselfish devotion to his country, of the wealth he
had poured out like water in its service, of the many
weary marches he had made, the battles he had fought,
the deadly perils he had encountered, to give it peace
and freedom ? And all for what ? To be driven forth

from the soil he had conquered, and the peace he had
won, a penniless man and an outlaw! And then, perhaps, other thoughts came to him. Might he not yet
retrieve his fortunes? This man Maxwell, who was coming against him, would in his hands be but as a child in
the grasp of a giant. Having crushed him, might he not
sound the border slogan, rally the whole West to his side,
and in one day dismember the country which had so un-
gratefully requited his unselfish fidelity? Doubtless he
might have done so; and perhaps such thoughts came
to him, for a tempting devil is ever at our ears in our
hours of extremest trial. But this devil did not know
John Sevier. He might be an outlaw; he might be a
penniless wanderer in the land he loved; and even worse
might yet befall him, for there was no limit to the
malice of his enemies; but through it all he would
stand erect and say, as Jackson said at a later period,
"I will die in the last ditch before I will see this
Union disunited!"

Possibly these were his thoughts while he sat there,
by his smoldering camp-fire, till far into the cold gray
of the winter morning. But suddenly, with the first
streak of dawn, there came an explosion of a regiment
of rifles; and, springing upon his horse, Sevier saw
his men fleeing like frightened deer in all directions.
Then he spurred his horse into the thick-falling snow,
and, for the first time in his life, turned his back upon
his enemies.

A heavy snow-storm had set in at midnight, and to

thaw out their chilled limbs Sevier's pickets had repaired
to the nearest camp-fires. This had allowed Maxwell to
approach unperceived, under cover of the snow and the
darkness; and, unwilling to fire upon Sevier's troops, he
had, when morning dawned, ordered his men to discharge their pieces in the air. Sevier's men aroused
thus suddenly from sleep, taken by surprise and unwilling to fight, fled without firing a rifle, which ended this
Quaker battle.

Said Parmenas Taylor, who was one of Maxwell's men,
and subsequently, with Sevier, one of Governor Blount's
Council: "We did not go there to fight. Neither party
intended to do that. Many on both sides were unarmed,
and some who had guns did not even load them. Most
of us went to prevent mischief, and did not intend to let
the neighbors kill one another. Our men shot into the
air, and Sevier's into the corners of the house. As to
the storm of snow keeping the men from taking a sure
aim, it is all a mistake. Both sides had the best marks-
men in the world, who had often killed a deer, and shot
it in the head, too, when a heavier snow was falling.
The men did not try to hit anybody. They could easily
have done so if they had been enemies."

As Sevier rode away from this bloodless field he
was met by messengers from the border, who had been
sent to apprise him that the Indians were moving upon
the western settlements in great numbers. "In a moment," says Dr. Ramsey, "Sevier was himself again,
elastic, brave, energetic, daring, and patriotic. At the

head of a body of mounted riflemen he was at once upon the frontier to guard and protect its most defenseless points." His property was lost, and he was an outlaw; but he had yet a life which he might give to his countrymen.

CHAPTER VIII.

SEVIER AS AN OUTLAW.

"EIGHT or nine thousand people had crossed the [Holston] river and settled upon lands now within the counties of Greene and Hawkins; others had crossed the French Broad; and yet others, not a few, were settled between Clinch River and Cumberland Mountain. All of these were there in violation of the treaty of Hopewell. And yet they were there by treaties with the Indians, and by connivance and sanction of the State. By Sevier's treaty at Dumplin Creek these lands were granted to the white people for settlement and homes. The State of North Carolina had issued grants to her citizens to settle upon these lands. Under authorities and sanctions of this character these thousands of hardy and industrious farmers had gone there; were busily preparing their homes there. They displaced no Indian, they seized no one's cabin or field; they found it an almost 'howling wilderness,' and they hastened to change the whole face of Nature by the opening of farms and building of houses. But now these Indians complain; they allege that these settlers have trespassed upon Indian territory, and demand their expulsion."* North Carolina listened to these complaints, and, coolly repudiating her own official grants and her promises of protection to the settlers, she ordered a portion of these people off the lands they had in good faith occupied. And by a most curious logic she drew a line between them. Those north of the French Broad and Holston she would keep faith with; those south of those rivers, holding their lands by precisely the same title, she would abandon to the savage mercy provided for them by the treaty of Hopewell.

As near as can be ascertained, the people south of those rivers now numbered about three thousand, of whom not far from seven hundred were men inured to frontier life, and expert with the rifle. The country they occupied is comprised within the present counties of Blount and Sevier, Tennessee—a most beautiful region, watered by numerous streams, and interspersed with wooded hills and grassy valleys, where vegetation grows in rank luxuriance, and the soil yields most abundant rewards to the husbandman. All over this delightful region could now be seen the clearings of the white settler. At first a solitary cabin went up in the midst of a dense forest; then other cabins gathered about it, and the whole were inclosed in stout palisades, capable of resisting any small body of Indians. Then far and near the great trees were felled or girdled, the ground was broken up and planted,

---

* Putnam's "History of Middle Tennessee," p. 344.

and soon the whole clearing blossomed with the harvest. These places were called "stations." Not a vestige of one of them at this time remains, but the site of many is indicated by the smiling hamlets and villages that now dot the whole of this enchanting region.

Within the walls of these log fortresses the settler made his home ; but of necessity he went forth into the open country to till his fields and care for his cattle. But he never did this without his trusty dog and his rifle beside him. Though nominally at peace with the whites, the Cherokees knew that these people were delivered over to their tender mercy by the treaty of Hopewell. They avoided any attack in considerable numbers, from fear of provoking a conflict with Nolichucky Jack and his rifle-men, but they hung about the stations in small bodies, and never omitted a safe opportunity to commit a theft or do a murder. Hence, when one settler plowed his field, another stood guard over him in some commanding position from which he could observe an approaching enemy. Often were they driven to seek refuge for days within the walls of the stations, and on one or two occasions the more exposed were forced to abandon their homes, and fall back for brief periods upon the older set-tlements ; but there never was any permanent ebb in the tide of population. The retreating settler soon returned, re-enforced by other immigrants, and gradually he ex-tended his clearings down those fertile valleys till he beheld the rising smoke of the Cherokee wigwams on the spot where, time out of mind, had been the great council-

house of the nation. And even here only force had
stayed the settler's steps, for he belonged to a race
which has no watchword but "Forward!" whose encroaching spirit is one of the instrumentalities by which
Providence is girdling the globe with law and civilization.

In consequence of these encroachments the whole of
that wide district had now become one broad battle-field,
where the white man had met the red, and both had
gone down to a swift destruction. The traveler to-day
will scarcely come upon a spring, or a ford, or a wooded
path among the hills in all that region, which had not,
at the time whereof I am writing, been the scene of
some savage atrocity, or some heroic exploit of the white
settler battling for his home and the lives of his wife and
children. So long as the State of Franklin existed, the
conflict had not been so very unequal; but that State
was now dissolved, and these settlers—abandoned by
North Carolina and outlawed by the General Government—were left a mere handful of seven hundred, to
cope with twelve thousand infuriated savages, who now,
in overpowering numbers, were said to be moving down
upon them. But the settlers were not altogether abandoned, for Nolichucky Jack was hastening to their
rescue. He rode almost alone, a proscribed and penniless man, bringing nothing but the sword he carried and
the horse he bestrode; but in his very name there was
terror to these savages. So the settlers took heart as
they gathered behind their log walls, and listened for the

rapid tread of horses' feet which should announce his coming.

Sevier rode almost alone, for his designs had become known, and—to employ his own words—his "enemies were making use of every diabolical plan in their power" to balk his intention of giving succor to the threatened settlers. As has been mentioned, Joseph Martin, the concocter of the treaty of Hopewell, had succeeded General Shelby in command of the troops acting under North Carolina. He relished no better than Shelby the holding of a divided command—the acting as general of a skeleton brigade, while a mere private citizen held control of the actual military strength of the district. It was not for this that he had plotted the overthrow of Sevier, nor would his ambition be satisfied with the mere shadow without the substance of authority. He had been appointed to Sevier's position, but he could not fill it without gaining over to himself Sevier's followers, and driving their beloved leader from the Territory. He was subtle, sleek, and sinuous; and burrowing underground seems to have been the mode to which he naturally resorted to attain his objects. And, indeed, in no other way could he accomplish his present purpose, for Sevier was so firmly rooted in the affections of the people that any open assault upon him would surely recoil upon himself, as it had upon Tipton, whose friends were fewer now than at the beginning.

Martin's plans were furthered by the fact that there had arisen "a new king in Egypt, who knew not

Joseph "—Governor Caswell having been succeeded by Samuel Johnston, a worthy man, but wholly ignorant of western affairs, and only anxious to end the discontent in the speediest manner possible. From him Martin secured permission to remove all the militia officers lately appointed by North Carolina, with the sole exception of the colonels—Tipton, Maxwell, and Hutchins— and to reinstate in their places Sevier's captains, or such others as might be elected by the men themselves. This was restoring the old organization, excepting only its head, Sevier; and Martin counted confidently upon thereby gaining full control of the military strength of the Territory. It was, in truth, a master-stroke of policy; but it failed for lack of co-operation on the part of Sevier's captains. Those scarred veterans looked askance at the brand-new parchments which greeted them by their old titles. They had probably never heard of the play of "Hamlet" with the part of Hamlet omitted; but they put the same thought into their vernacular language, and said to one another, "Who can ride the bay mare but our old commander?" Having said this, they tossed the parchments aside, and thought no more of General Martin.

This was the condition of affairs when, on the evening of March 15, 1788, Sevier rode into the little town of Greeneville, on his rapid way to the border. Though the county-seat of Greene County, and the recent capital of the State of Franklin, Greeneville was then not much of a town. It was merely a score of log-cabins, clustered around a court-house also of logs, and without windows, or other than a single opening, in which hung a plank door on stout wooden hinges. Opposite to this imposing temple of justice was a log-cabin somewhat larger than the rest, and having before it, perched upon a tall pole, a huge sign—a yellow sun rising over red mountains, and casting its mellow rays upon the name of "Thomas Hughes, Innkeeper." Beneath this sign, and beyond the rays of the aforesaid rising sun, was a smaller board, which announced to all comers, "Entertainment for Man and Beast," at the moderate rate of "one shilling for diet, fourpence for lodging, sixpence for pasture and stable, eightpence for corn per gallon, and sixpence per half-pint for liquor." There being eight shillings in a North Carolina dollar, it will be seen from these "tavern rates" that any one with but a moderate supply of legal currency could then take his ease in a backwoods inn for an almost indefinite period.

Before this rude hostelry Sevier now alighted with the one hundred and fifty men who had followed him from Washington County, and here he was met by a number of his captains, who apprised him of the new tactics which Martin had adopted, and of a report, everywhere industriously circulated, that any officer or man serving under him was to be expressly outlawed by North Carolina. Sevier heard the tidings without emotion, for he was a man who took Fortune's ordinary "buffets and rewards with equal thanks"; but instantly he decided to give all the aid he could to the designs of his enemy. As soon as his men had somewhat refreshed themselves he called them all about him, and dispatched nearly the whole troop in various directions to call his old captains together for a conference upon the ensuing Friday. The emergency, he said, was pressing; every man must turn out, for he conceived the settlements to be in imminent danger.

They came, to the number of about three hundred—nearly all of Sevier's late subalterns—clad in linsey leggins and buckskin hunting-shirts, and mounted on fleet horses, every man having his sword by his side, his pistols or hunting-knife in his belt, and his trusty rifle slung to the pommel of his saddle. They were all of stalwart frame, strong and wiry, with bronzed faces, resolute looks, and a certain cool and dauntless bearing, which showed them familiar with battle and with victory. Such another body of men it would have been hard to find even in those days, and west of the Alleghanies. One glance at them was enough to account for Sevier's amazing exploits in border warfare; and the greeting they gave him proclaimed that, though now a proscribed and branded man, Nolichucky Jack was still the uncrowned king of the backwoods.

It was early March, and the morning was cold, but no building in the little town would hold the concourse, so they gathered in the open air, under the great trees which grew about the court-house. Each man upon his horse, they ranged themselves in silence, several men deep, around Sevier and Cocke and Kennedy, till they

16

formed a circle, in the center of which were the three generals, and on the circumference the hundred and fifty men who had shared in the recent bloodless battle. Kennedy was the first to speak. Briefly he explained the situation—the service offered by Martin, the outlawry threatened by North Carolina. Each man was free to do as he pleased; but, as for him, he had fought and bled with his general, and, let North Carolina do her worst, he should not desert his old commander. The feeling in his words found a responsive chord in the breast of every man present, and at once there went up a shout from every throat that rang through the old woods and was echoed back from the distant mountains. Then the men crowded more closely around their leader, each one with some expression of unwavering devotion.

Sevier was a man of the keenest sensibilities, and he must have felt deeply these tokens of attachment. It is said that he sat his horse for some time in silence, and that when he spoke his speech had none of his usual rapid and energetic utterance. He thanked the men for their devotion to him, and he hoped the time would soon come when he might again lead them against the enemy; but now, it was better that they should part. They were in the presence of a peril greater than any which had yet confronted the settlements, and division in the country might be attended with disastrous consequences; therefore, it was his wish that each man should accept the commission offered him by North Carolina, rejoin and recruit his company, and make his men ready for the struggle that was impending. He himself, with the few who were with him, would go on to the frontier, where the French Broad settlers, without hope of other aid than his, were threatened with speedy extermination. However, he knew the border settlers, and he had confidence that with them he could beat off the Cherokees. If the Creeks should rise, Georgia would call for volunteers, and then, as he was a general in the army of that State, his old comrades might again serve under him without violating any law whatever. Now, it was best that every man should return to his home, and quietly submit to the rule of North Carolina. As for himself, his first duty was to stand by the French Broad settlers. That done, some way would be opened by which he might be of further service to his country. The sky over his head was now dark, but the sun was in the heavens, and it might rise unclouded on the morrow.

This is the substance of what Sevier said to his officers, when denied so much as a single volunteer by North Carolina. Even then he could have rallied the whole West to his support; but he preferred to send his men to their homes, and to go himself, almost alone, to meet, with but a handful, a whole nation of savages. If this is ambition, then is it ambition that would lift a more ordinary man than Sevier to the altitude of a hero.

The men knew their leader, and his tone and manner convinced them that he had taken an irrevocable resolution ; so they attempted neither remonstrance nor entreaty, but with moistened eyes and quivering lips they

gathered about him, each one to say some last word at
parting.   One after another he took them by the hand,
and then without another word he waved his sword to
his hundred and fifty men, and turned his horse's head
to the westward.   Among the troop that followed him
were some of his old officers who were resolved to share
his fortunes, whatever they might be.   Among these
were Kennedy, his recent brigadier; Cozby, one of his
oldest subalterns ; Hubbard, the slayer of Untoola ; and
Evans, who had left his company of two hundred with
Robertson, and hurried over the Cumberland Mountain
as soon as he heard of the misfortunes of his old commander.   Others were moving out from the circle in
front of the court-house when Sevier halted his horse,
and, turning to them, asked that none should attempt
to follow him.   Thereupon Kennedy requested that he
might go on to see if more force were not needed at the
front ; if it were not, he would at once return and
accept the colonel's commission already tendered him
by North Carolina.   This Kennedy said and did ; but
the others said nothing — Cozby and Evans, because
they had resolved not to leave their old leader ; Hubbard, because being with Sevier he would be the sooner
within rifle-shot of the Cherokees.*

Of this gathering Martin soon heard, and about it he
wrote to the Governor of North Carolina as follows :
He dates his letter " Long Island (near the junction of

---

* From conversations with Dr. Ramsey.

the North and South Forks of the Holston) 24th March, 1788." In it he says:

"SIR: The confusion of this country induces me to lay before your Excellency, by express, our present situation, which is truly alarming. I sent, on Saturday last, to Sevier and his party, requiring them to lay down their arms, and submit to the laws of North Carolina, but can get no answer, only from Colonel Joseph Hardin, which I forward; though I know that on Friday last they met in convention, to concert some plan. The bearer of my express to them informs me that he understood that Sevier had gone toward the French Broad since the 10th instant; that Colonel Kennedy, with several others, had gone the same way to carry on an expedition against the Cherokee Indians, which, I am well assured, wish to be at peace—except the Chickamauga party, which could be easily driven out of that country if your Excellency should recommend it. I am somewhat doubtful that Sevier and his party are embodying, under the color of an Indian expedition, to amuse us, and that their real object is to make an attack on the citizens of this State; to prevent which, I have ordered the different colonels to have their men in good order, until I can hear from your Excellency; at which time, I hope, you will give me directions in what manner to proceed in this uncommon and critical situation, for which I shall wait till the return of the express before I shall take any decisive steps.

"Should the Franks still persist to oppose the laws
of this State, would it not be well to order General
McDowell to give some assistance—as a few men from
there will convince them that North Carolina is determined to protect her citizens?"

Three days only prior to dispatching this letter to
Governor Johnston, this same Martin wrote to General
Kennedy as follows:

"I am greatly distressed and alarmed at the late proceedings of our countrymen and friends, and must beg
your friendly interposition, in order to bring about a
reconciliation, which, you well know, was my object in
accepting the brigadier's commission. I am, perhaps, as
little afraid of stepping forth in the field of action as any
other man; but I would be sorry to imbrue my hands in
the blood of my countrymen and friends, and will take
every method in my power to prevent anything of that
nature. In our present situation, nothing will do but a
submission to the laws of North Carolina, which I most
earnestly recommend to the people. You well know this
is the only way to bring about a separation, and also a
reconciliation for our worthy friend [Sevier], whose
situation at this time is very disagreeable. I most
sensibly feel for him, and will go very great lengths
to serve him. Pray see him often, and give him all the
comfort you can.

"I am told that a certain officer [Tipton] says that

if I issue an order for a reconciliation, that it shall not be obeyed; but I shall let that gentleman know I am not to be trifled with. Pray write me all what the people will do, and whether you will accept your commission, which I hope you will. Have the militia immediately officered and prepared for action, as I expect a general Indian war shortly. Please give my best respects to the people in general. Tell them my object is reconciliation, not war."

Hypocrisy is said to be "the homage that vice pays to virtue." Of this character was the tribute which this man paid to Sevier. A comparison of the two letters is enough to show his deep duplicity, for in every particular one letter contradicts the other. As subsequent events show, Martin's sole motive in writing to Kennedy was to detach him from Sevier; his aim in addressing the Governor was to prepare that official's mind for proceeding against the Franklin leader on a charge of high treason; hence Martin's insinuation that Sevier was levying troops to attack the citizens—a charge which he must have known to be outrageously false.

But, ignorant of these designs of his enemies, Sevier rode rapidly on to Houston's Station. Every step of his way was an ovation, and, despite his every effort to prevent it, before he had crossed the French Broad his troop had been augmented by about a hundred of his old soldiers, who, whether he would or not, insisted upon marching with him against the enemy. But when he

had once forded that river, the people went wild with
excitement. They flocked about him wherever he went,
strong men weeping, anxious women clasping him in
their arms, and little children clinging to his knees—for
had he not come to deliver them from a great danger?
Said an old man of ninety-seven to me in 1880 : " He
was a great man, was 'Chucky Jack. I remember him
right well, sir. I was a boy of five years when he came
across the French Broad to fight the Indians. We all
went out to greet him. He shook hands with dad, and
gave him some orders, for dad had fit under him ; then
he bent over his saddle and kissed mother, and asked dad
to lift me up that he might kiss me, too. Dad put me
up on the saddle, and 'Chucky Jack took me in his arms,
patted me on the head, and said that I should soon grow
up to be as brave a man as my father. Ah ! sir, I shall
never forget that." When time had razed about everything else from the old man's brain, and he could no
longer recognize even his own children, he vividly remembered 'Chucky Jack, and his taking him up in his
arms and speaking kind words to him !

The Cherokees had not yet appeared in the settlements, but the traders had come in, reporting that the
whole nation was about to go upon the war-path. The
Indians had heard of the overthrow of Sevier, and
counted upon an easy conquest of the French Broad settlements. That effected, they proposed to move forward and drive every settler beyond the Big Pigeon—
the eastern limit of their hunting-grounds, as defined

by the treaty of Hopewell. On arriving at the settlements, it was probable they would break into small parties, and attack simultaneously every one of the scattered stations. Sevier took his measures accordingly. The weaker stations he ordered to be abandoned, and the people to gather together in the stronger ones. The defenses of these were strengthened, and garrisons detailed for them, no man of which was to leave his post except at the call of the commander. He, with a select body of about four hundred men, well mounted, was to stand ready to meet any attack in force, or to invade the Indian country, as circumstances might dictate. In all previous conflicts, invasion had proved the most effective mode of driving back the enemy. His own wigwam threatened, the Cherokee would leave the settler in peace, and hasten to the defense of his wife and children. The success of such movements depended upon boldness and celerity, but those were the characteristics of Sevier's warfare. His heaviest blows were always struck in the heart of the enemy's country, and often when he was encompassed by twenty times his own numbers.

His preparations were now speedily made, and soon the whole region south of the French Broad was a fortified camp, in which each man had his post, and every one his allotted duty. Boys of fifteen were enrolled, and even women took to molding bullets and practicing with the rifle. But they were of the "home-guard," intended to act only in repulsing some determined assault upon the stations. Thus they stood to their arms, the whole of the scattered settlements; but nearly two months rolled away before they had any hostile tidings from the Cherokees. The Indians had probably heard of Sevier's presence among the settlers, and had deferred the intended attack till they could make it in irresistible numbers.

Meanwhile, the commissioners appointed by Congress, by an act of October 26, 1787, to treat with the Creeks, had not yet met those Indians. The Creeks continued to be troublesome, and Georgia was fast embodying troops to march into their country, exterminate the "perfidious nation," or to make peace with them on no "other terms than a total surrender of their country and themselves." This the Governor communicated to Sevier in a letter dated February 19, 1788, but which Sevier did not receive till early in April. Sevier's answer is here given, because it shows that at this time he had become fully apprised of the machinations of his enemies. It was as follows:

"FRANKLIN, *April* 10, 1788.

"SIR: Yours of the 19th of February I had the honor to receive. In our present confused condition of affairs, I am not able to reply with that accuracy and satisfaction to your Excellency I could wish. Our country is, at this time, almost in a state of anarchy, occasioned, as we suggest, by the North Carolinians stimulating a party to act in a hostile manner against us. . . . It is with great pleasure I inform you that a great num-

ber of our people discover a ready disposition to aid your
State against your savage enemies ; and, let matters occur as they may, if I am spared, I purpose joining your
army with a considerable number of volunteers, to act in
concert with you against the Creeks, though many of our
enemies are making use of every diabolical plan in their
power in order to destroy our laudable intention.

"I beg your Excellency will be so obliging as to advise us from time to time of your intended operations ;
and, should your campaign be procrastinated until the
fall season, I am of opinion you will get a much greater
number of men from this country."

The first tidings from the Cherokees was an atrocious
deed, at which the blood curdles. A settler named Kirk
had built his cabin on the south side of Little River,
about twelve miles from the present site of Knoxville.
It was surrounded by the usual stockade, but was far too
weak to resist attack from any considerable body of Indians. Kirk had been warned to repair to some one of
the larger stations, but he considered himself in no danger, being on good terms with the Indians, and having
always treated them with extreme kindness and hospitality ; so he continued to occupy his exposed position,
with his mother, his wife, and nine children, all under
fifteen years of age. His eldest son, a lad of sixteen, was
away with Sevier at Hunter's Station.

One morning in early May, Kirk had occasion to visit
a neighbor a few miles distant, and in his absence there

came to his cabin an Indian named Slim Tom, with
whom the family was well acquainted. He asked for
food ; it was given him, and he went away with many
expressions of gratitude. This gratitude he showed by
returning in about half an hour with fifty painted savages. I need not detail what followed. Not one was
spared—the aged grandmother, nor the young babe at
the breast. All were remorselessly butchered ; and when
Kirk returned, a few hours later, he beheld them—all
who bore his name except the stripling I have mentioned
—stretched, bloody and disfigured, on the grass in the
door-yard of his dwelling.

The mingled grief, and horror, and rage of this
man—thus at one blow bereft of mother, and wife, and
children—can only be conceived of by the imagination.
Almost crazed by the calamity, he left his dead unburied
on the ground, and with the speed of a deer rushed for
help to Sevier at Hunter's Station. Sevier had heard
such tales before, but this was one of peculiar atrocity.
Instantly he sent out mounted scouts to ascertain if this
was an isolated raid or an organized attack by a party
belonging to a larger body, which had separated, and
spread itself among the scattered settlements. At night
the scouts returned, reporting no other trace of Indians
except the trail of the murderers, which they had followed to the Little Tennessee, where it still went southward.

Gathering his men together to the number of about
four hundred, Sevier set out on the following morning

for the heart of the Indian country; and with him went young Kirk, and, as second in command, the Major Hubbard who was known as "the Indian-slayer." He followed the trail of the murderers, and so rapid was his march that early on the ensuing day he was fifty miles away, on the banks of the Hiwassee. Here he came upon a large town, filled with warriors, among whom the murderers of the Kirk family had taken refuge. Without a moment's delay, Sevier rode into this town, and then began the work of retribution. Panic-stricken, the Indians soon fled, but numbers were shot down in the street of the town, and as they were attempting to escape by the river. Before noon every hut and every wigwam in the place was a mass of smoking cinders.

Then Sevier turned his face toward the Little Tennessee and Tellico, where were the homes of Old Tassel, John Watts, and twelve hundred Ottari warriors. The towns were well-nigh deserted, but such men as were in them were either shot down or driven back to the mountains; then the torch was applied to half a dozen villages, and soon all that was left of them were so many heaps of smoldering ruin. The small number of men he encountered satisfied Sevier that the bulk of the Ottari were away upon a raid against the settlements; and leaving Hubbard and about two hundred men to complete the destruction he had begun, he hastened back with the remainder of his force to Hunter's Station.

Hubbard was encamped on the south side of the Little Tennessee, and on the northern bank, near a

17

small stream still called Abraham's Creek, lived an
old Indian named Abraham, who was known far and
near as the friend of the white settlers. Before hostilities began he had said that, if his nation went to war, he
should remain at home, and not lift a hand against his
white brothers. Sevier was no sooner away than Hubbard sent a messenger to this friendly Indian, inviting
him to cross the river to his camp. Abraham came with
his son, and then Hubbard asked them to go to Old
Tassel, and invite him to come there to a talk, for the
whites desired to be at peace with the Cherokees. This
they did ; and soon the Cherokee king appeared on the
opposite bank of the river with five of his principal chieftains—probably all of the " head-men " who were not
away on the war-path. On seeing them, Hubbard raised
a white flag, and invited them over to his encampment.

The Old Tassel knew Hubbard, and it is doubtful if
he would have trusted him had he not supposed that
Sevier was with the soldiery. It was generally known
that Sevier had been leading the troops, and this ac-
counted for the general panic which had everywhere
been seen among the Cherokees. They feared the
Franklin leader, but they trusted him implicitly. Old
Tassel was anxious for peace, and, unsuspicious of treachery, he now crossed the river with his chieftains. He
was met in a friendly manner by Hubbard, who told him
that Sevier was away, but would soon return, and meanwhile he and the chieftains had better wait for him in

an Indian cabin, which stood near the bank of the river.

The chieftains and the friendly Abraham had no sooner entered this cabin than a number of armed settlers noiselessly surrounded the building, so that escape from it became impossible. Then Hubbard and young Kirk entered the cabin, the latter with a naked tomahawk in his hand—the same savage weapon which had slaughtered his mother, his brothers and sisters, and his aged grandmother. Hubbard folded his arms and looked at the Indians, in his glance the vengeful hate which had come to be the ruling element in his nature. But the lad did not wait for this signal. Instantly raising the tomahawk, he buried it in the brain of the nearest Indian, as he sat on the ground at one extremity of the half circle in which they had formed themselves. The others, seeing from this the fate which awaited them, cast their eyes upon the ground, and, without a word, bowed their heads to the stroke which had slaughtered their comrade. Soon their bodies were dragged from the hut and thrown unburied upon a pile of *débris* on the bank of the river. Thus ingloriously perished the peace-loving Rayetayah—known among the whites as Old Tassel—an able man, and by far the best king who within historic times had ruled over the Cherokees.

Words can not describe the indignation and horror of Sevier when, returning on the following day, he learned that this dastardly deed had been committed. Bitterly he upbraided Hubbard and young Kirk, and the settlers

who had abetted the atrocity. The answer of Hubbard
and the others is not recorded ; but it is said that young
Kirk told Sevier that, had he suffered at the murderous
hands of the Indians as he had suffered, he would have
done as he had done. Sevier was merely a volunteer
leader, with only such power as was given him by the
settlers. Almost unanimously they approved of Kirk's
deed as an act of retributive justice, and therefore Sevier
was powerless to punish it.

There were not wanting enemies of Sevier who
charged him with complicity in this crime, and with
being conveniently absent to escape its responsibility ;
but this was indignantly denied by Hubbard, who assumed the entire odium of the deed, and boasted that he
would do the like again had one of his neighbors a like
provocation. Writing on this subject, the historian Haywood says : "Sevier never acted with cruelty before or
since ; he often commanded ; he was never accused of
inhumanity : he could not have given his consent on this
occasion. Considering existing circumstances, he could
not maintain as much authority now as at other times ;
he was proscribed and driven from his home. . . . They
[the settlers] consulted only the exasperated feelings of
the moment, and had never been instructed in the rules
of refined warfare."

This ill-advised and atrocious crime would naturally
inflame the passions of the Cherokees to the highest
pitch of frenzy. The bulk of the nation felt deeply
wronged by the continued encroachments of the settlers ;

but this, with one or two impatient outbreaks, they had
borne for six years, restrained by the pacific counsels of
Old Tassel, and by a fear of Nolichucky Jack and his
four thousand riflemen. But now the blood of their
leading chieftains had been most wickedly shed, and
blood for blood was the cardinal doctrine of their religion
—one of whose chief tenets was that the warrior who
lost his life in avenging the slaughter of a kinsman was
at once translated to the happy hunting-grounds, there
to be a mighty chief forever. The head chieftain of the
tribe was regarded as not merely the kinsman but the
father of the whole people. The lifting of a hand against
him was instant death to the most redoubtable warrior ;
how much worse was his treacherous murder by a hated
enemy ! The killing of Old Tassel was, therefore, a personal wrong to every Cherokee, and the avenging of it a
religious duty, which, if he failed to perform, the celes-
tial hunting-ground would be closed against him forever.
Hence, this one deed had created a nation of fanatics,
who would rush into battle regardless of death, and intent only on the slaughter of the settlers. Moreover, the
Cherokees would be sure to be secretly re-enforced by the
Creeks, and abundantly supplied with arms and ammunition by the Spaniards, who now were intensely exasperated against the settlers because of Robertson's decided
rejection of their overtures for an alliance. Hard beset
as he was, the intrepid pioneer had refused their proposals, disdainfully saying : "The Spaniards are devils ;
and the worst devil among them is the half-Spaniard,

half-Frenchman, half-Scotchman, and altogether Creek scoundrel—McGillivray!"

Thus had the unwise killing of Old Tassel greatly increased the difficulty of the task which Sevier had undertaken. Never before, it seems to me, were the odds so largely against him; not when, with but forty men, he repulsed Old Oconostota, nor when, with only nine hundred and fifty, he scaled and carried the rugged escarpment of King's Mountain: For active operations he had in reality but about two hundred and fifty men—the veterans who had voluntarily followed him from the older counties. The seven hundred others were settlers, who, though zealous, brave, and ready to fight to the death, were an unstable force—with him to-day but away to-morrow—drawn off by the first rumor of danger to the station which held their wives and children. Never, at any one time, was Sevier at the head of more than four hundred.

But, surrounded by such disheartening circumstances, never once did Sevier's courage fail him, never once did he call one of his old comrades to his aid, or ask for help from the older counties. His genius seemed to rise with the occasion, and a careful study of his life fails to exhibit him ever so truly great as when, a proscribed and ruined man, he forgot his own interests, and, without hope of pay or fame or other reward, he threw himself, almost alone, a forlorn hope between those outlawed settlers and their certain destruction. He seems to have regarded his self-imposed and herculean task

simply as a duty ; and he went about it with cheerful deliberation, adjusting his means to his ends with a sort of
mathematical precision which made success a foregone
conclusion.   This exact forecasting of results, this
ability to achieve great ends with small means, were
the most characteristic traits of Sevier's military
genius.   They enabled him, with never more than a
thousand men, to do a great work in American
history.

Now for five long months Sevier was every day in the
saddle—sometimes with forty men, sometimes with four
hundred—striking blow after blow, and with every blow
totally discomfiting the enemy.   Recorded in detail, his
exploits in this campaign would fill a volume.   I can recount only a few—just enough to show the character of
the conflict.

After seeing that the bodies of Old Tassel and his
chieftains had received decent burial, Sevier led his
troop rapidly back to Hunter's Station, for he knew that,
as soon as the Cherokees had made their first wail over
the dead, the whole nation would swarm upon the settlements.   His first step was to dispatch messengers to the
various stations, warning them to be on their guard, to
observe strict discipline, and on no account to venture
out either singly or in small parties without the utmost
caution.   If threatened with attack, they were to apprise
him at once by swift messengers, and to this end he
should keep them advised of his movements.   It had
been well had his instructions been observed ; but with

most men familiarity with danger breeds a contempt of it, and it was so with these settlers.

It was not long before all of the scattered stations were attacked almost simultaneously; and then Sevier became well-nigh ubiquitous, hastening from one to another, and from all driving off the savages before they had done any material damage. Then came a lull in the savage operations. It began to be thought that the Indians had withdrawn into their own country, and a party of twenty-one settlers ventured across the Little Tennessee, on a scouting expedition. Incautiously they entered an open field, when they were suddenly surrounded by a large body of savages. Sixteen of the settlers were shot on the spot, one was wounded and taken prisoner, and the remaining four were chased to the gates of the fort on the present site of Knoxville. Then the Indians turned back to make an assault on Houston Station.

Five families were housed at this fort—all told, perhaps forty persons, only ten of whom could handle a rifle. With the first alarm, one of the riflemen was sent off to Sevier, while the others essayed to defend the place till his arrival. The Indians quickly surrounded them, and soon it rained bullets on the little inclosure. One of the garrison incautiously exposed himself for a moment, and in that moment an Indian ball pierced his brain, and sent him to the great accounting. But the remaining eight fought on, the men firing and the women loading the rifles and molding the bullets. Their fire was rapid, and their aim certain, and many a savage fell never to rise again ; but the Indians fought with a desperation never before shown by the Cherokees. At length the filling between the logs was shot away, and every now and then a ball came into the building, and in dangerous proximity to the occupants. A young woman, subsequently the wife of Senior S. Doak, D. D., was kneeling by the fire, molding bullets, when an Indian ball passed over her head, and, bounding back from the wall, fell at her feet. It was flattened by the blow, and catching it up she molded it anew, and, handing it to the nearest rifleman, said : "Here is a ball run out of Indian lead ; send it back to them as quickly as possible. It is their own ; let them have it in welcome !" The conflict lasted for nearly an hour, when, discouraged with their loss of life, the Indians suddenly drew off from the station.

Sevier was twenty-five miles away, but, setting out at once, he met the Indians on their retreat. They numbered over a hundred, and only a few men were with him ; but they no sooner sounded his well-known yell than the savages broke and scattered in all directions. Sevier determined on pursuit, for he had meanwhile heard of the massacre at the Little Tennessee, and such deeds he always punished by a speedy invasion. Going on to the station, he sent out messengers to call in his men, and on the following day, with Captain Evans and about two hundred men, he invaded the Indian country, laying waste all in his pathway. At Chilhowee he met a

large force of savages, whom he at once attacked and
routed, killing thirteen outright, who were left on the
ground, while a larger number of wounded were borne
away by the Indians.   Then he returned again to the
protection of the settlements.

For more than a month the fight was around every
station, and everywhere at the critical time appeared
Sevier with his little band of riflemen.   Day and night
he was in motion, and it is said that now for one whole
week he never for one hour was out of his saddle.
Few lives were lost among the settlers, for they had
learned caution ; but the bones of many a Cherokee were
left to bleach in the summer's sun far away from the
resting-places of his ancestors.   The upper hunting-
grounds are pleasant in the dreams of the untutored
savage ; but the instinct of life is strong in him, and
'Chucky Jack the Cherokees had long regarded as under
the special protection of the Invisible Powers.   It was
they who turned aside the bullets which were aimed at
him, and fighting with him was therefore merely a struggle with destiny.   The contest was hopeless ; so at last,
beaten and crest-fallen, John Watts, Double-Head, and
the Bloody Fellow drew off their dispirited followers,
and led them back to their mountain fastnesses.

They had no sooner gone than Sevier resolved upon
another invasion of their country.   The Cherokees must
be made to feel the full bitterness of the war they had
brought upon the settlers ; and, taking with him only
Cozby and Evans, and a hundred and forty men, he

plunged at once into the heart of the Cherokee nation. It seems foolhardy in the extreme, this onslaught of but a handful upon three thousand infuriated savages; but Sevier knew his soldiers, and they knew him, and every one of them believed in his invincibility. It was just such apparently desperate enterprises that had given the Cherokees the superstitious belief that Sevier was under supernatural protection. Sevier knew this, and counted upon it as an auxiliary more potent than a thousand rifles.

Crossing the Little Tennessee under the cover of night, Sevier made a rapid march to the tall Unakas, and, scaling them, fell with fire and sword upon the Valley towns, where dwelt fully one third of the Cherokee nation. He spread havoc and death through all that region, shooting down every man he met, and taking none prisoners. Everywhere his route was marked by smoking villages; and everywhere, without making so much as a single stand, the Indians fled before him. Then, the work of destruction finished, he turned his face homeward.

He had now been ten days in the Indian country, and he knew that the whole nation would rise in his rear and attempt to intercept his march to the settlements. Destiny might be on his side, but here, the Cherokees saw, was a chance to take destiny at a disadvantage, amid rugged defiles and mountain-passes, where ten men might bar the way of a hundred. John Watts was a half-breed, and less superstitious than his people. The

eagle of the pale-faces was in a trap, and, if he could but
capture or destroy him, it was certain, now that Old Tas-
sell was dead, that he—John Watts, at the age of thirty-
five—would become the *archimagus* of the nation.   It
was the highest object that could be presented to Cherokee ambition; so Watts called in his warriors to the
number of eight hundred, and lay in wait for Sevier at
the point where he would attempt to recross the Unakas.
But Sevier had counted on this contingency, and he
moved with extreme caution as he approached the foot
of the mountains.

The usual route was by a narrow pass along the bank
of the Little Tennessee, where it breaks through the lofty
range amid scenery that is grand beyond description.
The river here flows over a rocky channel, lined with
precipitous cliffs, under which the path winds for a
fourth of a mile, only wide enough for a single horseman.   Here Watts had posted his men, concealed among
the rocks, three hundred on one side of the river and
two hundred on the other, while another force of two
hundred lay in wait at the outlet of the defile.   Hemmed
in on one hand by the tall cliffs, on the other by the deep
and rapid river, the moment the white men entered the
pass they would be a broad target for the Indian rifles;
and, if any ran the gantlet in safety, they would be
mown down by the two hundred who were lying in ambush at the outlet beyond.   Thus destruction to all
would have been certain; not a man who entered that
narrow pass would have lived to tell the story.   The

route was the one Sevier would naturally have taken ; but, to make sure of his falling into the trap, Watts placed another hundred men some distance in advance of the pass, with orders to fall back on Sevier's approach, and thus lure him on to destruction. Then, sure of his prey, Watts waited the approach of Sevier, not dreaming that he would attempt to climb the steep and rugged mountain on horseback.

But the cunning of Watts overreached itself, and served merely to warn Sevier of his danger. It is probable that he would not have essayed the perilous passage under any circumstances, for he was as cautious as he was bold ; but, experienced as he was in Indian tactics, this decoy party plainly disclosed to him the ambuscade. Paying no sort of attention to the retreating Indians, and striking at once for the foot of the mountain, Sevier led his men up its precipitous side, over slippery rocks and fallen trees, and through tangled undergrowth, where never before horseman had traveled. They moved rapidly, but often had to dismount to cut their way or to help their horses up some steep acclivity ; and it was between sunset and dark before they stood upon the summit of the mountain. Here they halted for a while to rest their jaded beasts ; but it was not long before they began the equally toilsome descent of the northern slope. Evans was one of the most trusted of Sevier's captains, and he was placed in the rear, that being the position requiring the greatest vigilance. Now, when Evans had gone about two hundred yards down the mountain, one of his

18

men requested permission to return for some small article he had left behind at the halting-place on the summit. At the summit the man heard the forward glide of a large body moving through the underbrush, and, hastening to Sevier, apprised him of the danger. At once every rifleman was ordered to dismount and unsling his rifle, in readiness for immediate action.

Thus they went down the mountain, in momentary expectation of attack, leading their horses, and picking their way among rocks and precipices, with no light but that of the dying moon struggling through flying clouds and through the thick, overhanging branches of the forest. At their every step they heard the steady glide of the eight hundred savages; but, unmolested, they at last reached the foot of the mountain. Here the country was still broken by ravines and encumbered with rocks and matted undergrowth. It was no fit field for a battle; therefore every man was ordered to mount, and they sped away to an open place about ten miles distant, on the plains of Tellico. Here the riflemen went into camp, and, a double force of sentinels being placed to guard against surprise, they cooked their suppers, and then, overpowered with fatigue, sank into such sleep as is apt to follow a day of toilsome marching. But no sleep came to Sevier. Soon the sentries reported that the Indians were cautiously encircling the encampment; but he let his men sleep on, while he, with only Cozby and Evans, walked the picket-rounds all the night, intent upon every sound that came from the near-by forest. He

expected an attack just before day, when men sleep the
most soundly ; but the morning came without any alarm
from the savages.   They were eight hundred to his one
hundred and forty ; but their hearts failed them.   John
Watts could not inspirit them to an attack, and soon Sevier led his force unmolested back to the settlements,
with not a man of it so much as wounded.

Chagrined at this second escape of the great eagle of
the pale-faces, John Watts now made a determined effort
to arouse the Cherokees for another descent upon the
settlements.   Should a great nation, he said, be beaten
back by a handful of white men ?   What was 'Chucky
Jack more than other men that the bullets should dodge
him ?   North Carolina had outlawed him ;   the Great
Council of the pale-faces was against him ; and should
he — one outlawed man — make women of the entire
Cherokee people ?   No ! let the whole nation rise, and
drive these white men beyond the Big Pigeon ;   and let
them not rest, day or night, till they had taken vengeance for the murder of Old Tassel.

And the whole nation rose, and fell again in overwhelming numbers upon the French Broad settlements.
Again, and for three long months, the whole region was
a battle-field, and again was Sevier everywhere perform-
ing prodigies of valor.   From station to station he rode
by night and by day, and everywhere he rode there were
battle and victory.   His exploits during this period can
be likened only to those of some knight-errant of the
middle ages ; but neither in history nor in fiction do I

know of anything that equals this marvelous campaign
of the border hero ! The fame of it crossed the rivers,
and awoke a thrill of pride among the old soldiers, who
adored him ; and it even swept over the mountains,
and became subject of comment by the two journals
which then shed a dim political light upon benighted
North Carolina. One of these,* published at Raleigh,
had the following account of one of his exploits,
and, as it is characteristic of them all, it is here
copied :

"On the 21st of September a large body of the enemy, not less than two hundred, attacked Sherrell's Station late in the evening. Sevier that day, with forty
horsemen, was out ranging, and came on the Indians'
trail, making toward the inhabitants ; he immediately
advanced after them, and opportunely arrived before the
fort when the Indians were carrying on a furious attack.
On coming in view of the place, he drew up his troop in
close order, made known his intention in a short speech
to relieve the garrison or fall in the attempt, and asked
who was willing to follow him. All gave unanimous
consent ; and, at a given signal, made a charge on the
enemy as they were busily employed in setting fire to a
barn and other out-buildings. The Indians gave way
and immediately retired from the place, and the gallant
little band of heroes reached the fort, to the great joy of
the besieged. This exploit was performed under cover

---

* "North Carolina State Gazette."

of the night, and, conformably to the Governor of Franklin's usual good fortune, not a man of his party was hurt."

Before this period, Sevier's old comrades along the Holston and Watauga had clamored to be led to his aid ; but this Governor Johnston could not permit, for it would be an infraction of the treaty of Hopewell. At last, however, he, in a manner, gave way to the pressure by consenting to an expedition against the Chickamaugas. These Indians were Cherokees, and had been active in the attacks on the French Broad settlers ; but they were a horde of lawless banditti, with a hand against every man, and war upon them was at any time justifiable ; besides, Martin had said to the Governor that they could " be easily driven out of that country."

Accordingly, Martin called his men together, to the number of about four hundred and fifty, for a descent upon the Chickamaugas. The settlers rendezvoused at White's Fort, now Knoxville — nearly all of them old soldiers of Sevier, and under such of his former officers as Colonels Love and Kennedy. They were a fine body of men, trained to Indian fighting ; and as they passed through the French Broad country the hearts of the settlers must have beat high with hope, for with less than half the number of these same men Sevier had put to rout the two thousand Chickamaugas. Surely with such a force Martin would be able to make short work of the pestiferous gang, and thus relieve the settlements from their midnight marauding.

Martin crossed the Hiwassee, and then marched directly to the Chickamauga towns on the Tennessee, near the present site of Chattanooga. On his approach the Indians deserted the nearest town, and fell back to the point where the river breaks through the Cumberland Mountain. Here they made a stand, and were attacked by the troops in an open field between the bluff and the river. Martin's men fought desperately, but, being badly led, were soon driven back with the loss of three of their bravest captains, who fell mortally wounded. Martin attempted to rally them to a second attack, but all but sixty refused his lead; and thus the expedition resulted in disastrous failure, not because the men would not fight, but because they would not with him as their leader. Then he led them ingloriously back to their homes, and the expedition had no further result than to inspirit the Cherokees to a renewed attack upon the settlers. Colonel Joseph Brown, subsequently an officer under Jackson, but then a boy of sixteen, and a prisoner among the Chickamaugas, speaks as follows of this event and its consequences, in a narrative he wrote at the request of General Zollicoffer, of Nashville, and which is now in possession of the Tennessee Historical Society: "At one time a Colonel Martin got to Chattanooga, within twenty miles of where I lived; but the Indians killed three of his captains, and he killed only one Shawnee and one negro. No Cherokees were killed; but they raised an army of three thousand men—borrowing one thousand Creeks, to go with fifteen hundred

Cherokees on foot, and five hundred mounted Cherokees, many of whom were half-breeds and dressed like white men. They kept [these last] ahead of the army, and white men who met them thought them a scouting party of whites, and were by this scheme readily taken prisoners. Several men were taken in this way the day they got to Gillespie's Fort. Their object in raising the army was to drive all the whites from the south side of the French Broad."

This new invasion also Sevier beat back ; and, having done so, he made another of his unexampled raids into the Indian country, going on this occasion down the Coosa River as far as the present town of Rome, in Georgia. Again he returned without the loss of a man, either killed or wounded.

This last invasion, more wide-spread in destructiveness than the previous ones, broke completely the spirit of the Cherokees. Even John Watts, the most indomitable of their chieftains, said to his warriors : "The wind and the fire fight for the great eagle of the pale-faces. We can no longer contend with him. From his high station in the clouds he sees our exposed places ; and when he swoops down, his hot breath blasts our corn-fields and consumes our wigwams. His flight is like the wind ; his blow like the thunderbolt. Who can stand before him ? He claims the French Broad lands. He will be our friend if we let his people plant their corn in peace. He speaks well. Let it be so ; for it is the voice of the Great Spirit."

This was the end of the war upon the French Broad settlers. It had lasted actively for five months, the settlers having to meet not less than ten times their own number of well-armed and infuriated savages. Having thus secured peace to the border, Sevier, in the latter part of October, returned to his family, from whom he had now been separated for more than half a year. In this period he had not only saved the French Broad settlers, but had rolled back an invasion from North Carolina, which, had it been successful, would have brought upon the frontier the whole strength of the Southwestern Indians. He had done this; and yet, at this very time, as we shall soon see, North Carolina was lending her aid to a plot for his destruction.

CHAPTER IX.

WHILE the fame of Sevier was thus ringing throughout the eastern counties, and all men were watching in enthusiastic admiration the unequaled valor and amazing generalship by which he beat back and finally subdued the infuriated Cherokees, it seems incredible that one man could be found, within hearing of his deeds, who could construe them into treason against North Carolina. But, nevertheless, it was so ; and that man was the Governor of that Commonwealth. Martin had followed up his insinuation that Sevier was levying troops to war upon the citizens by letters to Governor Johnston, in which he made adroit misrepresentations of Sevier's conduct, charging him with barbarous and inhuman acts (such as the killing of Old Tassel), and with making unprovoked war upon the Indians, when they desired to be at peace with the white people. Technically, Sevier may have been an insurgent, both against North Carolina and the United States, inasmuch as he was obstructing the execution of the treaty of Hopewell ; but, to listen to such a charge, the Governor had to forget that blood is thicker than water, and to shut his eyes to the fact that every blow struck by Sevier was in the interest of humanity. He heard Martin's falsehoods in silence from March until late in July, and then he wrote that worthy as follows :

"Sevier, from the state of his conduct set forth in your letter, is incorrigible, and I fear we shall have no peace in your quarter till he is proceeded against to the last extremity."

At the same time the Governor gave directions for Sevier's arrest, in the following letter to Judge David Campbell of the Superior Court :

"HILLSBOROUGH, 29*th July*, 1788.

"SIR : It has been represented to the Executive that John Sevier, who styles himself Captain-General of the State of Franklin, has been guilty of high treason, in levying troops to oppose the laws and government of this State, and has, with an armed force, put to death several good citizens. If these facts shall appear to you by the affidavit of credible persons, you will issue your warrant to apprehend the said John Sevier, and in case he can not be sufficiently secured for trial in the district of Washington, order him to be committed to the public gaol" [over the mountains].

Well knowing that Sevier did not style himself "Captain-General of the State of Franklin," and had not "with an armed force put to death several good citizens," Judge Campbell promptly refused to issue the required order of arrest, giving his reasons to the Governor. These reasons do not appear to have been satisfactory to that functionary, for he at once gave similar instructions to Judge Spencer, who resided over the mountains, but was about to proceed to Jonesboro to hold a session of court in connection with Campbell. The North Carolina judge issued the warrant, and it was in readiness for execution when, after more than six months' absence, Sevier returned to his family.

At home, Sevier found that his wife had recovered his negroes, paid his debts, and got his domestic affairs generally into a satisfactory condition. Court was then in session, and, after a few days spent at home, he visited the county-seat, to meet his old friends and acquaintances. He was cordially greeted by all, and he heard nothing of the warrant, because its issue had been kept a profound secret among the few who were plotting his destruction. No attempt was made to arrest him while he was in Jonesboro, for his enemies well knew that the effort made publicly would be futile, and might result in bloodshed. He must be taken unawares, suddenly, and under cover of night, or the whole country would rise for his protection. Hence, they watched for an opportunity to take him secretly, and hurry him over the mountains before tidings of his arrest could get abroad among the people. Such an opportunity soon presented itself. Both Tipton and Martin were at Jonesboro—the

latter holding a muster of his recently defeated militia—
but Sevier was unsuspicious of danger. He appeared
openly in all public places, and late in the evening rode a
short distance out of town to spend the night with a
friend. There he would be remote from all assistance,
and could be easily captured.

Sevier had no sooner gone than Tipton got together
eight or ten desperadoes for the purpose of arresting
him; and, having seen this done, Martin hastened to the
house of a Colonel Robinson, one of Sevier's friends, that
he might be able to show an *alibi*, and thus escape the
odium of the transaction. As Tipton rode out of town
with his squad, he met Colonel Love, a friend of Sevier's,
but then second in command to Tipton in the militia of
Washington County. Tipton invited Love to join them,
and he went along in hopes to prevent bloodshed. The
party silently surrounded the house where Sevier was,
and about the break of day rapped at the door for admit-
tance. The lady of the house soon appeared, and, seeing
Tipton and his armed *posse*, she conjectured the object
of their visit, and, planting herself in the doorway, refused to admit them. Then ensued an unseemly struggle between the lady and Tipton, which caused an uproar loud enough to arouse Sevier, who slept in a remote
part of the dwelling. Gathering at once that his enemies were in pursuit of him, Sevier hastily threw on his
clothing, and passed out of the rear door. He soon encountered Colonel Love, and, taking him by the hand,
said, "I surrender to you." Love led him to where

Tipton was still struggling with the lady of the house. A drawn pistol was in Tipton's hand, but whether he had threatened to use it upon the lady is not stated. In a towering rage he now turned upon Sevier and threatened to shoot him. Love prevented this, and after a time quieted the irascible gentleman. Then Sevier's horse was brought up, and he was led away from the house. Soon afterward iron handcuffs were placed upon him, and Tipton left him under guard of a deputy-sheriff and two of the desperadoes, with orders to convey him at once to Morganton, and lower down in North Carolina, if it should seem to be necessary to prevent a rescue.

Tipton had no sooner gone than Love persuaded the deputy-sheriff to remove the handcuffs from Sevier, and to send to his wife a message, which Sevier had written, apprising her of his arrest, and requesting her to forward to him some money and clothing. Love remained with the party until these articles were received, and then returned to his home.

The sheriff's party set out at once for North Carolina, and encamped that night on the summit of the Iron Mountains. Here one of the guards named Gorley informed Sevier that they were instructed to kill him, and that George French, the other guard, would doubtless attempt it before they were out of the mountains. Sevier was unarmed and at their mercy, and he determined to make his escape at the first possible moment. The opportunity presented itself on the following morning,

19

and, putting spurs to his horse, he broke away into the forest. French was better mounted than Sevier, and the latter's horse soon became entangled in the branches of a tree, which had been thrown down by a hurricane. While he was in this position French overtook him, and, drawing his pistol, discharged it so near to Sevier's face that he was burned by the powder. But the discharge was harmless; for, fortunately, the bullet had fallen out of the barrel in the act of drawing the weapon. By this time the other guards had come up, and the deputy-sheriff pledged his word that no further assault should be made upon Sevier if he did not again attempt to escape. Without further incident the party arrived at Morganton, and Sevier was delivered into the custody of William Morrison, the Sheriff of Burke County.

That the guards had instructions to murder Sevier was generally believed by his friends; but it should be borne in mind that the charge rested solely upon the unsupported word of a characterless desperado. Violent and reckless as Tipton was, there are no grounds for the belief that he would instigate a deliberate murder; therefore the order, if such there were, must have emanated from Martin, whose smooth villainy might have been equal to such an atrocity.

Meanwhile, tidings of the capture of Sevier became noised abroad among the frontier people. Such excitement was never known in Jonesboro as when the dwellers there were told in the early morning that Nolichucky Jack had been kidnapped overnight, placed in irons, and spirited over the mountains, to be tried for high treason by the State authorities of North Carolina. To quote the somewhat high-flown language of a document of the period : "Had the destroying angel passed through the land, and destroyed the first-born in every dwelling, the feelings of the hardy frontiersmen would not have been more aroused! Had the chiefs and warriors of the whole Cherokee nation fallen upon and butchered the defenseless settlers, the spirit of retaliation and revenge would not have been more strongly awakened in their bosoms! They had suffered with him, fought under him; with him shared the dangers and privations of a frontier life; and they were not the spirits to remain inactive when their friend was in danger."

Sevier was the idol of the frontier people. His captivating manners, generous public spirit, great personal bravery, and high soldierly qualities, had won him the admiration and love of every man, woman, and child in the Territory. For years, without pay or reward, he had stood sentinel over their homes, had guided them through terrible dangers, and led them to wonderful victories; and now, when a hand that should have been friendly was lifted against his life, every man felt it as a blow aimed at his own person, an outrage that could be wiped out only in blood. So every one thought and felt as he shouldered his trusty rifle and hurried to the rendezvous to which all resorted in times of danger. The tidings had flown with the wind; men came together as

if by instinct, and before nightfall of the second day
fully two thousand dauntless backwoodsmen, armed to
the teeth, had gathered at Jonesboro, determined to
rescue their beloved commander, or "to leave their
bones to bleach on the sand-hills of North Carolina."
For a time it seemed as if nothing could hinder a hostile invasion of the "mother-State," and the bloodshed and lasting animosity that would inevitably have
followed.

But wiser and more moderate counsels at last prevailed. Among the two thousand who assembled at
Jonesboro were Judge Campbell, Generals Cocke and
Kennedy, Major Cozby, Captain Evans, the sons of
Sevier, and nearly all of his former captains. The
people were accustomed to follow these men, and they
now assented cordially to the suggestion of Cozby that
the leading officers should retire to some quiet spot,
and concert measures suited to the emergency. Accordingly, about a hundred met in the court-house some
hours after dark, with closed door and windows. Campbell was the first to speak. He advised moderation, and
the avoiding of any act that would bring about a collision
with North Carolina ; but his voice was soon drowned by
cries of "Down with North Carolina !" "We want a
collision with her !" "We have too long submitted to
her tyranny !" and other exclamations of a similar character. Amid this uproar Cozby mounted upon one of
the benches and waved his hand for silence. He was a
man of huge frame, marked and swarthy features, and

an air of inflexible resolution. He seldom spoke, and when he did speak his sentences were short and pithy, and his words had something of the ping that follows the leap of the rifle-bullet. Owing partly to the decided friendship of Sevier, and partly to Cozby's own character, his opinions had much weight with his fellow-officers. He now said that moderation and conciliation would be wasted upon North Carolina; that she had thrown down the gauntlet, and the western men would take it up, if they had a spark of manhood in them; yet he would not advise a resort to open force to rescue their general. No doubt such a course would succeed, but it would bring about a collision disastrous to both sides. Better, sometimes, than open force was secret stratagem. Give him the general's fast mare, and half a dozen men of his own selection, and he would undertake to have their leader back within a week; or, failing to do it, he would put North Carolina to the expense of burying James Cozby.

"How will you do it?" inquired a number of voices.

"I don't know; and, if I did know, I wouldn't tell you," answered Cozby; "but I will do it, if I have to set fire to Morganton, and rake the general out from the cinders!"

"I'll be one of your men!" now cried Captain Evans, and his words were echoed in a chorus of nearly all present. Cozby declined the volunteered aid, remarking that his men were already chosen and his plan formed,

subject only to such alteration as might be forced upon
him by circumstances. All he asked of those present was
absolute secrecy. This was assented to by the whole assembly, and then the meeting broke up, and the outside
gathering dispersed to their homes, wondering much
what could be the secret plan that their captains had
adopted for the rescue of their beloved leader.

The enterprise was desperate in the extreme, and altogether worthy of all that is known of Cozby; but it is
said not to have originated with him, but with the heroic
woman who for thirty-five years was the honored wife of
John Sevier. The plan of it could have originated only
in a most heroic soul, altogether devoted to Sevier, and
such a soul had Catherine Sherrill. There is a tradition
of her in the family, which, as it illustrates her character, may be appropriately related in this connection. It
is said that in the first year of her married life she went
one day with a poor neighbor to obtain for her some provisions from the smoke-house of her husband's dwelling on the Nolichucky. Her hand was upon the wooden
latch of the smoke-house door, and she was about to
open it, when she was arrested by a sudden cry from the
woman with her, who fell upon her knees, threw her
arms about her feet, and burst into an hysterical fit of
weeping. The woman was the wife of a wretched rene-
gade—a desperate Tory and horse-thief—named Dyke,
who dared not appear by daylight in the settlements.
For an entire year he had neglected his wife and children, between whom and starvation nothing had stood

but the bounty of Sevier, whose unstinted hand was ever open to the needy and unfortunate. Regularly during all of that time the wife of Dyke had come to Catherine for the daily food of herself and her little ones, and she was there now for her accustomed measure of meal and flitch of bacon.

With her hand still upon the smoke-house door, Catherine turned, and, bending her eyes in inquiring surprise upon the weeping woman, asked, " What is the matter ? " " O madam ! " sobbed the woman, still clasping her feet, " I can not tell you, for I love my husband. He has fallen into bad ways; but he was once very good and kind to me." Then her speech was broken by another hysterical fit of weeping. Catherine tried to soothe her, spoke to her gentle words of hope and encouragement, and soon the woman found speech again. " O madam ! " she said, " you are so good, so kind, how can I let any harm come to you or your husband ? " " My husband ! " cried Catherine ; " what of my husband ? What danger threatens him ? Speak, woman ! " In her look and tone was that which would brook no denial. The woman hesitated, as if torn by conflicting emotions ; but then, awed into speech by the intense passion of Catherine, she told her in broken sentences that her husband Dyke had returned to the settlement, and was at that moment, with half a dozen other desperadoes, concealed in her cabin, where she had overheard them plan the murder of Sevier, while he slept that very night with unfastened doors in his unguarded dwelling.

Within an hour the ruffians were captured, and before the sun arose upon another day Dyke had gone to give account for a worse than wasted life to a higher than human tribunal. With tears Catherine pleaded for his life, and for her sake, and that of the ruffian's unhappy wife, Sevier would have saved him. But his fate was taken out of Sevier's hands by some of the settlers, who broke at midnight into the cabin where the ruffian was confined, and hanged him to a near-by tree. It was on the eve of King's Mountain, and the exasperation against the Tories was at its highest.* That turning battle of the Revolution would not have been fought, had Sevier fallen by the hands of these ruffians. So, on what seem to us trivial events, often hang consequences which are felt far along the centuries.

Thus was Sevier's life saved by the devotion of his wife; and now again she came to his aid when it was again endangered. She no sooner knew of his capture than she conceived a plan for his rescue, and, sending for Cozby, she besought him to join two of Sevier's sons in carrying it into execution. To this Cozby promptly assented; but, deeming a force of three men somewhat too weak to storm an entire State, he chose three more—Captain Nathaniel Evans, already mentioned, and Jesse Greene and John Gibson, favorite captains of Sevier,

---

* This account, written by her father, the late Col. A. W. Putnam, of Nashville, was communicated to me by Mrs. Julia P. Perkins, a great-grand-daughter of John Sevier and Catherine Sherrill.

and men of tried coolness and daring. When the Jonesboro meeting broke up, these six men rode rapidly off to
Sevier's home on the Nolichucky. There they passed
the night, and early on the following morning, with the
blessing and Godspeed of the "Bonnie Kate," they set
out on their hazardous expedition. Not many hours
later Colonel Love descried a party of half a dozen finely
mounted men, leading Sevier's favorite mare, and climb-
ing rapidly the mountain-path which the prisoner and
his guard had taken on their way to Morganton. The
presence of the led animal disclosed to Love the object
of the expedition ; but he kept his own counsel, and let
them ride on unmolested.

In the height of the excitement there were threats of
hanging Tipton ; and, had not that gentleman remained
for a time in seclusion, it is probable that violence would
have been done him. As it was, he escaped summary
justice only in consequence of the moderate counsels of
the most influential of Sevier's friends. Martin, who
had been the prime mover in the outrage, was not visited
with the same public indignation ; for, like the mole, he
had burrowed underground. However, he was soon to
learn that men who work in the dark, seeking their ends
by tortuous means, though they seem to have eyes, are,
like the mole, really stricken with blindness.

At Morganton Sevier was met by Major Joseph
McDowell, who had fought by his side at King's Mountain, and by General Charles McDowell, who, when driven
from his home in the Revolution, had found an asylum

with Sevier on the Nolichucky. These gentlemen showed him every attention; and, indeed, he was treated with great consideration by all in the neighborhood, the sheriff going so far as to let him visit, unattended, a brother-in-law who resided some miles distant, on his simple parole that he would return on the day set for his trial.

The court was in session, and in a few days the trial came on, amid such a gathering as had never before been seen in North Carolina. Far and near the news had spread, and many thousands came together to witness what was regarded as by far the most important political event that had occurred in the State since the proclamation of peace with Great Britain. The rude log court-house could not contain the great concourse of people, and the court sat with open doors and windows, much the larger part of the auditory being gathered outside in the court-yard.

The trial had begun when Cozby and his companions arrived on the outskirts of Morganton. There they halted, and, concealing four of the horses in a clump of bushes, left them there near the roadside, all saddled and bridled, in charge of the young Seviers, and Captains Greene and Gibson. Then Cozby and Evans, disguised as countrymen, entered the town, riding their horses and leading Sevier's celebrated racing animal. Proceeding as near to the court-house as they deemed prudent, they dismounted, and, tethering their horses to the limb of a tree, hid their rifles among its branches.

Then they mingled with the crowd, their capacious hunting-shirts concealing the small arsenal of side-arms which they had provided for use in an emergency. Their plan was to effect the rescue by strategem ; but, that failing, to fire the town, and, in the consequent hurry and alarm, to burst the doors where Sevier was confined, and bear him off in the confusion.

Loitering along on foot, they now approached the door of the court-house, Evans still leading the mare, which had been negligently curried, to resemble more nearly the horse of a countryman. Arrived at the court-house, Evans threw the reins loosely over the neck of the animal, and stood with her directly before the open door, and in plain view from the interior of the building. He gazed leisurely around, as if an idle spectator of events, while Cozby entered the court-room, and, elbowing his way up the crowded aisle, halted directly before the judge's bench, and only a few feet from where his beloved leader sat, surrounded by the court officials, but as "cool and undaunted as when charging the hosts of Wynca on the Lookout Mountain." Soon Cozby caught Sevier's eye, and, by a significant gesture, directed his attention to his favorite horse, which stood impatiently pawing the ground at the doorway. With one glance Sevier took in the situation. A tear, it is said, moistened his cheek, for he saw that daring spirits were at hand, who had periled their lives for his rescue. Seeing that he was understood, Cozby now pressed still nearer to the bench, and in the quick, energetic tone which was peculiar-

iar to him, said to the judge, "Aren't you about done
with that man?"

The question, and the tone and manner of the speaker, drew all eyes upon him in amazement. For a few
moments—as Cozby had intended—all was confusion.
Taking instant advantage of this, Sevier sprang from
among the officers, and, the crowd parting instinctively
to the right and left, with a few bounds he was upon the
back of his horse, and speeding away on the only road
toward the mountains. Judge, lawyers, and spectators
now rushed from the court-room, and in the confusion
Cozby and Evans regained their horses and followed
their leader. The outside crowd was composed mainly
of a mass of "white trash," who have come into the
world for some as yet unascertained reason. They are
the most stupid of created things, but they can appreciate a horse-race; and now they sent up shout after shout
as Sevier sped away, followed by the sheriff's officers.
The latter rode as if the fate of North Carolina hung
upon the capture of the fugitive, but they could not out-
strip the wind; the mare did that, and in a few moments
she had Sevier at the rendezvous, where, with one wild
shout, his rescuers closed in behind him and bore him
off in safety. In two hours he was twenty miles away,
at the house of a friend, in the seclusion of the Alleghanies.*

---

* This account of Sevier's rescue is taken from the narrative of
William Smith, in the "Annals of Tennessee," supplemented by personal
conversations with Dr. J. G. M. Ramsey.

Among the crowd who witnessed the rescue, cheering they knew not why, was, it is said, "a tall, lank, uncouth-looking young man, with long locks of hair hanging over his face, and a cue down his back, tied in an eel-skin." "His dress was singular, and his manners and deportment those of a rough backwoodsman."* His name was Andrew Jackson; and he was then on his way to establish himself as an attorney in Robertson's colony, on the Cumberland.

Here I may as well anticipate events to record the tragic fate that befell Judge Spencer, who had issued the warrant for Sevier's arrest. Returning to North Carolina, he was seized with a severe illness, and, when only partly recovered from it, he one day ventured to take a seat in the open air of the court-yard in front of his dwelling. Attired from head to foot in red flannel, he was enjoying the morning breeze, when he was suddenly approached by a deadly enemy, who, unmindful of his weak condition, and without one word of warning, set upon him furiously. The judge defended himself as well as he could, and uttered loud cries for help; but no help came, and soon he fell prostrate to the ground, lifeless. Thus ingloriously perished this jurist —done to death by the beak and talons of a "turkey-gobbler." Scientists attributed the disaster to the red flannel which he wore, and to the shock resulting from the sudden assault; but the common people always

---

* Albert Gallatin.

maintained that it was owing to his having consented to the arrest of John Sevier.*

Never was such rejoicing known beyond the Alleghanies as when news arrived that Nolichucky Jack had been rescued from the clutches of his enemies. As the tidings flew from hamlet to hamlet, the whole Territory broke into a blaze of bonfires and illuminations, and soon the entire country came together—men, women, and children—to Sevier's home, on the Nolichucky. The whole district took a long holiday, and it seemed as if the people would never give over their rejoicing. While he was in peril, they had thought of Sevier's vast services to them, of his recent heroic defense of the French Broad settlers; and his danger had endeared him to them the more strongly. The malice of his enemies had only deepened the attachment of his friends. His name now acquired a sort of electrical force which prostrated all opposition; and henceforth for twenty-seven years, whether in office or out of office, he held undisputed sway over the backwoods. He was still a branded and outlawed man; but, in the teeth of this proscription, the people of Greene County, at their first election, chose him as their State senator; and from that time forth honor after honor was heaped upon him by the whole backwoods people. They falsified the common adage that "republics are ungrateful."

Sevier was still under indictment, and liable to in-

---

* Communicated by Hon. W. A. Henderson, of Knoxville.

stant arrest and trial for high treason ; but at the first session of the Legislature, in November, 1789, he repaired to Fayetteville to demand the seat to which he had been elected. It could not be accorded to him until his disqualifications had been removed, and at once one of his friends, Mr. Amy, the senator from Hawkins County, introduced a resolution withdrawing the charge of alleged treason, and restoring him to the rights of citizenship. The resolution was opposed by Tipton, who was still a member of the Senate, and it was warmly advocated by Mr. Amy—so warmly that Tipton took strong offense at his words, and became so much infuriated that a hostile collision was with difficulty prevented. The debate was consequently adjourned to the ensuing day, and the evening was passed in reconciling the two gentlemen.

Colonel Roddy, of Greene County, censured Amy for exasperating Tipton, and begged him, in continuing the debate, to use language that would "soothe his feelings." Amy probably declined to pick his words, for it was finally agreed that Roddy should continue the discussion on the following day. Accordingly, Roddy resumed the debate, but he had not proceeded far in his speech before Tipton became again so much infuriated that he sprang from his seat, and, rushing upon Roddy, seized him by the throat, while Amy cried out to Roddy, "Soothe him, colonel—soothe him !" The echo of the House was, "Smooth him ! smooth him !" which indicated the sympathies of the members. A challenge to a duel resulted, but friends interfered, and the matter was settled amicably.

Robertson was a "silent member," with so little confidence in his oratorical ability that on all occasions he addressed the Senate in written memorials; but now it is said that the confusion had no sooner subsided than he rose to his feet, and in a strain of impassioned eloquence depicted the great services of Sevier, and his amazing sacrifices for the State and the western country. The legislators had done a great wrong in inflicting upon him outlawry. By doing so they had disgraced the State and themselves, and if they had a vestige of self-respect they would make haste to blot out the record of their misdoing. As for John Sevier, he was not to be judged by men who brought bar-room manners into the hall of the Senate, and disgraced it by brawls unseemly even in a tavern. Upon such men he should waste no words, but to the other gentlemen he would say that, if they had a proper regard for their own characters, they would at once repeal the act which outlawed John Sevier, and restore him to the citizenship his whole life had so highly honored. The motion being put by the Speaker, the resolution was passed unanimously — Tipton not voting.* At once Sevier took his seat, amid the universal congratulations of the members.

To this same Legislature Martin presented a claim for

---

* From conversations with Dr. J. G. M. Ramsey.

compensation for the officers and men who had been engaged in the recent abortive Chickamauga expedition. The claim was a novel one, for during eighteen years the over-mountain settlers had defended themselves at their own cost and charges. It met strong opposition; but was at last passed, with the proviso that the money should be raised from taxes levied upon Washington District. Thus were the settlers made to pay their own war expenses—not directly and voluntarily, as under Sevier, but indirectly and by enforced taxation.

The claim had one good result : it disgusted the legislators with Joseph Martin, whom they at once removed from his position as brigadier-general of the western militia. What became of him I do not know, but from this date he disappears from border history. Having done this act of retributive justice, the same Legislature proceeded at once to commission Sevier as brigadier-general, and to place him in supreme military command beyond the mountains. A sudden change of fortune truly : one day a branded outlaw, in peril of his life; the next, in supreme command, and elevated to it by his very enemies ! Henceforth, honors crowded thickly upon Sevier. Soon a convention of the people ratified the new Federal Constitution, and North Carolina became once more a member of the Union. She was entitled to four representatives in Congress, one of whom was apportioned by the General Assembly to the counties beyond the Alleghanies. The election occurred in the ensuing March, and Sevier was put in nomination without a competitor, as no one would run against him. He was unanimously elected, and in the following June took his seat in Congress, the first representative from the great valley of the Mississippi.

CHAPTER X.

THE State of Franklin went out of existence with the expiration of Sevier's term of office, on March 1, 1788; and this event left the settlers south of the French Broad and Holston in an anomalous and dangerous position. They had been an organized county under Franklin; but, though North Carolina had issued grants to the settlers for their lands, she now refused to exercise jurisdiction over them, or to in any way recognize their existence. The United' States also gave them no sort of recognition; or, rather, Congress did by the treaty of Hopewell admit that they were intruders upon Cherokee territory, and, in express terms, hand them over to the tender mercy of the savages. Therefore, these people, numbering as they did about one eighth of the whole Watauga population, were now existing without either law or protection. We have seen how the savages moved against them as soon as Sevier had relinquished command of the Franklin militia; and how, acting only as a private citizen, he then saved them from destruction.

That peril was no sooner passed than they were exposed
to as great a danger ; and from that, too, they were to be
rescued by their beloved leader.

The war with the Cherokees ended in October, 1788,
and at once there began to swarm into the French Broad
settlements very many disorderly characters, who had
been driven out from the older districts.   They herded
generally in the forest, but they prowled around the stations, committing theft and sometimes murder, and before the close of the year had become so numerous that
there was little security for life or property in the district.   In this emergency the settlers applied again to
Sevier for assistance.   He was now an officer of North
Carolina, and consequently could afford them no personal
aid ; but he did what was quite as effectual by showing
them how to protect themselves.   As once before he had
done for the Watauga settlers, so now for these exposed
borderers Sevier framed a form of civil government, by
which they might become an independent community—
a little republic, on the confines of a larger one, and
wedged in between it and two hostile Indian nations.
These "Articles of Association" cover less than two octavo pages, but they contain everything that was necessary for the efficient civil and military government of the
outlawed settlements.   Of themselves they are sufficient
evidence of the remarkable ability of Sevier as a civil
organizer.   They were signed by all the settlers, who for
that purpose met together at the house of Isaac Thomas,
of whom I have had occasion to make mention in a

previous volume. The brave scout had named the little collection of log-cabins, which had clustered about his own, Sevierville; and the place is now one of the most beautiful villages in all that picturesque country. The government then organized was sufficient to rescue the district from anarchy and violence; and under it law, order, and a proper administration of justice were maintained until 1794, when the United States erected the district into a county, and gave it the name of Sevier, in honor of its deliverer and organizer.

The authority of North Carolina was now acknowledged throughout the western counties; but the western people had by no means returned to a hearty allegiance to the older government. They still felt their former antipathy to the "Tar-heel Commonwealth" and its "sand-hill" majority; and they regarded with mingled distrust and aversion the legislators whose unwise acts had introduced such disorder among them, and subjected them to so much hazard. With the French Broad settlers they heartily sympathized, and they considered their treatment by North Carolina as not only unjust but a political blunder; and in the same category they classed the act by which the Legislature decreed that the soldiers of Martin's abortive Chickamauga expedition should be paid in certificates redeemable only in payment for taxes in Washington District. Such parsimony was regarded as contemptible; but it was seen to be dangerous when the Legislature, from avowed economy, repealed the act for the support of the garrison which Sevier had placed at the mouth of Elk River to protect Robertson from the murderous raids of the Creeks and Chickamaugas. Next to Sevier, Robertson was more beloved than any man on the border, and, though it was many years since they had seen his face, this exposure of him to renewed attack, in order to save a few paltry dollars, excited among the Watauga settlers intense and universal indignation. Moved by these motives, the western people again clamored for separation from North Carolina, and prayed that, if they could not be allowed to form themselves into a separate State, they might be taken under the wing of the General Government, which now was a body having force and vitality, with Washington himself as its executive.

At the same time that these sentiments were entertained beyond the mountains, the North Carolina Legislature awoke to the fact that the western counties were an inconvenient, expensive, and troublesome appendage, and that it was for the interest of both sections that the two should be no longer united. Accordingly, the Assembly proceeded to mature a plan for a peaceable separation, and soon passed an act, in pursuance of which, on the 25th of February, 1790, North Carolina ceded to the United States all her territory west of the Alleghanies. On the 2d of April of the same year, Congress accepted the cession; and, on the 7th of August following, it enacted an ordinance erecting the ceded district into the "Territory southwest of the River Ohio," and making provision for its government.

On the same day Washington nominated as Governor of the new Territory, William Blount, one of the few men of any talent whom North Carolina contributed to the Revolution. He had been a member of the North Carolina Senate and of Congress, a deputy from North Carolina to the convention which framed the Constitution, and he had commended himself to the western people by a strenuous opposition to the treaty of Hopewell. He was of an English family of some rank and wealth, which at an early day had settled in the country, and was also a gentleman of good address, courtly manners, kindly feeling, and commanding presence. With some weaknesses, he was a man of worth and ability. His relations with Washington were very friendly, and doubtless to this fact his appointment is to be attributed. With Blount were associated, as Territorial judges, David Campbell and Joseph Anderson, the first of whom had been on the bench of the Superior Court of both Franklin and North Carolina. To John Sevier Washington gave the rank of brigadier-general in the United States army, with command of the militia of Washington District; and he gave a like rank, and the command of the Cumberland militia, to James Robertson.

Thus was the government of the new Territory organized; these five men being supreme, each in his own department, and the five embodying in themselves all legislative, civil, and military powers. But it was provided in the ordinance that, whenever there were five thousand free adult males resident in the Territory, there should be added to them a Legislative Council and a House of Representatives, to originate and enact laws. And it was also provided that, whenever by actual census the total population should number sixty thousand free whites, the Territory should be admitted as an independent State into the Union.

A peal of rejoicing was heard everywhere upon the "western waters" when this action of Congress was announced in the Territory; and the general joy was increased when, early in October, the new Governor arrived upon the Watauga, and it became generally known that all the civil and military officials of the late State of Franklin were to be retained in their positions. People saw in this the hand of John Sevier, and they recognized the fact that he was to be again the "power behind the throne," as he had been before, while Robertson was nominally the "head-man" at Watauga.

Only ten days subsequent to this came tidings that President Washington had concluded a treaty at New York with McGillivray and twenty-eight of the principal chiefs of the Creek nation, by which the machinations of Spain would be at last thwarted, and the war-cloud dispelled which had so long hung ominously over the entire border. It only remained to obtain from the Cherokees a cession of the lands occupied by the settlers south of the French Broad and Holston, to secure permanent peace and prosperity to the western country; and soon it was announced that the Governor had dispatched a messenger to Echota, inviting the Cherokees to meet him at a conference, and that they had agreed to come for a "talk" to White's Fort, on the Holston, in the following May.

In these various events the people saw an augury of peaceful times, in which, no longer hampered by North Carolina, they might speedily attain to such a growth in numbers and wealth as would entitle them to rank as a State on equal terms with the older members of the Union. And this auspicious future they attributed to John Sevier, though it is evident that in some of these events he had no hand whatever. His popularity rose to an astonishing degree—higher, if possible, than when his life was endangered by the animosity of North Carolina ; and, had Blount attempted to conduct his administration without him, which he did not, the attempt would doubtless have been a failure. The popular feeling is illustrated by a trifling incident which is said to have occurred to Blount himself on his first entrance into the Territory. It is related that, riding with a small escort into the town of Jonesboro, he dismounted at the one log-tavern, and applied to the landlord for his best rooms, saying that he was the new Governor. The boniface, it is said, eyed him leisurely from head to foot— from cocked hat and "store-clothes" to high-top boots— and then coolly remarked : "You can have my best rooms, sir, if you've the money to pay for them ; but, as for your being the Governor, it ain't so ! We've got a Governor already, and his name is John Sevier ; and let me caution you, sir, that it won't be healthy to go 'round

21

here usurpin' his office. We've heard the United States has put some ruffle-shirted fellow over us; but we don't care a d—n for the United States! We've got a Governor now, just as good a one as we want; and I tell you, sir, his name is John Sevier."

Whether the story be true or not, the Governor had the good sense to act upon its moral. Had he done otherwise, he would have found it impossible to restrain the people, under the strong provocations they soon received from the Spaniards and the Indians.

The conference with the Cherokees did not occur in the following May, owing to the fact that the Indians were fearful to come unarmed to the treaty-ground as was the custom. The recent ill-advised slaughter of Old Tassel had made them suspicious of treachery, and many of the chieftains of the interior towns refused to trust themselves in the power of the whites. To allay their apprehensions, Robertson, in whom all the tribes had the utmost confidence, was sent among them, and he succeeded in inducing the attendance of the principal chiefs and warriors at White's Fort, in the latter part of June, 1791. White's Fort was then on the extreme frontier, and as it afterward rose to prominence as the future Knoxville, and became for many years the seat of both the Territorial and State governments, it requires a few words of description.

The place was first visited by white men in the summer of 1787. Then a couple of Revolutionary soldiers, named James White and James Conner, from Iredell

County, North Carolina, came upon it one day as they were exploring for a spot on which to locate the land-warrants they had received from the State in return for their services in the war. They had reached a point on the northern bank of the Holston, about four miles below the mouth of the French Broad, when their steps were arrested by the beauty of the scene which was every-where spread around them. They were at the summit of a low ridge that sloped abruptly down to the river, which here flowed in a turbid stream, a hundred and fifty yards in width, but broken by a small island, clad in green, and covered with giant oaks and poplars, tow-ering a hundred feet and more into the air. On the river's opposite bank was a range of lofty hills, that rose in grassy slopes from the water's edge, but soon broke into perpendicular cliffs whose summits bore the forest growth of many centuries. Everywhere was seen this primitive forest, interspersed with a dense foliage of laurel and rhododendron, which loaded with perfume all the atmosphere. No sound broke the primeval stillness save the voice of the birds that were singing their morn-ing hymn among the trees, and the low murmur of a little streamlet which, fed by numerous springs, poured its clear waters into the turbid river through a deep ra-vine not a hundred yards away. The dense growth of deciduous trees indicated a deep, rich soil, and the many springs that bubbled up along the margin of the narrow stream would furnish an inexhaustible supply of pure water for a settlement. These features marked the spot as an appropriate site for the home of which these men were in quest; and, moreover, the summit on which they stood was Nature's own location for a fort, and without a fort no frontier hamlet could then be safe from the murderous attacks of the Indians.

The location decided upon, these men set about the erection of the log fortress which was to protect their intended settlement. It covered a triangular piece of ground of about half an acre. At each corner was built a cabin of hewn logs a foot or more square, the ends mortised, and the logs fitted closely one upon the other, so as to form a wall impenetrable to rifle-bullets. Two of these cabins were of two stories, the upper story projecting about two feet beyond the lower, and pierced with port-holes, from which the settler could see and repel an enemy should he scale the stockade, or approach near enough to fire the buildings. The stockade filled the intervening spaces between the cabins, and was of timber a foot square and eight feet long, imbedded firmly in the ground, the upper ends sharpened, and the whole set so closely together as to be impervious to small-arms. A wide gate, hung on stout wooden hinges, and secured by heavy hickory bars, opened toward the little stream, and from it a path led down to one of the many springs along its border. Though of rude construction, and not very imposing in appearance, the fort was altogether impregnable to any attack from such desultory warriors as the Indians, unless they should come upon it in overpowering numbers, or by a regular siege starve out the garrison. It was on the model of the one built fifteen years before by John Sevier, at Watauga; which original fortress was the prototype of a thousand others subsequently erected beyond the Alleghanies.

Having built the fort, the two veterans set to work felling the trees about the barrack and clearing the ground of stumps, to prevent their becoming hiding-places for savage assailants; and then they planted the cleared land in corn, and went away for their families. They returned with them the same year, and with the family of another Revolutionary soldier took up their abode in the fort; and thus was formed the nucleus of the first capital of the great State of Tennessee.

The growth of a backwoods town at this period was not what it is now, when steam and electricity have annihilated distance, and the iron road bears to the remotest border all the appliances of a high civilization. Life on the frontier was then totally destitute of the luxuries, and but scantily furnished with the comforts, which are now considered essential to cultivated existence. For years the houses were of rough logs, with puncheon floors and unglazed windows; and the settler's fare was of as primitive a description. Pounded corn was his only bread, his only meat the game brought down by his rifle. He planted flax, and this his wife spun and wove into garments for herself and her children; but his own clothing was seldom other than the deer-skin leggins and hunting-shirt of the aborigines. This was the way of life of the first settlers of Knoxville.

But they did not long remain there alone. Soon other families gathered into the fort, and then others clustered around its walls, but near enough to find it a refuge in case of an attack from the Indians. Among the first-comers were James King, Hugh Dunlap, Samuel and Nathaniel Cowan, Joseph Greer, John Chisholm, John and Arthur Crozier, Charles McClung, and Francis A. Ramsey, many of which names are now, at the distance of a century, borne by the most prominent citizens of the present city of more than twenty thousand inhabitants. The surrounding country also soon came to be settled by a thriving farming population, among whom were such men as James Cozby, the heroic rescuer of Sevier, and John Adair, lately the patriotic entry-taker of the Watauga District; and they helped to make White's Fort an important trading and agricultural center. This was its condition when it was chosen as the ground upon which to hold the treaty with the Cherokees; and this event decided its future, for it brought it to the notice of the Government officials, and led them to select it as the capital of the new Territory.

The treaty was held at the foot of what is now Water Street, and under the tall trees which then shaded the banks of the Holston. Fully twelve hundred Cherokees gathered upon the ground, and from far and near came all the white settlers. None wore arms; and it was curious to see the whites, who had only recently met these painted savages in deadly conflict, now fraternizing with them as if their relations had always been friendly. The Governor's tent was pitched on a gentle knoll near the river; and, standing there in full dress—with gilded sword and epaulets, and three-cornered hat bedizened with gold lace—he gave audience to the dusky delegates. One by one, to the number of forty-one, they were presented to him, and each one was received with as much courtesy as if he had been the representative of a civilized monarchy; for the Governor was a man fond of ceremony, and fully believed that a considerable display of "fuss and feathers" was needed to impress a due sense of white prowess upon the savage imagination. But a trifling incident which occurred on the first day of the gathering should have taught him differently. Two men then came together on the treaty-ground who had not met before for ten years. The two were clad in buckskin hunting-shirts and homespun trousers, with none of the Governor's tinsel decorations; but they were no sooner seen together on the grounds than the Governor's marquee was deserted, and the chieftains gathered about them with hand-shaking and every manifestation of friendship. The two men were Sevier and Robertson.

On the 2d of July the treaty was concluded. It guaranteed perpetual peace and friendship between the whites and Cherokees; and, in consideration of certain valuable goods, and an annual payment of one thousand dollars in money, it secured from the Indians the cession of all lands lying north of "the ridge which divides the waters running into Little River from those running into

the [Little] Tennessee." This did not convey to the
United States all the lands which had been settled upon
south of the French Broad and Holston; but the chieftains could not be prevailed upon to make any further
extension of the line, and the settlement was acquiesced
in as the best that could be done in the circumstances.
Moreover, the United States Government was anxious to
be in friendly relations with both the Creeks and Cherokees, pending the negotiation which was still going on
with Spain for the opening of the Mississippi.

These Indians occupied the territory between the
Spanish and American settlements. The Spaniards were
in high favor with most of the chiefs and warriors; they
had for a long time traded with them, and they had
pledged to them the protection of the Spanish king
against the encroaching progress of the Americans. This
intercourse the Spanish Government had fostered, because these Indians were ready instruments for harassing
the settlers; and ceaseless secret warfare was to be the
policy of Spain until she could force the Western people
to secede from the Union. The Government of Washington had penetrated the designs of Spain, and it aimed
to frustrate them by a policy of "masterly activity."
Its officers were instructed to treat the Spaniards with
courtesy, and to act only on the defensive toward the
Indians, who were to be detached from the Spanish alli-
ances if possible. This had now been done in express
terms by treaty, first with the Creeks and now with the
Cherokees, both of whom had acknowledged themselves

to be "under the protection of the United States, and of no other sovereign whatsoever."

But these Indians were faithless and treacherous. They might at any moment violate the treaty, and come upon the frontier settlements in overpowering numbers; therefore, as Sevier was restricted by the Government from pursuing his favorite policy of invading their country, he must put his own country into the best posture for defense. To this end he built a cordon of block-houses along the frontier; and he removed his own residence to the extreme western border, where he could act without delay as the emergency demanded. He built a station about five miles south of White's Fort, and among the people he had so recently saved from destruction. His house he located near a beautiful spring, which gushes from one of the spurs of Bay's Mountain, and in the midst of a hilly and picturesque country. It was of logs, like his residence upon the Nolichucky; but it was commodious and comfortable, and much better adapted to the region than a more pretentious dwelling. This removal of Sevier, from an old-settled and secure district to one that was new and constantly exposed to raids from the savages, denoted the same forgetfulness of self which had led him twenty years before to cast in his lot with the Watauga settlers.

The removal of Sevier led to the departure of Blount from Watauga, where he had at first made his residence, and his locating nearer the "general of the forces." He chose White's Fort as his residence, and built there at

first a plain log-cabin, on a gentle knoll, about a quarter
of a mile west of the fort, and near the grounds now occupied by the university.

The coming of the Governor gave the place an importance it had not possessed before. It became at once the
capital of the Territory ; a court-house went up, and a
jail — both of logs, and the latter only fourteen feet
square—and it received the name of Knoxville, in honor
of General Knox, then the Secretary of War. Settlers
also flocked into it, and it was not long before the town
could boast of a post-office, with a mail arriving twice a
month from the seaboard ; and a newspaper, which appeared as often, to scatter the news of the world among
the secluded backwoods.

To this primitive region Sevier removed his family,
and the Governor his wife—the gentle and accomplished
Mary Grainger. In his humble log-cabin the Governor
held such state as he could ; and there, too, Mary Grainger dispensed such numberless graces as charmed alike
the rude frontiersman and the still ruder aborigines.
But a rude log-cabin was not a suitable dwelling for this
gentle lady ; therefore, being a man of abundant means,
the Governor planned and erected for her a more commodious mansion. It was located on the slope between
the fort and the river, and when built was as pretentious
a dwelling as could be found anywhere west of the seaboard. The frame was of oak, covered with planed
weather-boarding ; and the house was surrounded by a
well-kept garden, which was the delight of all beholders.

It looked down upon a log court-house, a log jail, and a score of log dwellings, which, with the log barrack already mentioned, composed the capital of the vast Territory over which Governor Blount now held dominion.

One by one the old log-cabins have been torn down to make room for more stately structures ; and to-day only one of them remains, a sad, dilapidated memorial of the simple tastes and frugal lives of the past century. This sole survivor of a by-gone time was in its day the home of one of the most influential citizens of Knoxville. He was a God-fearing man, with a large family, and he planned to build a two-storied dwelling with room and verge enough for his numerous progeny. But when the logs were upon the ground, and the structure had risen a short distance above the first story, he said to the friends who were aiding in its erection : "Why should I have a house so much better than my neighbors ? And, besides, shall I not be tempting Providence if I build such a tower of Babel as this will be if we carry it up a full second story ?" So the cabin rose no higher than it was, and thus it has remained to this day, except that a descendant of the patriarch, less humble of spirit than his progenitor, years ago covered its naked ugliness with a coat of rough weather-boarding.

In his framed house the Governor lived freely, and even elegantly, and dispensed the liberal hospitality so natural in the olden time to the well-born and well-bred Carolina gentleman. Levees and receptions were frequent, and the mansion was often crowded with strangers, drawn to the frontier by business, pleasure, or curiosity, from all parts of the Union. The style of hospitality was, of necessity, below that of Philadelphia and other of the older cities; but in the condition of things it was not less expensive to the liberal host, who was forced to draw all his luxuries and elegancies from long distances on pack-horses or clumsy ox-wagons. The visitor, however, whoever he was, rich or poor, white man or red, was sure of a cordial welcome, and none ever went away without speaking in honest praise of the hearty good feeling of the gentlemanly Governor, and the genuine grace and goodness of his accomplished lady.

But the old mansion was built in troublous times, and its new coat of paint was scarcely dry when it narrowly escaped a fiery baptism. For the Cherokees had risen, and were marching on the settlements. Concession and conciliation had been of no avail. The treaty of Holston was not a year old when they fell upon Robertson, and now John Watts and the Bloody Fellow were impatient to engage in a shooting-match with Nolichucky Jack's riflemen. They knew the orders of his Government—that in case of attack he should simply defend the settlements, and under no circumstances invade the Indian country. They knew this, and also that in the fort at Knoxville were stored three hundred muskets and a large amount of ammunition, under guard of but two invalid soldiers, while Sevier was twenty miles away on the extreme frontier, and the Governor was at Watauga. The muskets and gunpowder were too glittering a prize for the Cherokees to resist, with Nolichucky Jack so far away, and under orders not to pursue them into the Indian country.

So it came to pass that, soon after the solitary cannon of the fort announced the sunrise on the morning of September 25, 1793, a horseman, covered with foam, rode in hot haste into the quiet town, crying out: "The Cherokees are coming! A thousand strong! Not ten miles away! Every man to the barrack!"

They fled to the fort, the men leaving the plow in the furrow, the women the morning hoe-cake unbaked before the fire, and there they made ready, as well as they could, to meet and repel so overwhelming a force of the enemy. James White, the pioneer settler, a man now somewhat beyond his prime, but an able soldier, took command of the forty settlers who had gathered within the fort, and the little band prepared to defend themselves to the last extremity.

The fire-arms were unboxed, put in order, and set beside the port-holes, and every soul—even the women and older children—was put at work molding bullets and loading muskets. The women and children were to load while the men were to fire, and thus the effective force of the garrison was augmented to a hundred. There was no haste or noise, but all worked for dear life, for well each one knew that his life was at stake—for the savages spared neither sex nor age; if the fort were taken, it would be an indiscriminate massacre.

22

So the hours wore away—one hour, two hours—and the watchman on the lookout saw as yet no sign of the savages. Then another horseman rode up also in hot haste, his horse, too, covered with the foam and dust of hard riding. He reported the Cherokees fifteen hundred strong, at Cavet's, scarcely eight miles away. They had halted there, set fire to the stables, and would no doubt massacre the thirteen men, women, and children who were at the station. Was not this a prophecy of the fate that awaited the little garrison? This they all thought, but not a soul gave his thought expression. With firm, fixed eyes they looked into one another's faces, and what these looks said was, "If we must die, we will sell our lives as dearly as possible!"

Then other anxious hours wore away, till the sun began to sink below the hills, but still the watchman on the lookout called, at regular intervals, "Nothing yet of the red-skins." What did it mean—this delay of the savages? At nightfall the veteran White called a council, and asked every man this question. The majority thought that the Indians, true to their usual tactics, were waiting for the darkness to cover their movements, and that they would be upon the fort by midnight. White himself was of that opinion, and he asked, "But what can we do—forty men against a thousand?"

The answer of all was that they could die, but they would sell their lives as dearly as possible. But White had no thought of dying any sooner than might be

absolutely necessary. And he believed that what can
not be effected by force can sometimes be accomplished
by stratagem. A mile to the west, by the route the
savages would approach, is a high ridge, which was then
covered with a dense growth of oak and poplar. White
proposed that all the men in the fort, except two of
the oldest, should repair there when the night was somewhat advanced, and, concealed among the trees, in a
line about twenty yards apart, await the coming of the
Indians. When the advance of the savages was within
short musket-range of the most remote of the garrison,
he should fire, and that should be the signal for each
man to take deliberate aim and bring down an enemy.
Then, without waiting to notice so much as the effect of
his discharge, every man should make his way as quickly
as he could to the fort, which, if the Indians should
come on, they would defend to the last extremity. But
it was thought that the sudden attack in the woods
would throw the enemy into confusion ; that he would
expect a formidable ambuscade, and would seek his own
safety in flight, leaving the fort unmolested.

It was a hazardous plan ; but those brave men put it
into execution. All night long they waited there, resting upon their muskets ; but no savage yell broke the
stillness of their vigil, and in the morning another horseman came, announcing that the Indians, after destroying Cavet's, had turned suddenly southward. They were
then in full retreat to the Tellico, and close at their heels
was Nolichucky Jack, the Nemesis of the Cherokees !

This the savages knew, and hence their sudden flight to their mountain fastnesses.

For several months the people had been greatly exasperated over the repeated outrages of the savages, and time and again they had called upon Sevier and the Governor to allow them to invade the Indian country; but, in compliance with their instructions, both these officers had been obliged to refuse all such requests. The Governor, however, had addressed the Secretary of War on the subject; but the latter had replied, declining to be led into a useless and expensive war. The encroachments of the settlers were, in his opinion, the cause of the savage outrages. Let those cease, and the Governor would have no more border murders.

This statement of the subject did not meet the views of the border settlers. They at once enrolled themselves, and were about to march upon the Cherokees, when the Governor issued a proclamation calling upon them to desist and return to their homes. This they did, on hearing that orders had been given to a company of cavalry to range between the Holston and the Little River. In the midst of this excitement we have the first tidings from Colonel John Tipton since the decease of the State of Franklin. Under date of March 23, 1793, the "Knoxville Gazette" has this paragraph in relation to that gentleman: "Much has been said about the attempts and determination of Colonel John Tipton to raise a body of men, regardless of law and the orders of the Government, to destroy the Cherokee towns. Only five men appeared at his rendezvous—Jonesboro—instead of his boasted nine hundred. They passed through Jonesboro, marched to a still-house [a groggery] a few miles below, and returned. This affords a pleasing proof of the good sense of the people." And it also showed that Colonel Tipton had not recovered the popularity he had lost in consequence of his course toward John Sevier.

In the exasperated state of the public mind it was not difficult for Sevier to collect, within twenty-four hours, a body of six hundred horsemen to invade the Indian country. It was reported to him by James Carey, one of the United States interpreters residing with the Cherokees, that "the impression was prevalent among the Indians that the reason the Americans did not retaliate, but bore patiently the injuries they had received from them, was the posture of their negotiations with foreign powers, and their fear of offending them. If it were not for this, the Americans certainly would not be offering and begging peace in return for murders, robberies, and bloodshed, daily committed on their citizens."

It was neither wise nor safe to let the daring inroad of John Watts against the very capital of the Territory go unpunished. This was the unanimous sentiment of the people, and, his action being now authorized by the Secretary of the Territorial Government, Sevier proceeded to deal a sudden and destructive blow against the very heart of the Creek and Cherokee nations. He

swept through the Cherokee country, leaving a trail of
blackened ruin behind him; and then he pressed on into
the country of the Creeks, not slackening his pace till
he arrived near the present town of Rome, Georgia,
where he found the combined Creek and Cherokee forces
drawn up to dispute the passage of the Hightower
River. The rest is best told in Sevier's own report to
the Governor: "In the afternoon of the 17th inst."
(October), he writes, "we arrived at the forks of Coosa
and Hightower Rivers. Colonel Kelly was ordered, with
a part of the Knox regiment, to endeavor to cross the
Hightower. The Creeks and a number of Cherokees
had intrenched themselves to obstruct the passage.
Colonel Kelly and his party passed down the river,
half a mile below the ford, and began to cross at a
private place, where there was no ford. Himself and
a few others swam over the river. The Indians, discovering this movement, immediately left their in-
trenchments, and ran down the river to oppose their
passage, expecting, as I suppose, that the whole intended
crossing at the lower place. Captain Evans immediately, with his company of mounted infantry, strained
his horses back to the upper ford and began to cross
the river. Very few had got to the south bank before
the Indians, discovering their mistake, returned and
received them furiously at the rising of the bank.
An engagement instantly took place, and became very
warm, and, notwithstanding the enemy were at least four
to one in numbers, besides having the advantage of situa-

tion, Captain Evans with his heroic company put them in a short time entirely to flight. . . . Their encampment fell into our hands, with a number of their guns, which were of the Spanish sort. . . . The party flogged at Hightower were those which had been out with Watts. We took and destroyed three hundred beeves, which must distress them very much. Many women and children might have been taken ; but, from motives of humanity, I did not encourage it to be done, and several taken were suffered to make their escape. Your Excellency knows the disposition of many who were out on this expedition, and can readily account for this conduct."

In Evans's "heroic company" was a son of James White, the pioneer of Knoxville, who subsequently rose to eminence as Judge Hugh Lawson White. The Indians were making a determined stand under King-Fisher, one of their most distinguished warriors, when young White leveled his rifle, and the formidable champion fell mortally wounded. This decided the battle, for the Indians immediately broke and fled.

Sevier now turned his face homeward, destroying every town and village in his way. This invasion, which is called the campaign of Etowah, completely broke the spirit of the Indians, and never again, during the life of Sevier, did they venture to attack in force the French Broad and Holston settlements.

CHAPTER XI.

THE hostility of the Indians continued after their crushing defeat at Etowah, but they never again, until 1812, mustered in force for a general attack upon the border. For a time they made inroads upon the settlements in small gangs, which, stealing at midnight upon some solitary cabin, would be miles away by the morning; but gradually even these raids ceased, for the fast-increasing population soon gave Sevier so considerable a body of troops that he was able to patrol every hamlet and every by-path in the Territory. The campaign of Etowah taught the Indians that Sevier could be made to resume his former policy of carrying the war into the enemy's country. This the Cherokees were too wise to invite, when he would now be backed by such a force as could be drawn from a population of at least fifty thousand; therefore, they beat their "spears into pruning-hooks," exchanged their tomahawks for broad-axes, and with these set about the felling of the forest. Soon afterward Robertson broke up the nest of the Chickamauga bandits, and then the whole Cherokee nation took to peaceful ways. They planted and sowed and gathered into barns, beginning thus that career of civilization in which they have made such commendable progress in their new home west of the Mississippi. From this time forward, for twenty years, peace and Nolichucky Jack reigned upon the border. It was a patriarchal "reign," such as never before or since has been known in this country; but, before briefly considering it, it seems necessary to take a short survey of the way of life of the people who were the pioneers of civilization beyond the Alleghanies.

The present State of Tennessee covers an area of 42,050 square miles, but at the period of which I write the Indian title had been extinguished to less than one sixth of this surface. Civilized man occupied only two detached portions of it: the first, an irregular parallelogram of about five thousand square miles, extending southwesterly from the present town of Bristol to the high ridge south of Little River; and the second, an oblong tract of about two thousand square miles, extending some forty miles up and down the Cumberland, on either side of the town of Nashville. The remainder of this vast region was either in permanent occupation by the savages or frequently resorted to by them as a hunting-ground; and they were estimated to number not far from a hundred and fifty thousand, of whom at least twenty thousand were warriors. These Indians were the immediate neighbors of the settlers; but beyond the Mississippi was an unknown myriad, in friendly alliance with the others, and who also were by nature and instinct the enemies of the white race. Very high of courage and resolute of purpose must the people have been who in the space of twenty years could not only wrest from so superior a force the fairest portion of their possessions, but could reduce them to a state of vassalage in which the various tribes were content to own these intruding strangers as lords paramount over the fields which, time out of mind, had held the graves of their ancestors.

And yet the people who achieved such astonishing results had no permanent military organization; they occupied scattered plantations, which, in most cases, they tilled with their own hands, and their warlike expeditions were merely episodes in their lives. Their military operations being over, they returned to their homes, and resumed the axe and the plow with which they were subduing the wilderness. They were mostly an agricultural people, having no large towns, and very few villages. Jonesboro, their largest settlement, contained not more than a hundred log-cabins; and Knoxville, when it had been for three years the capital of the Territory, numbered only thirty houses, only one of which had required a trained mechanic for its construction. The place was little more than a farming hamlet—the center of an agricultural district, having a radius of about fifteen miles, and a total population of not exceeding five hundred, some of whom, like John Sevier, had their homes upon their plantations, but kept up a town residence on account of official duties, or because it brought them more closely in contact with the outside world. But both town and country dwellings were models of rustic simplicity, and often men who wielded a wide influence had their abode in cabins that would now be thought unsuitable domiciles for any one above a day-laborer. The father of Hugh Lawson White was the wealthiest man in the Knoxville district; but that eminent jurist learned to read by the light of a hickory-fire, and studied law in a small log office, having a puncheon floor, and not a pane of glass in its two narrow windows.

Nearly all of these original cabins have crumbled away, but from the few that remain it is easy, with the help of tradition, to reconstruct the life that was led by the early pioneers. At the time of which I am writing, the traveler could not journey a mile in any direction along the valleys of the Holston or Watauga without coming upon a few acres of clearing, inclosed within a brush fence, in the midst of which was a one-story cabin of unhewed logs, about twenty feet square, roofed with split poplar, and having, going up on the outside, a huge chimney of sticks and clay. Its windows would be "glazed" with coarse paper, made transparent by a smearing of bear's grease; and at night they would be protected by heavy shutters, stoutly barred, as were the doors, to keep out intruders. Over the doorway, both in front and rear, was a narrow opening to serve as a lookout and port-hole in case of attack; and, until John Sevier brought permanent peace to the border, the man of the house never opened his door of a morning till he had clambered to this opening to see that no savage enemy was lurking about his dwelling.

On one side, the house was flanked by a small patch of inclosed ground, growing the ordinary garden vegetables, and on the other by a log-barn, or a few ricks of hay or corn-fodder. Beyond the house stretched a broad field of plowed land, mostly in Indian corn, though, if the farmer was but a recent immigrant from the older settlements, it might contain a sprinkling of wheat, rye, oats, and other edibles; for this soil will produce whatever grows in the temperate regions. But, let it contain what it might during the farmer's first season, by his second it would be pretty sure to be monopolized by the native cereal—for corn was the one best adapted to the condition and wants of the pioneer. No other grew so fast, matured so quickly, or yielded so abundantly, and hence, from both choice and necessity, it was the food most cultivated by the early settler. "Without it," says Dr. Ramsey, "the frontier settlements could not have been formed and maintained. It was the principal bread of that robust race of men— giants in miniature—which, half a century since, was seen on the frontier."

Beyond the little clearing stretched an almost unbroken forest; but threading it here and there were foot-traces and bridle-paths and narrow wagon-roads, encumbered, perhaps, with stumps, and in the rainy season hub-deep in mud, but leading to where some

similar dwelling occupied a similar clearing. The dwellings were within rifle-sound of one another, and so the
pioneer was not without social life and neighbors, whom
he probably valued the more from the fact that there
were not very many of them.

Nor was the pioneer without intercourse with the
world. If he lived upon or near a highway, a stream
of human life flowed past his door almost daily, either
in bands of hunters following the fast-retreating deer
and buffalo, or in long cavalcades of immigrants wend-
ing their slow way in clumsy, covered wagons to homes
still farther to the westward. From these new-comers
the settlers received tidings from the outside world—
"news" which had of necessity grown old on its journey of two or three months from the seaboard.

The settler's life was anything but lonely. In this
genial climate, where man seems exempt from the general
law "In the sweat of thy face shalt thou eat bread,"
there is a long season after harvest, and again after
planting, when the farmer has next to nothing to do.
These seasons the pioneers devoted to friendly intercourse with their neighbors, and numberless were their
social gatherings. They came together for quilting-
bees and dancing-shindies, for shooting-matches and
corn-shuckings; and these were often scenes of unrestrained mirth and jollity, but always of innocent and
hearty enjoyment. Corn-shuckings were favorite gatherings, for they brought together the young and old of
both sexes; and the husking and shelling of the corn

23

did not in any way interfere with the free flow of conversation. Scarcely a winter evening passed but the neighbors dropped in upon one another—for a mile in a new country is not nearly so long as a mile in an old one. It is not difficult to imagine one of these gatherings, or to conjecture what would be the prominent topics of conversation on such occasions. They were not theological. Such subjects afforded no chance for discussion, for all were "Hard-shell Baptists," who had formulated the whole duty of man into the one phrase, "Love thy neighbor, and hate the Cherokees." They were not political; for here, too, all thought alike, and had embodied their political principles in one tenet, "Nolichucky Jack, first and last and all the time." Neither of these subjects would engage their attention. Their talk would be of the dangers they had passed and the obstacles they had overcome in their more than twenty years' struggle with the savages and the wilderness. Then, as he sat by the broad, open fire-place, while the younger people were gathered around, "a-shucking of the corn"—

"Dad would take down his Deckard,
    And tell the stirring tale,
How 'Chucky Jack, the hero,
    Led on the Indian trail;
How silently we followed
    Where he did lead the way,
Till the savage camp we sighted
    At the dawning of the day.

Then 'Chucky Jack dismounted,
  And gave the Indian yell,
And down we swooped upon 'em
  Like devils out of hell.
The bullets they did rattle,
  About our ranks like hail;
It was the sort of battle
  At which the brave might quail:
But through it all our leader,
  A-waving of his blade,
Rode 'mid the fire and slaughter
  As cool as on parade;
Though many a savage marksman,
  All through the bloody strife,
Had poised his deadly rifle
  For the taking of his life:
But never yet was molded
  The bullet for his breast,
For there's a better fate awaiting
  Our hero of the West."

They were a fine race of men and women; but they
lived in deeds, not words, and so have left but scanty
records from which to construct their histories. Their
lives, their very names, are being fast hidden under the
gathering mold of a century. Even the children who
listened to their stirring tales of danger and deliverance
are old men now, from whose minds are rapidly fad-
ing the feeble impressions of those early days; but
with them all still linger vivid traditions of the in-

veterate hostility between the white settlers and the Cherokees, a considerable portion of which once powerful nation still hovered along the border when Tennessee was admitted to the Union.

Few of these old people now remain; but here and there one may be seen among the Tennessee mountains, tottering along under the weight of almost a century. I have met about a score of them, and some of the traditions I have gathered from them will bear repetition, as they cast light upon the lives led by the early settlers. One old lady, "high up near Clinch Mountain," told me that her mother used to relate how, when her father and his two brothers were at work in the field, she had to stand guard over them with a rifle. She would perch herself upon the roof of the little cabin, or, more often, on a knoll on the outskirts of the clearing, whence she could see in all directions. One day a score of savages came upon the three men and one woman, and were all put to flight, except two, who were left upon the ground unfit for military duty. The same old lady was well acquainted with the famous Parson Cummins, who wielded the sword of the Lord and of Gideon, and was in the habit of taking his rifle into his pulpit, and looking carefully to its priming before he became too much engrossed in reminding the Lord of what he ought to do for the frontier people.

An aged patriarch whom I met in the vicinity of Knoxville knew well Major James Cozby, of Knox County, who had endeared himself to all in the Territory by his

heroic rescue of Sevier from the clutches of the North
Carolinians. Cozby was, he said, a man of iron mold,
standing "six feet and over in his stockings," and of so
huge a frame that even those stalwart mountaineers
seemed striplings beside him. His dress was that common to the region—trousers of ordinary linsey, dyed a
dingy red with the inner bark of the butternut, and his
coat the famous buckskin hunting-shirt, open in front,
and displaying a breast seamed all over with scars.
When my informant knew him he had retired from
the dangerous trade of killing Cherokees, and taken to
the more peaceful pursuit of practicing upon the bodies
of his white neighbors. He was a physician of the old
school—one of the kill-or-cure persuasion—but, with the
help of fresh air and out-door exercise, he managed to
keep the country in a very healthy condition. Far and
near, through rain and sleet and heat and cold, and at
all hours of the day and night, he journeyed on his healing mission, and he was always a welcome guest at every
fireside—for he carried the children safely through the
whooping-cough and the measles, and was never known
to demand a dollar for his services. If a patient was
able and willing to pay, it was very well; if he was
not, it was equally as well—or rather, it was better, because it helped to swell the account which the worthy
physician was rolling up of good deeds done in the
body.

With his other rare qualities the doctor was an admirable narrator—none told a story more picturesquely;

and it may be regretted that one so competent to be the historian of Sevier's campaigns should have devoted all of his later years to dispensing calomel and ipecacuanha among his neighbors. He was fond of relating how, on one occasion, he outwitted a band of Cherokees, who had surrounded his house after nightfall, determined to rid the tribe of one of its worst enemies. His domestic animals having given the usual signs of unrest by which they warned the whites of the approach of the savages, he looked through a port-hole, and saw obscurely a band of twenty stealthily secreting themselves in the adjoining woods and fence-corners. No one was in the house with him but his wife and several small children, the oldest of whom could only just make out to lift a musket; but Cozby barricaded the door, put out the fire, primed his two rifles afresh, and, with his wife at one port-hole and himself at the other, spent the night in giving orders in a loud voice to his platoon of—small children. The *ruse* succeeded; the savages were held at bay, and with the first streak of dawn he had the satisfaction to see them steal silently away into the forest, without so much as firing a rifle.

Cozby used also to relate some of the many exploits which entitle the women of the border to a rank among heroines. Among others was the story of a widow, who, having lost her husband in the wars, resisted all entreaties to repair with her two little ones to the fort, but stood her ground alone in the forest, scooping a bed for her children under the floor of her cabin, and standing guard over them, night after night, with a well-primed rifle, till the very savages, in admiration of her intrepidity, passed her on their midnight raids, and left her to till her little clearing in safety.

And he also told of the wife of George Mann, whose house, about twelve miles above Knoxville, was once surrounded at dead of night by a band of twenty-five Cherokees. Hearing a noise at his stables, Mr. Mann went out to ascertain the cause, when he was shot down and scalped by the savages. Uncertain of the fate of her husband, the wife locked the door, and with a rifle in her hand—which only that morning she had learned how to use—she seated herself by the entrance, and waited in silent expectation, surrounded by her sleeping children. Soon she heard approaching footsteps. Was it the neighbors, aroused by the firing, coming to the rescue? No! for, as she listened more intently, she recognized voices in a strange tongue. They were the Indians, thirsty for slaughter. The truth flashed upon her—her husband had been killed, and she was left to cope single-handed with a horde of savages, made the more savage by the blood they had tasted.

She made no sound, but firmly grasped the rifle and leveled it carefully at the crevice of the door. Soon stealthy steps moved along the wall, and the door was pressed against by a heavy force; in a moment it yielded and partly opened. A savage was there on his hands and knees, another was behind him, and still another, and a dark group was in the background. Instantly she pulled the trigger. The first savage rolled heavily to the ground, the second yelled with pain, and then the rest, hastily gathering up their dead and dying comrades, fled toward the stables. Those they set on fire; but they did not venture to again attack the house so heroically defended.*

Other narratives as thrilling as the foregoing are contained in the "Knoxville Gazette," a file of which has been most kindly submitted to my inspection by the Tennessee Historical Society, of Nashville. This journal was started by George Roulstone, November 5, 1791, and was the first newspaper published beyond the Alleghanies. It was a small sheet, and the editor seldom ventured to express an opinion, but confined himself to the easier task of chronicling passing events. He was the first postmaster of Knoxville, to which office was sent much of the mail matter for the district east, and all of it for the country west, of the Holston. The mail arrived but twice a month, and on "post-day" half the town gathered round the log post-office, to receive their letters—if they had any— and to cheaply glean the news from the postman. He traveled on horseback, and, though the schedule time was thirty miles a day, he never made the journey from Philadelphia in less than thirty days, and often he was as long as fifty on the way. Infrequent as were the mail

---

* This incident is also narrated in Ramsey's "Annals of Tennessee," page 639.

arrivals at Knoxville, there was absolutely no official
mode of distributing letters received at that office for
places within a radius of a hundred miles. But any
horseman who was passing from one settlement to another would carry letters in his saddle-bags; and then
they were passed from hand to hand until they reached
their destination. Official dispatches were often transmitted in this manner, and generally with safety.

The receiving of a letter was a great event in a
neighborhood, and often months passed without one
coming to the smaller villages; and, when one did arrive, it was the signal for the gathering together of
all the neighbors to listen to its reading. The rates
of postage were very high; and, as the United States
Government did not recognize the coon-skin currency
of Tennessee, letters were often detained in the offices
for months, because the recipient could not get together
enough "Continental" to pay the postage.

But, poor as was the postal service, it was superior
to the facilities for traveling. There were few roads,
and those few were simply avenues cut through the
forest, and so encumbered with stumps, and perhaps
with fallen trees, that passing over them was dangerous and well-nigh impossible. A journey then from
Knoxville to Philadelphia was equivalent to a voyage
now from New York to China, and involved about as
much preparation. Friends came together to take a
solemn leave of the traveler, to drink his health in
bumpers of punch, and to wish him "God-speed" on

his journey. If he happened to be a public man, his going would be mentioned in the newspaper, and prayer might be offered up for his safety by the clergyman at church on Sunday.

These clergymen were of a peculiar class—one which has disappeared altogether from the older sections of this country, and is now only rarely seen in the mining districts and back settlements of the West. Most of them were illiterate ; but some had considerable talent, and all were earnest, God-fearing men, always ready to

> "Prove their doctrine orthodox
> By apostolic blows and knocks."

Till the advent of Bishop Asbury, of the Methodist Episcopal Church, in 1788, they were, almost without exception, of the "Hard-shell" Baptist persuasion, and firm believers in immersion, plenary inspiration, election, predestination, and reprobation. Their theory of morals was condensed into one phrase : "Thus saith the Lord." What he commands is right ; what he forbids is wrong ; and the Bible is his infallible word. A faith how simple, and yet how sublime!

Their Sunday meetings were often seasons of great religious interest, and always of social union, when neighbors came together in a friendly way and cultivated a spirit of kindliness and good-fellowship. The meeting-house was usually of logs, located at a cross-roads or on some conspicuous plot in a settlement, and

around it were a few acres devoted to the abode of the
dead.   Great trees—the walnut, the poplar, and the lo-
cust—shaded the little inclosure, and gave it in summer
a picturesque beauty.   To this church all resorted, for the
Sabbath was universally observed.   On this day all work
was suspended, and high and low, rich and poor, arrayed
in their Sunday best, wended their way, on foot or horseback, through the quiet woods, to the house of prayer.
The men were clad in clean shirts and "boughten
clothes," the women in starched cotton gowns and new
silk hats or sun-bonnets, and all met on the rough
benches inside, or — when some "powerful" preacher
made the house to overflow—upon the grass outside the
rude edifice.   Then the preacher would give out the
hymn, and Old Hundred—sung by several hundred
voices — would rise upon the air, and, mingling with
the music of the birds, float away among the neighboring trees, till the whole forest echoed with the
melody.

"What a blessing," says Wilberforce, "is Sunday,
interposed between the days of the week like the divine path of the Israelites through Jordan!"   No institution has contributed so much to the welfare of
the human race.   To it, more than to anything else,
are due the peace and good order of every civilized community.   Where it is neglected, are found ignorance,
vice, disorder, and crime ; where it is observed, peace
prevails, good morals are promoted, vice is suppressed,
the poor are elevated, and the nation prospers.   It was

the influence of the Sabbath, and of the earnest men who ministered in those rude sanctuaries, that enabled Sevier and his compatriots to mold restless backwoodsmen into order-loving citizens, and to plant a healthy, robust, manly civilization beyond the Alleghanies.

Meanwhile population had flowed into the Territory with amazing rapidity, and Knoxville, its capital, had become a center of great activity. Though the giant trees still stood in and about it in primeval grandeur, the place wore more of a civilized appearance. Broad streets had been laid out, better buildings had gone up, and several marts of merchandise had been opened, which dispensed the substantial necessities, and the not so necessary luxuries, of the entire world among these rustic people of the backwoods. In the "Knoxville Gazette" of August 11, 1792, James Miller announces that he will receive, in exchange for all descriptions of dry-goods and groceries, "bear, deer, otter, wildcat, muskrat, mink, fox, and raccoon skins, and all kinds of fur whatever; besides beeswax, linsey, and 700 linen"; and in the same journal Nathaniel and Samuel Cowan make a somewhat similar announcement. These last were the great traders of the district; and, what is singular, at the distance of nearly a century, their lineal descendants are the principal merchants of all that wide region, doing a business during our recent civil war which is said to have mounted into the millions. If the gentlemen presiding over the present palatial establishment, which covers the

half of a city square, could see the commercial edifice of
their great - grandfathers, they would, no doubt, open
their eyes wide in wonderment. For it was a wonderful
store — a genuine curiosity-shop—in which was to be
found everything that grows in the air, on the earth,
and in the waters under the earth, including clean consciences and brave, manly hearts, that beat kindly to
everything human. In it there were dry-goods and groceries ; crockery and hardware ; drugs and dyestuffs ;
guns and ammunition ; hats, caps, and brogans ; coffee
from Brazil, and tea from China ; choice wines from Ma-
deira, and sparkling champagnes from France—or, more
probably, from Connecticut, and the product of vines
growing on the trees of some apple-orchard. There was
food also for the mind : books and stationery—slates,
pencils, and a coarse foolscap paper, considered cheap at
five dollars a ream. The principal books were the Bible,
Watts's and Rippon's Hymns, the "Pilgrim's Progress,"
Baxter's "Saints' Everlasting Rest," and Dillworth's
"Spelling-Book"—for the American "Grammatical In-
stitute" (the first edition of Webster's Speller), though
published more than a dozen years before, had not yet
been adopted by the literary magnates of the backwoods ;
and, consequently, like our English cousins, they still
put "u" into *honor* and *endeavor*.

All these things could be found in the store of the
Messrs. Cowan, and many more of which I have not seen
an inventory, and consequently can not make positive
enumeration. And all these products of the earth, air,
24

and sea were to be had by the frontier people for a fair amount of peltries or legal currency.

Let no one consider that the inventory of a country trader's shop is beneath the dignity of history. Such things mark the progress of a people in civilization; and we are beginning to learn that not from the bulletins of battles, with their ghastly record of broken bones and broken hearts, should we construct the annals of a country, but from its newspapers, the scenery its people looked upon, the habitations they dwelt in, and the traditions they have handed down to their children of their peaceful deeds, their ways of life, their habits of thought, and their views upon the stirring questions which in their time agitated the nation. Civilized man is not now a mailed warrior, astride of a prancing steed, with lance in rest, ready to do battle to all comers. He is a home-keeping individual, going about in every-day clothes, and with an eye to the main chance; but, nevertheless, he is courteous to his friends, loving to his wife, affectionate to his children, has some vague notions of his political rights, and entertains a reasonable hope that, by doing justly, loving mercy, and being regular at church and prayer-meeting, he will finally get to even a better country than this is. Of much such a character was the population which at this time tenanted the Western backwoods. They could fight, but they loved peaceful ways; and their greatest conquest was that which they achieved over the wilderness.

The well-filled warehouses of James Miller and the

Messrs. Cowan, and the grist-mill of good Captain White, of honorable memory, drew crowds to Knoxville; but greater crowds resorted there at the sessions of court and of the Legislature. Then many thousands came together till they overflowed the four spacious taverns, and were forced to camp out upon the vacant lots, under the trees, or in the clumsy covered wagons which are still to be seen in that region. Not many years ago I met a very old gentleman who had, when a young boy, been present on one of these occasions. He thought it was in 1796, when Sevier was first elected Governor, and had come to Knoxville to attend the session of the first State Legislature. Of this, however, he was not certain; but he vividly remembered the circumstances of the occasion.

The old gentleman said that his father lived some miles in the country, but he had fought under and voted for Sevier, and he was bound to see him open his first Legislature. However, he was a thrifty man, and, in order to hit two birds with one stone, he loaded his farm-wagon with "truck," to exchange at Cowan's store for tea and coffee and "boughten goods" generally. This he did overnight, and with the first streak of dawn he put his span of barbered mules to the wagon and set out for the capital—he and his wife perched upon a high seat in front, and the boy behind, astride of the bag of corn which was to feed the animals.

The mules were "nimble critters," and they got the wagon to town by ten in the morning; but the place was already filled with a great crowd, all clad in their Sun-

day clothes, who had come to witness the imposing cere-
monies of the occasion. The women were mostly arrayed
in calico or linsey gowns, Quaker hats, or sun-bonnets,
with neatly crimped caps, fastened underneath the chin
by a narrow ribbon ; and the men wore linsey trousers,
and hunting-shirts of the same material, or of clean
buckskin, from the breast-pocket of which protruded—
for that occasion only—a flaming red bandana. The
shoes of all were polished into looking-glasses, with a
mixture of soot and swine's grease ; and even the ugly
slouched hats of the men had taken on a holiday appearance. It was an orderly, good-natured crowd, bound to
have a good time, and to get its money's worth in a sight
of the Governor and the high officials of the new Commonwealth.

But the boy gave little heed to the people, for his
mind was soon engrossed in looking at the wonderful
things in Cowan's store, to which his father had bent his
steps as soon as he had securely tethered his mules—
having in mind to get through with the serious business
of the day before he gave attention to its holiday attrac-
tions. He had scarcely finished his traffic for "store-
goods," when a great commotion was heard in the street,
with a mingled chorus of cheers and the Tennessee yells
with which these people were accustomed to go into battle. Every one rushed in hot haste out-of-doors, and the
boy, being like Zaccheus short of stature, clambered
upon the horse-block in front of the warehouse, where he
could see over the heads of the multitude.

The street was lined on both sides by an eager crowd, and beyond, toward the river, a cavalcade of horsemen was approaching. One who rode slightly in advance of the others was the object of especial attention. He no sooner came in sight, than cheer after cheer went up from the waiting throng, rending the air, and making the leaves upon the old trees to tremble. He rode a magnificent horse, and he sat him as if he had been born in a saddle. He was a man somewhat above fifty; but his form was erect, his eye undimmed, and his natural force not yet abated. He had a genial look and an indescribable charm of manner, and when he spoke, as he occasionally did, to a by-stander, his eye actually beamed with kindliness. He asked about the health of a wife or child, or—with a merry twinkle in his eye—when the next young soldier was to be expected. But in all this, though there might be jest, there was no trace of the demagogue, but a hearty sincerity which drew all hearts to him irresistibly. As he passed along, the women dropped courtesies, and the men took off their hats, but there were no boisterous demonstrations. Their cheers they reserved till he was well on his way, and there was no longer any chance of their catching his glance of recognition. For this was Nolichucky Jack, their new Governor, and the idol of these people.

Riding on his right, and as nearly abreast of Sevier as the latter's high-mettled horse would allow of, was an older and shorter man, somewhat stout, and with grizzled, mole-colored hair. His head was bent slightly

forward, so that the boy could see only his heavy eye-
brows. He seemed absorbed in himself, and scarcely
conscious of what was going on around him; but the
lad observed that he had prominent features, and a face
darkened and reddened by exposure, and that the people
paid him much attention. His dress was not so neat
and well-fitting as Sevier's, and indeed he seemed altogether careless of his personal appearance, as if he had
more important things to think about. "And he had,"
said the old gentleman, "for that was Robertson, the
pioneer of Watauga, the founder of Nashville, and the
man who, for fifteen years, with never a thousand men,
had fought the whole Creek and Cherokee nations."

There were some twenty or thirty in the party of
horsemen; but none of the others did the old gentleman
particularly remember, except one, in a high cocked
hat, who rode a short way in the rear of Sevier—a slight,
erect, wiry man, of about thirty years, who sat his horse
as if about to charge upon an enemy. "I needn't tell
you how he looked," said the old gentleman, "for that
was Andrew Jackson, and his face is better known than
any other man's in America, except George Washington's."

The crowd closed in on the rear of the Governor and
his party, and the boy and his father followed to witness the opening of the Legislature. Soon the proces-
sion passed the new brick house of Major McLellan, a
son-in-law of Sevier, in the wooden wing of which the
Legislature was shortly afterward to hold its sessions,

and then it moved on to the little log court-house in which the wisdom of the State was to assemble. Here Sevier dismounted and led the way into the building; and then the legislators filed in and took their seats upon the rude plank benches. Many of them were men who, had they lived in an older community, would have had pages devoted to their exploits, but now their names are scarcely to be read except upon the map of Tennessee. The backwoods people were too busy to write history, and the State has been chary of her monuments; but she has tried to perpetuate the memory of her greatest worthies by giving their names to her various counties. There are to be found the names of many of the men who listened to the inaugural address of the new Governor.

Soon Sevier mounted the platform at the end of the room, and delivered the address which is to be found in its proper place on one of the following pages. It was very brief, but it might be taken as a model for all similar documents. When he rose he was greeted by tumultuous cheering, and a like demonstration followed when he had ceased speaking. All this the boy saw and heard, for the doors and windows were open, and when he told me of it, eighty-three years afterward, he added, while his eye lighted up with an almost youthful enthusiasm : "He was a great man, sir ; I don't know that the country has had any greater ; it certainly has had none who was so much beloved by the people. He was their idol. To them his smile was a benediction; his word, an inspiration; the touch of his hand, an anointing; and yet, sir, this great State, which he created, lets him sleep in a distant grave, without so much as the simplest monument!"

So far as I know, only two of the old buildings which looked down on these scenes are now remaining. One of them is the brick dwelling of Major McLellan, in the wooden wing of which were held the subsequent sessions of the Legislature. When it was built, this house was regarded by the country people as one of the seven wonders of the world, and from far and near they came to see such a monstrous pile of brick and mortar; but to eyes accustomed to modern architecture it is a most unsightly structure. It is now occupied as a negro boarding-house. Of more inviting appearance is the wooden building which was the residence of William Blount, while he was the Governor of the Territory. It shows its age, but is still in good preservation, and still surrounded by a well-kept garden, which one can easily see may have been a delight to all beholders, making the attractive mansion still more attractive. Not many years ago I wandered through its half-vacant rooms, and, as I looked about upon its dingy walls and smoke-begrimed rafters, there rose up before me a vision of that by-gone time—of the genial old Governor and his gentle lady, and of all the brave men and beautiful women who once made the glad music of life resound through its deserted chambers. And now, where are they? Silence, death's music, is over and around them;

but a beauty and a fragrance went out from their lives which have floated down to us, and will be felt by many coming generations.   Men die, but their deeds live after them ; and the deeds of these men will live when much of later history is forgotten.

CHAPTER XII.

THE NEW COMMONWEALTH.

POPULATION in the State of Franklin was at a standstill during its brief and troubled existence. It contained thirty thousand people in 1784, and it was estimated to have no more when Sevier went out of office in March, 1788. And this was during a period when an unparalleled tide of emigration was sweeping over the Alleghanies. But this tide sought the more northern territory which, though equally exposed to savage invasion, was not torn in a like manner by civil dissension. In 1783 the population of Kentucky was estimated at twelve thousand, and by the spring of 1784 at twenty thousand.* In 1784, thirty thousand immigrants are said to have come into the Territory from Virginia and North Carolina,† while 19,889 passed Muskingum, going down the Ohio to Kentucky, between August 1, 1786, and May 15, 1789.‡ In 1790

---

* Monette's "Valley of the Mississippi," vol. ii, p. 143.
† Albach's "Western Annals," p. 419.
‡ "Columbian Magazine," January, 1790.

the population of Kentucky, by actual enumeration, was 73,677, while it was not till 1793 that the 5,000 adult males were found in the Southwest Territory, which, by the provisions of the Ordinance of 1787, were to entitle it to a Territorial Legislature.

This Legislature came together on the fourth Monday of February, 1794, and its first act was to nominate ten persons, from among whom Congress was to choose five, to serve as a Legislative Council. Among the five thus selected by Congress was John Sevier. This Council, with the Governor and the House of Delegates, constituted the first General Assembly for the Southwest Territory, which met in the ensuing August. The minutes of the session show that Sevier took at once, and as a thing of course, an active part in the business of legislation. Being appointed by the Council to confer with the House of Representatives as to the order to be observed in the transaction of business, he reported the following "rules of decorum" for the government of the Legislature, and they are here quoted as a curious illustration of the primitive character of the legislators, who stood in need of such instructions.

1. When the Speaker is in the chair, every member may sit in his place with his head covered.

2. Every member shall come into the House uncovered, and shall continue so at all times but when he sits in his place.

3. No member on coming into the House, or removing from his place, shall pass between the Speaker and

a member speaking, nor shall any member go across the House, or from one part thereof to the other, while another is speaking.

4. When any member stands to speak, he shall stand in his place uncovered, and address himself to the Speaker; but he shall not proceed to speak until permitted so to do by the Speaker, which permission shall be signified by naming the member.

5. When any member is speaking, no other shall stand or interrupt him; but when he is done speaking, and has taken his seat, any other member may rise, observing the rules.

6. When the Speaker desires to address himself to the House, he shall rise, and be heard without interruption, and the member then speaking shall take his seat.

7. When any motion shall be before the House, and not perfectly understood, the Speaker may explain, but shall not attempt to sway the House by arguments or debate.

8. He that digresseth from the subject, to fall on the person of any member, shall be suppressed by the Speaker.

10. Exceptions taken to offensive words, to be taken the same day they shall be spoken, and before the member who spoke them shall go out of the House.

18. Upon adjournment, no member shall presume to move until the Speaker arises and goes before.

The above rules were adopted on the second day of

the session, and by the fourth day bills had been reported to regulate the militia of the Territory; to establish judicial courts; to make provision for the poor; declaring what property should be liable to taxation; to levy a tax for the support of government for 1794; and for the relief of such persons in the militia as had been disabled by wounds, or rendered incapable of procuring, for themselves and families, subsistence; and providing for the widows and orphans of such as had died. The paternity of the last bill is attributed directly to Sevier; the speedy enactment of the others was no doubt largely due to the surprising energy that he was accustomed to infuse into any business with which he was connected.

Among other acts passed by this Legislature was one incorporating Blount College, which subsequently became the University of Tennessee, and has still a flourishing existence. The session lasted thirty-seven days, the members coming together at seven o'clock in the morning, and remaining in session so long as they could see without candles. The Council assembled in the fort, or in the large room of the village tavern; the Representatives met in a one-story log building, about twenty feet by thirty, which had been erected for a land-office. The probable expenses of the Territory for 1794, which had been ordered to be ascertained, were reported as "two thousand, three hundred and ninety dollars"! Before their adjournment the two Houses concurred in a resolution requesting "the Gov-

ernor to direct that, when the census is taken next
June, the sense of the people may at that time be inquired into, how far it may be their wish for admission into the Union as a State."

The census which was held in pursuance of this
resolution disclosed the fact that there were 77,262 people in the Territory, of whom nearly sixty-seven thousand were whites, and that, consequently, it was entitled
to admission into the Union as a State.   Accordingly, a
convention was held at Knoxville on the 11th of January, 1796, and a constitution adopted for a new State,
to be called Tennessee.   Writs of election were then
issued, which resulted in the choice of John Sevier as
Governor.   There was no opposing candidate.   Thus,
after twelve years of varied fortune, was it shown that
Sevier was still the unanimous choice of the people.
Until now they had not been able to express their will;
but from this time forward, to the day of his death, he
was in name, as well as in fact, their leader.   The administration of Blount had been universally satisfactory,
but the people did not so much as consider his name for
the office which general opinion recognized as belonging
of right to the man who for more than twenty years had
been the chief stay and bulwark of the Territory.   However, on the assembling of the Legislature in the following March, Blount was elected one of the Senators of the
new State in Congress, William Cocke being made his
associate Senator ; and Andrew Jackson, who had for
some years been United States District Attorney in

Robertson's colony on the Cumberland, was chosen as Representative in the Lower House of Congress.

Sevier's first message to the Legislature on the assembling of the two Houses is a model of brevity, and well worthy of preservation. It was as follows:

" Gentlemen of the Senate and House of Representatives:

"The high and honorable appointment conferred upon me by the free suffrage of my countrymen fills my breast with gratitude, which, I trust, my future life will manifest. I take this early opportunity to express, through you, my thanks in the strongest terms of acknowledgment. I shall labor to discharge with fidelity the trust reposed in me; and, if such my exertions should prove satisfactory, the first wish of my heart will be gratified.

"Gentlemen: accept of my best wishes for your individual and public happiness; and, relying upon your wisdom and patriotism, I have no doubt but the result of your deliberations will give permanency and success to our new system of government, so wisely calculated to secure the liberty and advance the happiness and prosperity of our fellow-citizens.

"JOHN SEVIER."

The machinery of the new State was now in full operation, and it soon became apparent that the people beyond the mountains had entered upon a new and more prosperous era. Their history of twenty-six years had been a stormy one, in which, on several occasions, their very existence had depended upon the soldierly abilities of John Sevier; but now this remarkable man was to display qualities equally as notable, but of a totally opposite character. He was to be even greater in peace than he had been in war; and the autocratic power which he wielded by virtue of his wonderful popularity was to be exerted altogether for the public good. He saw that the prosperity of the new State depended upon peace, internal and external; and this he determined to secure by extending absolute justice to all men—red as well as white—who had their homes within the limits of his Commonwealth. The exercise of his peace policy he began upon his personal enemies. Among his first appointments were those of John Tipton, James Stuart, and Robert Blair as magistrates of Washington County, and the same John Tipton and John Blair as commissioners for the town of Jonesboro—all of which persons had for a long time been his personal and political enemies.

In his efforts to preserve peace with the Indians, Sevier was aided by a recent treaty between the United States and Spain, by which the latter power had conceded the navigation of the Mississippi, and relinquished her "protection" over the Southwestern Indians.*

---

* This Spanish imbroglio, which for ten years endangered the existence of the newly-formed Union, is one of the most interesting chapters in American history; and I shall attempt to relate it in a life of Robertson, which I purpose to write in another volume.

The condition of the settlers south of the French Broad and Holston was still not in every way satisfactory. A portion of their lands had been acquired by the United States under the treaty of Holston, but, no land-office having yet been opened, the settlers had not secured a legal title ; a portion also was still held by the Cherokees, and the settlers, holding these last only by right of occupancy, were fearful of future disturbances. Having their welfare in mind, Sevier soon addressed the following message to the Legislature :

" Mr. Speaker and Gentlemen of the Legislature :

" Permit me to remark to your honorable body that, as our Senators are about to proceed to the Federal Legislature, it may not be inexpedient to remind them of the necessity of taking under consideration the embarrassed situation which claimants are under to lands south of the line concluded on in the treaty of Holston, and now within the Indian boundary.

" In my humble opinion, it is a matter of great public importance, and particularly interesting to the State and to individuals, to either have the Indian claims extinguished, or the adventurers compensated for their lands.

" I have no doubt you will take the premises under due deliberation, and give your Senators such instructions as you, in your wisdom, may deem necessary and advisable.　　　　　JOHN SEVIER."

On the eve of the adjournment of this first Legislature the Governor also brought to its attention the condition of the frontier, advising friendship with the Indians as the best defense and security of the settlers. He also noticed the fact that the soldiers in the late campaigns were still unpaid, and he proposed, with the approval of the Legislature, "to attend in person at the next session of Congress, to urge upon that body payment to the troops for their hazardous and toilsome services." To this the Legislature replied, expressing solicitude that Congress should not only provide for the defense of the frontier, but should also make full compensation to the troops heretofore employed in that service. But it dissuaded the Governor against attending upon Congress in person, and suggested that he should delegate the duty to the members of Congress from Tennessee.

Soon thereafter Tennessee was formally admitted by Congress as a State of the Union, and, in communicating this fact to the Legislature, Sevier said, "I have the pleasure of announcing to you, gentlemen, the admission of the State of Tennessee into the Federal Union, a circumstance pregnant with every prospect of peace, happiness, and opulence to our infant State.

"The period has at length arrived when the people of the Southwestern Territory may enjoy all the blessings and liberties of a free and independent republic."

To this end this man and these people had labored and struggled for twelve years, and it was but natural that they should now felicitate themselves upon having at last achieved the right of self-government.

Re-elected Governor in 1798, Sevier soon found his peace policy subjected to a severe strain in consequence of the encroachments of settlers upon the Cherokee lands west of the Clinch, and in the beautiful valley along Powell's River. Two companies of United States troops had been stationed at Knoxville for the purpose of preventing further encroachments, and the commander of these troops had issued a manifesto ordering all trespassers off the Indian lands. Many of the settlers had obeyed the order, and fallen back from the lands which had been conveyed to them by North Carolina; but the larger number had held their ground, and defied the United States soldiers to attempt their removal. Between Knoxville and Nashville and west of Clinch River stretched a wilderness several hundred miles in extent; and a large portion of this territory had been granted to her soldiers by North Carolina, though not one acre of it had been ceded by the Cherokees in any of their many treaties with either the State or the United States.

The disorder of the situation is graphically described by a young Englishman who journeyed over this wilderness in the summer of 1797. He was the Francis Baily who afterward rose to eminence as an astronomer, and became the founder and President of the Royal Astronomical Society. After detailing the incidents of his trip through the forest from Nashville, he says:

"It will be observed, by an inspection of the map,

that, from the time we took the Cumberland Mountains
to this place, we have been traveling within the Indian
country. The Indians keep their tract of land in full
sovereignty, and have not yet parted with their title to it
to the United States. But, soon after we leave the banks
of the Clinch River, we get once more within the limits
of the State of Tennessee. After refreshing ourselves at
the ferry, we continued our journey, intending to reach
this evening an encampment of men, women, and children, which was formed between this place and Knoxville.

"These people were waiting to set out to settle some
lands on the Tennessee River, but (as there lately had
been a dispute with the Indians with respect to the running the line which divided their territory from the
United States) they thought it best to wait the issue of
the negotiation which was pending. The limits of the
Indian territory had been fixed by the treaty of Holston ;
but, it being some years after ere the line was actually
run, they found (when they came to survey that part of
the country) that a number of inhabitants had encroached and settled on the Indian territory. This was
not at all to be wondered at, as it is almost impossible to
know where a line (drawn only upon paper) will actually
strike when it comes to be measured. As the United
States (agreeably to the policy which they have universally adopted) were determined that the Indians
should have no just cause of complaint, they ordered all
the families which had so encroached to remove within

the limits of the United States, and the President actually sent a detachment of the army into the country to enforce his commands.

"This was the bone of contention which was the subject of conversation in every place I went into. The inhabitants firmly opposed being removed from their settlements, and they were supported in their opposition by the encouragement of those who were within the limits of the United States, as they all hate the Indians, and think a little deviation from justice is a thing to be overlooked where their two interests clash with each other. So far does prejudice carry us! And I believe the inhabitants were prepared to defend themselves against the soldiery with the point of the sword. Happily, things did not come to these extremities, for it was discovered that the line which had been drawn by the surveyors was not agreeable to the treaty; that, if it had been drawn right, it would not have cut off any of the inhabitants of the State within the Indian limits. Accordingly, a representation of this case was made to the General Assembly at Knoxville, who forwarded a remonstrance to the President of the United States; and, at the same time, formed a number of resolutions indicative of their determination not to suffer the inhabitants to be turned out of their possession. Such was the state of the country when I was in it.

"We reached the encampment about sunset, and, having kindled a fire among them and turned our horses into the woods to search for pasture, went round to visit the different parties we saw there. They were scattered over a rising ground, near which were some fine springs of water. They seemed to lament their situation, in being deprived of going to settle the land which they had justly and fairly bought, and were so worked up by the apparent hardness of their case that, had things taken a contrary turn, I believe they would have forced their way by the point of the bayonet." *

Congress had passed an act imposing fines and forfeitures upon all who should attempt to take possession of any lands within the Indian boundary, and against this act the Legislature, at the instance of Sevier, had protested as follows : "This Legislature, ever willing to support the Constitution and laws of the United States, being impressed with a sense of the injury and grievances sustained by the citizens in consequence of the line of the treaty of Holston, and the act before mentioned, do earnestly request that the prohibitions preventing them to possess the lands before alluded to may be removed; that provision by law be made for extinguishing the Indian claim to said lands; that the owners and grantees of said lands may enter upon, occupy, and possess the same in a full and ample manner, and have every right, privilege, and advantage, which they are entitled to by constitutional laws."

---

* "Journal of a Tour in the Unsettled Parts of the United States of North America in 1796 and 1797." By the late Francis Baily, F. R. S., President of the Royal Astronomical Society. London, 1851.

As a result of the energetic measures taken by Sevier and the Legislature for the relief of the settlers, Congress appointed commissioners to hold a treaty with the Indians for the acquisition of the lands in the disputed territory. The commissioners did not enter upon their duties until the summer of 1798, and meanwhile it required all the address of Sevier to prevent an outbreak among the impatient settlers, who were encamped in the woods almost in sight of the lands to which they were entitled by legal purchase. Under date of Knoxville, April 23, 1798, he addressed to them a circular, in which he counseled against any "rash and imprudent" proceedings, predicted the early arrival of the treaty commissioners, and assured "his countrymen that nothing should be lacking that might tend to their present and future advantage."

The commissioners arrived at Knoxville in the following month, and arrangements were at once made for their meeting the Indian chiefs early in the succeeding July, at the Tellico block-house. The treaty-making power was vested solely in the United States commissioners; but Sevier appointed General James Robertson, James Stuart, and Lachlan McIntosh, agents to represent the State of Tennessee. They were to attend at the treaty to look after the interests of the settlers, and the Governor gave them written instructions on such points as he deemed of special importance. These points were :

1. "To obtain as wide an extinguishment of the

Cherokee claim, north of the Tennessee, as was attainable.

2. "An unimpeded communication of Holston and Clinch Rivers with the Tennessee; and the surrender of the west bank of the Clinch, opposite Southwest Point.

3. "To secure from future molestation the settlements as far as they have progressed on the northern and western borders of the State, and the connection of Hamilton and Miro Districts, then separated by a space of unextinguished hunting-ground, eighty miles wide.

4. "To examine into the nature and validity of the claim recently set up by the Cherokees to lands north of the [Little] Tennessee River. Does it rest upon original right? Is it derived from treaties? Is it founded only upon a temporary use and occupancy?"

The State agents and the United States commissioners met the Indians at the appointed time, and the following is the brief record which the historian Haywood makes of the proceedings:

"The council opened. The Bloody Fellow having prefaced the subject, delivered a paper which he stated to contain their final resolutions, which were a peremptory refusal to sell, and an absolute denial to permit the inhabitants to return to their homes." In other words, all the elaborate preparations, attended with great expense and trouble to both the State and the United States, were rendered nugatory by the obstinacy of a few badly disposed savages, who were madly intent upon war with the whites. Since the death of Old Tassel, there had been no generally acknowledged king of the Cherokees. Double-Head had held dominion over the northern portion of the tribe, John Watts over the southern; and without a war the contending claims of these rival chieftains could not be decided. Should a war with the whites occur, one of them would have a chance to win supremacy over the other, even if the nation should be defeated; therefore both were now opposed to any treaty whatever. They refused to negotiate on any terms; but Robertson, who had more weight with them than any one on the treaty-ground, persuaded them to meet the whites again in the following September.

They did so; and, Robertson not being able to attend, Sevier himself repaired to the treaty-ground. He had no sooner exchanged greetings and a few remarks with the Cherokee chieftains than they assented to such a treaty as was demanded by the whites. The circumstances were unchanged in every particular: there was the same rivalry between John Watts and Double-Head, and the same conviction that a war with the whites would bring about a settlement of their own disputes; but they no sooner came in contact with Sevier than they consented to a treaty which ceded to the whites the land already settled upon, and a much larger territory than had been demanded in the previous July. And this cession was secured by the pay-

26

ment of only five thousand dollars, with the promise of
an annuity of one thousand.

The arguments resorted to by Sevier to bring the
Indians to a reasonable settlement can only be conjectured. It is probable that the language he used to
them now was much the same he had employed on previous occasions, when he had told them that no man,
or body of men, had a right to appropriate as mere
hunting-grounds vast tracts of the earth's surface ; that
the Great Spirit had designed the soil for the men who
tilled it, and caused it to yield its natural fruits. This
the white man did ; and the Indian must resort to his
ways, or give place to his advance. There was no alternative. This continent was to be overspread with
civilization. It was manifest destiny, and whoever
should resist it would perish. He would be glad to
live at peace with the Cherokees ; but peace or war
was at their own election. If, however, they chose war,
they should remember that, when he struck, his blows
were heavy, and that he was now at the head of a hundred thousand, every man among them deadly sure with
the rifle.

The Cherokees chose peace, and never again, so long
as Sevier lived, did they dig up the hatchet. And, what
is more remarkable, from this time forward this man,
whom they had persistently fought for nearly twenty-five
years, became their most trusted counselor and friend.
In all disputes among themselves, they chose "'Chucky
Jack" as their umpire ; and when their rights were in-

vaded, or their lands encroached upon by the settlers—
which was not seldom—it was to the "great eagle of the
pale faces" that they turned for help and protection.
And they never appealed to him in vain. However
powerful might be their opponent, both they and he
were sure to receive exact and impartial justice at the
hands of the "good old Governor."

Up to this period a large part of the people had dwelt
in rude fortresses, termed stations, of which there were
two or three hundred within the limits of the Territory.
These stations were inclosed with palisades, and usually
contained cabins enough to house from fifty to two hundred people. This involved a certain crowding of the
population, which, in the midst of unbounded space, was
submitted to only because it was necessary to insure
safety from the savages. But, so soon as the absolute
ascendency of Sevier had secured permanent peace with
the Indians, the habits of the population, and the entire
aspect of the country, underwent a sudden change. The
fortified stations were abandoned, and here and there,
over the whole country, went up detached farm-houses,
nestling among wide-spreading trees, and overlooking
broad, cultivated fields, laden heavily with the golden
riches of a coming harvest. Towns and villages, too,
sprang up as if by magic, with dwellings no longer built of
rough logs, and intended only for security, but of painted
weather-boarding, with glazed windows, modeled, it may
be, after the wooden palace of Governor Blount, which
was the first framed dwelling west of the Alleghanies.

Thus it was that the stockade gave place to the neat and well-ordered village, in which the mechanic arts began to flourish, school-houses and churches to go up, and men to cultivate all the amenities and refinements of civilization. Immigration continued to flow into the country in such numbers that the census of 1800 showed the State to contain a population of not less than 105,682.

Thus, in the space of little more than twenty-five years, and in the face of appalling difficulties, had Sevier and his compatriots built up a great commonwealth in the heart of the Western wilderness. In the history of no other people is there any similar achievement. It was possible only to men of the Anglo-Saxon race, and to them only when given a leader as wise, as heroic, and as self-devoted as John Sevier.

CHAPTER XIII.

I AM not writing a history of Tennessee. The aim of this volume, and of the one which has preceded it, has been to recount the career of the remarkable man who was the founder and builder of that Commonwealth; and I have related the early history of the State only for the reason that his life was so interwoven with its early life that one can not be told without relating the other. The same remark applies to Sevier's subsequent career, for to the very last he was the soul of the Commonwealth he had created.

But we have now arrived at a period in his life, and in that of the State, when to both may be applied the saying, "Happy are the people whose annals are vacant." To this man, whose career had been until now one long struggle, and to this State, which was cradled in the midst of perils, nurtured amid external and internal strife, and time and again had been saved from destruction only by the single hand and brain of this one man, had come a season of repose—an unbroken period of peace and prosperity, barren of incident, and unruffled

by a single one of those striking events which form the
staple of most histories. To the State it was peace, and
such prosperity as was then unknown to any of the sixteen States, except the neighboring one of Kentucky;
and to Sevier it was peace and such abounding honor,
both at home and abroad, as was accorded to but few of
the men of his generation. We have seen that, when but
recently an outlaw, he was given by Washington sole
command of the men of Watauga; so now, in 1798, on
the recommendation of Washington, he was appointed by
President Adams a brigadier-general in the army that
was forming to resist the arrogant encroachments of
France. But the war-cloud passed away, and left Sevier
sitting in peace "under his own vine and fig-tree."
With a passing glance at him there, I will close this im-
perfect record of his life, which has been written in the
hope that it may recall to his countrymen the great
services he rendered to American freedom and Western
civilization.

At the close of Sevier's second term he was again
unanimously elected Governor, and then, having served
six consecutive years, he was, by the Constitution he had
helped to frame, not again eligible for the position till
the expiration of two years. During this interval the
office was filled by Archibald Roane; but at its close the
people again put Sevier in nomination, and he was again
elected without an opposing candidate. Two more unanimous elections succeeded, he serving another consecutive six years; and then, feeling old age coming upon

him, he declined any further nominations for the office. But the people would not dispense with his services. They at once elected him to Congress, and they kept him there by three successive elections, of the last of which he probably never heard, for it occurred while he was away in the Creek country, where he died at the age of seventy years, having been for fifty-two years—since he was a boy of eighteen—in the active service of his country.

During all of this long period Sevier was a leader of men, and a prime mover in the important events which occurred beyond the Alleghanies. For thirty years of this time he was engaged in almost constant warfare ; and, though his men were altogether volunteers, and he, until after the battle of King's Mountain, commanded without a commission, and merely as an elected leader, there never was known so much as a whisper of insubordination among them. Without fear or question they followed wherever he led, even upon the most desperate expeditions ; and the wave of his sword, the sound of his voice, was enough to transform the most timid among them into heroes.

And the sway of Sevier was as potent and undisputed in civil as in military affairs. Aided by North Carolina, a few factious and ambitious men had attempted for a time to undermine his authority, but their efforts were futile ; and, from the moment of his reconciliation to the "mother-State," all opposition to him ceased, and, no matter what official position he held, ever afterward he was

the autocrat of the backwoods. The Governors who succeeded him had only a nominal authority. So long as he
lived, he was the real seat of power. On all questions of
importance, the people asked, "What says the good old
Governor?" They might differ from him in opinion,
but when they did they questioned their own judgments,
and submitted cheerfully to his decisions. This they did
because experience had shown that he was always right.
The same genius which governed his military operations,
and made victory a foregone conclusion, enabled him to
forecast civil results, and to lead his people on by peaceful ways to prosperity and greatness.

A rule like his was never before or since known in
this country. It was made possible only by the peculiar
genius of Sevier, and the primitive character of the people he governed. Untrained in the military art and ignorant of governmental science, they were building up
a great empire. This they knew, and naturally they
looked to the man who had the ability to shield them
from danger and to guide them on the road to permanent
peace and prosperity. And it is Sevier's peculiar glory
that he did this without any thought of self—never once
looking to his own profit, or fame, or honor. It is said :
"Whosoever would become great among you shall be
your minister ; and whosoever would be first among you
shall be your bond-servant." Of this nature was Sevier's
greatness—dwarfed by no selfish ends, and inspired and
nourished wholly by a single regard for the good of
his fellow-men. This accounts for the fact that the

trans-Alleghany people were welded by him, as it were,
into one individual, with but one heart, one mind, and
one purpose; and these all centered in one great brain
and heart, which was the moving force of the whole.
They were the body, he was the soul; and, had it not
been so, Western civilization might have had a different
fate in the eighteenth century.

A little incident will illustrate Sevier's wonderful
popularity, and show how, in the remotest cabins, par-
ents spoke of him to their children with such unbounded
affection and admiration that the little ones came to regard him as some superior being—a sort of demi-god,
entitled to their unquestioning allegiance. I had the
anecdote from a gentleman of Knoxville,* who long ago
was told it by the old man who had been a party to the
occurrence. The aged countryman first saw Sevier when
he was a lad of some six or seven years, but he had heard
much of him from his very infancy, and his young imagination had magnified him into a sort of heroic demi-
god. One Sunday, when all the settlement had gathered
for religious services in the cross-roads meeting-house,
a hatless man rushed into the sacred building, shouting
that Nolichucky Jack was coming up the road on his
way to Virginia. At once the Sunday services were suspended, and every one turned out—even the minister.
They found the road lined with men and women, for the
news had spread far and wide, and all had come together

---

* Hon. William A. Henderson.

to welcome the idol of the people.   Soon Sevier came in
sight, walking his horse, and followed by a cavalcade of
gentlemen.   Nobody cheered or shouted, but all pressed
about him to get a look, a smile, a kindly word, or a nod
of recognition from their beloved Governor.   And these
he had for all, and all of them he called by name ; and
this, it is said, he could do to every man and woman in
the State, when they numbered more than a hundred
thousand.   The boy's father had been a soldier under
Sevier, and when the Governor came abreast of him he
halted his horse, and took the man and his wife by the
hand.   Then reaching down, and placing his hand on
the boy's head, he said : "And who have we here ? This
is a little fellow I have not seen."   That he was noticed
by so great a man made the boy inexpressibly proud and
happy ; but could this affable, unassuming gentleman be
the demi-god of his young imagination ?   This was the
thought that came to the boy, and he turned to his
father, saying, "Why, father, 'Chucky Jack is only a
man !"   But that was the wonder of the thing—how,
being only a man, he had managed to capture the hearts
of a whole people.

The devotion of the men of the border to Sevier is
without any parallel in American history.   His will was
literally their law, but it was law regulated by a kindness which sprang from a great, loving soul.   This all
men knew and respected ; and I think it may be said
that they refrained from strife, and violence, and crime,
less because it would subject them to punishment, than

because of the pain their misdoings would inflict upon
the heart of the "good old Governor." Though, as a
class, impatient of restraint, and of somewhat reckless
characteristics, crime was almost unknown among them.
For years there was no State's prison in the State, and
the jail at Knoxville—fourteen feet square—was seldom
afflicted with a tenant. There were courts, and judges,
and juries ; but Sevier was the court of last resort—the
supreme judge, the final jury. Was any one—white man
or red—aggrieved, he complained to the Governor ; did
two men differ, they submitted their controversy to him ;
were some of his old comrades in poverty or distress, they
appealed to their old commander, and he always found
some way to give them relief and assistance, though he
had impoverished himself in defending his country, and
was in his old age reduced to a meager pittance of a
thousand dollars a year.

But it must not be inferred from this that society beyond the mountains had reached that happy condition
wherein men have only minor differences, easily settled
by arbitration, and that courts of law had become entirely obsolete. The men of the backwoods had not altogether given over backbiting and bickering, torn down
their log temples of justice, and unanimously agreed to
submit all disputes to the decision of one man, whose
clear brain would rightly estimate and impartially weigh
both sides, and whose great heart would infallibly temper
justice with the gentle dews of mercy. It was not so.
It has not anywhere in this world been so since Adam

migrated from Eden, and Cain committed the first crime of which there is historical record ; and it will not be so for the next fifty thousand years, if the laws of heredity hold good, and universal man does not imbibe the spirit of the loving Christ, who came to earth to tell us that love is the grand motive power of the universe. Ever since man first transgressed the law, there have been legal tribunals, and they were to be found among these primitive people. But the courts sat only twice a year, and often their sessions were of not more than a week's duration. Their dockets were lean, and their rough benches deserted, because of the loving influence of one man, whose brotherly kindness had permeated the whole community. There were but seven lawyers in the entire Territory when it numbered nearly one hundred thousand people, and even they had caught some of Sevier's spirit, if the manifesto of one of them is any indication of the principles of the rest of the fraternity. I find this manifesto in the advertising columns of the "Knoxville Gazette," of April 6, 1793, and it deserves preservation. It is headed—

"FIAT JUSTITIA."

And it goes on to say : "Having adopted the above motto, as early as I had the honor of admission to the bar, I have covenanted with myself that I will never knowingly depart from it ; and on this foundation I have built a few maxims which afford my reflection an unspeakable satisfaction :

"I. I will practice law, because it offers me opportunities of being a more useful member of society.

"II. I will turn a deaf ear to no man because his purse is empty.

"III. I will advise no man beyond my comprehension of his cause.

"IV. I will lead none into law whom my conscience tells me should be kept out of it.

"V. I will never be unmindful of the cause of humanity, and this comprehends the fatherless and widow, and those who are in bondage.

"VI. I will be faithful to my client, but never so unfaithful to myself as to become a party to his crime.

"VII. In criminal cases I will not underrate my own abilities; for, if my client proves a rascal, his money is better in my hands, and, if not, I hold the option.

"VIII. I will never acknowledge the omnipotence of legislation, nor consider its acts to be law when against the spirit of the Constitution.

"IX. No man's greatness shall elevate him above the justice due to my client.

"X. I will not consent to a compromise when I conceive a verdict essential to my client's future reputation or protection; for of this he can not be a competent judge.

"XI. I will advise the turbulent with candor, and, if they persist in going to law against my advice, they must pardon me for volunteering it against them.

"XII. I will acknowledge every man's right to manage his own case if he pleases.

27

"The above are my rules of practice, and though I will not at this critical juncture promise to finish my business in person, I will, if the public service should require my removal hence, do everything in my power for those who like them; and endeavor to leave them in proper hands if I should be absent.

"WILLIAM TATHAM.

"KNOXVILLE, *March 23, 1793.*"

Sevier's justice knew neither rich nor poor, but his heart beat the warmest and his hand was the most open to those who had fallen by the way in the struggle of life, or had most severely felt the rough buffetings of poverty. So long as he had wealth it flowed out to such in abounding measure, and when he could no longer give of his substance he gave them himself—in his influence, his provident care, his never-ceasing effort to ameliorate their condition. Government, he said, should be the guardian of the poor, the widow, and the fatherless; and there is not one of his messages to the Legislature, that escaped the ravages of the Vandal fire which consumed Dr. Ramsey's dwelling during the Union occupation of Knoxville, which does not have some reference to the needs or make some suggestion for the benefit of the "less fortunate of our fellow-citizens," whom he recommends to their "paternal care and wisdom." One of these messages is now before me, and it so fully reveals the man, and clearly sketches the condition of the young Commonwealth, that I copy the entire document. It is

dated September 19, 1799, and, according to the custom
of the time, was delivered in person to the assembled
Senators and Representatives, who subsequently respond-
ed to it through the Speakers of the two Houses. The
message was as follows :

"*Mr. Speaker, and Gentlemen of the Senate and of the
House of Representatives :*

"It is with peculiar satisfaction that I have the
honor this day of meeting your august body in this
house, where I have the pleasure of informing you that
the State is blessed with peace and quietude—the fields
of the husbandman abundantly supplied with the fruits
of the earth, our harvests yielding to the laborer ample
satisfaction for his toils.

"The laws and regular decorum, so far as comes
within my knowledge, are duly observed and supported
throughout the government. Emigration and population are daily increasing, and I have no doubt that—
under the propitious hand of Providence, your patronage, and the wise and wholesome laws which you in your
wisdom may enact—our State will become more and
more respectable and conspicuous, and that its citizens
will enjoy all the happiness and comfort this human life,
in an ordinary course, can afford them.

"The poor and the distressed claim the first share of
your deliberations, and I have not the smallest doubt
your attention will be duly directed to them, and to
every other object worthy of legislative consideration.

Among other things, gentlemen, permit me again to remind you that the landed estates of your constituents, in general, appear to be verging on to a very precarious and doubtful situation, and should a timely interference be neglected it may become a subject of very great regret. I, therefore, beg leave to recommend that, so far as it may be consistent with the cession act and good public faith, you provide, in the most ample manner, for the security and peaceful enjoyment of all such property as may appear to be in jeopardy.

"I now proceed to enjoin on you the great necessity of promoting and encouraging manufactories, and establishing warehouses and inspections of various kinds. These will give a spring to industry, and enable the agricultural part of the community to export and dispose of all the surplus part of their bulky and heavy articles. Providence has blessed this State with a soil peculiarly calculated for the production of wheat, hemp, flax, cotton, tobacco, and indigo ; it abounds with ores and minerals, and has navigable rivers amply sufficient to enable us to export to the best of markets. This being the case, gentlemen, you will readily conceive how essentially necessary it is for the encouraging and promoting of all the advantages enumerated, that you lend to them your early legislative aid and patronage.

"Gentlemen of the Senate and House of Representatives, I am deeply and sensibly impressed with the honor conferred on me by my fellow-citizens, in electing me for a third time to preside as the Chief Magistrate of the

State. I earnestly wish I possessed greater abilities and talents to enable me to discharge the important duties, trust, and confidence they have reposed in me; but rest assured that, so far as I am able, nothing will be lacking or neglected by me that may tend toward the interest, welfare, and safety of the State. Before I close this address, I can not forbear requesting a harmony of measures in your councils, and that you unite in endeavoring to promote our dearest rights and interests. I have the fullest hope that by your wisdom and policy you will secure to our country the advantages and respect to which it is entitled, and has a right to enjoy.

" (Signed)   JOHN SEVIER."

To this address the House and Senate replied, through their Speakers, as follows :

" *To his Excellency* JOHN SEVIER, *Governor of the State of Tennessee.*

"SIR : It is with peculiar satisfaction that the Senate and House of Representatives have received your communication, announcing to them that our State is crowned with the blessings of peace and quietude ; that the toils of the husbandman are amply rewarded with abundant crops ; that the laws throughout the State are well and duly executed ; and that emigration and population are daily increasing. And we beg leave now to assure you that, under the directing hand of the all-seeing Providence, nothing on our part shall be wanting to increase the respectability of our rising State, and promote the welfare and happiness of our constituents.

"Receive, sir, our assurance that the matters and things contained in your address, and recommended to us as subjects of legislation, shall meet with that investigation and deliberation which the importance of the different subjects requires.

"We beg leave, sir, to express our gratification at being the witness of your being once more called, by the unanimous suffrage of the freemen of Tennessee, to the seat of Chief Magistrate of the State, and to express our public confidence that you will continue to execute the duties which appertain to your office with that firmness, judgment, and impartiality which have heretofore characterized you as the Chief Magistrate of Tennessee."

On the last day of the previous session of the Legislature, it made to Sevier an address, which is notable from its having been signed by William Blount, the former Governor of the Territory, and then Speaker of the Senate, and by James Stuart, the aforetime adherent of Tipton, and enemy of Sevier, who was Speaker of the House of Representatives. Of John Tipton himself all trace from this time (1798) disappears. Whether he had died, or had retired, like Cincinnatus, to his farm, I have not been able to discover. The address was as follows:

"*To* JOHN SEVIER, *Governor of the State of Tennessee:*
"The communications you have thought proper to

make to both Houses of the General Assembly, at the commencement and during the present session, afford additional proof of the care which hath always marked your official character since the first appointment to your present station.

"In the course of the present session the Legislature hath taken into consideration the subject of your several communications, and acted upon the same consistent with the exigency.

"The General Assembly, having finished the business before them, propose to adjourn this evening, without day."

These addresses exhibit the regard in which the "good old Governor" was held by the Tennessee Legislature. The trust and confidence of the people in him was shown by their six times choosing him unanimously their Governor, and by their subsequently electing him with the same unanimity, on three successive occasions, to the Congress of the United States. Such repeated and unanimous expressions of trust, esteem, and affection have never been accorded to any other public man in this country.

But this man, so universally beloved, was not without his enemies, and one of these was no less a personage than Andrew Jackson, subsequently President of the United States, but who at this time had achieved no particular distinction. Since 1788 Jackson had been in the practice of the law in Robertson's colony on the

Cumberland, and, observing his energy and fearless prose-
cution of offenders, and perhaps thinking well of his legal
ability, Sevier, in 1798, appointed him a Judge of the
Superior Court of Law and Equity of the newly formed
State. Their subsequent relations seem to have been
friendly until 1803, when the position of major-general
in the Tennessee militia was about to become vacant, and
Jackson made application for the appointment. The
office was an important one, inasmuch as, under the
Governor, the major-general had control of the entire
military force of the State.

To make sure of securing the position he coveted,
Jackson sought a personal interview with Sevier, and
pressed upon him his claims to the office. Naturally dis-
inclined to intrust duties so responsible to a man who
had no knowledge of the military art, nor any martial
experience beyond that to be gained in a bar-room brawl,
or a scrimmage at a cross-roads, the Governor received
Jackson's proposals with decided coolness. But the
cooler he grew the hotter became the applicant, and he
soon broke into the absurd gasconading which, according
to his biographers, he occasionally indulged in, even
when accumulated years should have taught him better
manners. He had been, prior to 1795, a private in one
or two Indian fights under Sampson Williams, a noted
captain of Robertson's, and he probably boasted of these
exploits, of which there are still traditions in Nashville.
This disgusted Sevier, who was embodied frankness, and
had a peculiarly sarcastic smile by which he put down

officious pretension. He said to Jackson that he had never heard of any of his military exploits, except his carrying away of another man's wife. The allusion was to the fact that not long before Jackson had escorted his future wife, then Mrs. Robards, to Natchez, to remove her from the persecution of a brutal husband. The event created a great scandal at the time, but there can be no question that the relations between Jackson and Mrs. Robards were innocent, and that she was justified in fleeing from her husband. To the end of his life Jackson was extremely sensitive to any disparaging allusions to his wife, and he now promptly challenged Sevier to a duel. Jackson was but thirty-six, Sevier nearly sixty —an age when even military men are exempted from the practice of human slaughter; but the custom of the time regarded dueling as the genteel mode of healing differences between gentlemen, and Sevier accepted the challenge, by writing Jackson the note which follows:

"KNOXVILLE, *October 2, 1803.*

"SIR: Yours to-day, by Andrew Whithe, Esq., I have received, and am pleased with the contents, so far as respects a personal interview.

"Your ungentlemanly and gasconading conduct of yesterday, and, indeed, at all other times heretofore, have unmasked you to me and to the world. The voice of the Assembly has made you a judge, and this alone renders you worthy of my notice, or that of any other gentleman. To the office I have respect, and this only makes you worthy of notice.

"I shall wait on you with pleasure at any time and place not within the State of Tennessee, attended by my friend, with pistols, presuming you know nothing about the use of any other arms. Georgia, Virginia, and North Carolina are in our vicinity, and we can easily repair to either of those places, and conveniently retire into the inoffending government. You can not mistake me or my meaning.

"Yours, etc., etc.,

"JOHN SEVIER.

"Hon. A. JACKSON."

To this Jackson replied that it was in the town of Knoxville that Sevier had taken the name of a lady "into" his polluted lips, and in the neighborhood of Knoxville he should atone for it, or he would publish him as "a coward and a poltroon."

Sevier then dispatched to Jackson his second, with a note, saying the gentleman would arrange upon a "time and place of rendezvous." No arrangement was made, for Jackson insisted on a meeting in the vicinity of Knoxville. Some correspondence ensued, which Sevier closed by a note in which he said: "An interview within the State you know I have denied. Anywhere outside, you have nothing to do but to name the place and I will the time. I have some regard for the laws of the State over which I have the honor to preside, although you, a judge, appear to have none." *

This closed the correspondence, but it did not pacify the irate Jackson, who soon afterward made an assault upon Sevier in the streets of Knoxville. Both were mounted, and Sevier was surrounded by about twenty horsemen. Jackson was much more thinly attended, and armed only with a cane and a brace of pistols; but, putting his cane in rest, like the lance of a plumed knight, he charged down upon Sevier most furiously. The latter dismounted to meet the assault; but a collision was prevented by the attending gentlemen, who soon pacified Jackson, and induced him to give his hand to the Governor.

But they never became friends, and, indeed, they could not well be, for they could not meet on any common ground of fraternity. Both were brave, honest, and intensely patriotic; but in all other respects they were as far asunder as the antipodes. Jackson was a born fighter, by his very nature aggressive, and delighting to struggle with men, either with arms or in the political arena; and it was this trait which made him, though essentially just, kind, and good, the best-hated man who has lived in this country. Sevier, on the contrary, though he had a genius for war, was by

---

* This correspondence appeared in full, some years ago, in the "Cincinnati Commercial"; and it is quoted entire by Professor Clayton, in his "History of Davidson County." Mr. Clayton has, however, I think, fallen into error in regard to some of the attending circumstances.

nature a man of peace and a lover of harmony. He
was kindly affectioned to all, high and low, white man
and red, and ever ready to sacrifice for the meanest,
rest, comfort, and property. Moreover, he had a strict
regard for decorum, was a born gentleman, actually
loathing the low sports and roistering gasconade to
which Jackson was at this time addicted. Sevier never
regained his respect for this man, who was so strangely
destined to rise to the highest station, and even in his
retired old age to control so absolutely the politics of this
country. When Jackson's fame was at its zenith, and
the country was ringing with his military successes,
Sevier would not admit that he had the ability to command, and, in a letter to his son, severely criticised
his conduct of the Creek campaign.*

But, though apparently reconciled to Sevier, Jackson's feeling toward him continued to be extremely
bitter. Soon after the events just narrated, his brother-
in-law, Donelson, was indicted for frauds in the sale of
lands, and at once Jackson charged that Sevier was
implicated in the transactions. The charge was speedily
disproved, and from the first the people knew it to be
absurd, for, with every ability and facility for making
money, Sevier was so poor that, but for his wife's excellent management of his plantation, he could not
have supported his family. But the charge showed
the *animus* of Jackson, who never forgot a friend or
forgave an enemy.

---

* See "Rear-Guard of the Revolution," page 314.

Sevier was poor. For more than twenty years his means had been exhaustively drawn upon for the equipment and support of the men who under him had fought for the country against both the British and the Indians; and the consequence was that, though free from debt, he had nothing but his plantation and a meager pittance of seven hundred and fifty dollars a year during his first term as Governor of Tennessee. He had rendered vast and vital services to the country, and at the sacrifice of about all he possessed, but he had never thought of asking remuneration from a government that was quite as poor as he was. Blount, who had just gone out of office as Governor of the Territory, had lived in a style of elegance not common to the backwoods; and it was but natural that Sevier should feel it incumbent upon him to support a town residence somewhat in harmony with the dignity of the new State. Accordingly, not realizing exactly how poor he was—as few men do who have been reduced from affluence to poverty—he bought a house-lot in Knoxville, and, soon after his first election as Governor, began the erection of a spacious brick mansion. However, when the building had arrived at the top of the basement story, he found himself in the position of the one in Scripture, who began to build, and was not able to finish. He had a horror of debt; so, like an honest man, he went no further, but, selling his lot and unfinished house, he paid off his workmen, and then, like Cincinnatus, retired to his farm, where he ever

28

afterward lived, making his home, when obliged to be in Knoxville on official business, with his son-in-law, Major McLellan, in the new brick house which has been mentioned. The unfinished house was bought by a Mr. John Park, and it is yet standing, and the property of his descendants. Mr. Park completed it after the plans of Sevier; but he used a somewhat differently colored brick in its construction, so that the line where Sevier left off and Park began was distinctly visible. That line has remained to this day, a speaking monument to the poverty, unflinching honesty, and democratic good sense of the first Governor of Tennessee.

Near the main road leading to Sevierville, and about five miles from the city of Knoxville, in a deserted and worn-out field, are the ruins of an old log station. During the war between Sevier and the Cherokees for the protection of the French Broad settlers, the place became the refuge of a number of families, and it had been a frontier post before Knoxville was settled. It was in a secluded and picturesque region, where a copious spring gushes forth from a spur of Bay's Mountain. The surrounding land was bought by Sevier when, about 1790, he took up his abode on the frontier, to be nearer to the hostile Indians. The buildings he at once enlarged, and he kept on adding to them year by year—one log-house being tacked to another—till the structure more resembled a hamlet than a single dwelling. Here he lived ever after his futile effort at building a town mansion, in a style of rustic sim-

plicity, going into town about every morning, and returning at night, and always on horseback, for to the very last
of his life he was never so much at home as when in
the saddle. He was a superb horseman, and always
rode a magnificent animal.

The principal apartment in the Governor's house
was the reception-room, which occupied the whole of one
of the cabins, and was furnished in a manner approaching to elegance, its puncheon floor being partly covered
on great occasions with an imported carpet, which had
been presented to the "Governor's wife," as the lady was
universally styled, by some one of her seaboard admirers.
But the precious rug never made its appearance except
to honor some distinguished guest—some high home
official or titled foreigner—whom curiosity or business
had brought into the backwoods. They had no sooner
gone than it was carefully dusted and rolled away to one
side of the room by Jeff and Susy, old servants, who
had been reared in the family. It was never known to
remain on the floor overnight but on the single occasion
when, in 1798, Louis Philippe and his brothers were on
a visit to the Governor.

In this primitive mansion Sevier kept open house
and entertained his guests in a style of genuine backwoods hospitality. His guests were numerous, for no
stranger came into the country without calling upon
the Governor, and his old companions in arms often so
thronged upon him that the house could not contain the
crowd, and some of them had to find lodgings in the

stables—which, however, was no great hardship, for the
Governor's barns were about as palatial as his dwelling.
Here, too, came the Indian chiefs—John Watts, Double
Head, and Esquetau (the Bloody Fellow), whom he
had so often and so severely punished—to stretch their
moccasins before the great wood-fire, eat of the Governor's venison, and ask his advice upon the important
affairs of their nation.   Dr. Ramsey, who lived near, and
knew Sevier well—he not dying till Ramsey was eighteen
years old—told me that the Indian chiefs were frequent
visitors, and he never knew a time when one or more of
Sevier's old soldiers were not quartered at the mansion ;
and that he thought none of them ever came to him with
a worn-out nag, broken down by a long journey, but the
Governor asked him, on his going away, to exchange his
old horse for one of his own blooded animals, of which
he always kept the largest and finest stud to be found
anywhere west of the Alleghanies.   "This was not
strange," said Dr. Ramsey, "for every man in the State
regarded the Governor as his personal friend, and looked
upon him and all that he had as public property ; and
in return the Governor considered all, especially the poor
and needy, as his children, and so entitled to all he
had of time, thought, and possessions."

The nearest neighbors of Sevier were his old compatriots and devoted friends, James White, James Cozby,
Francis A. Ramsey, the father of the historian, and the
John Adair of whom I have made honorable mention
in a previous volume.   With them and his family he

was a regular attendant on Sunday services, in a little stone church, at a hamlet called Lebanon, about half a mile distant from his dwelling. He had a pew of his own, but he usually sat with his tried and trusty friend Cozby, in a high-backed, old-fashioned enclosure, on the left of the aisle, and near the front entrance. On such occasions he doffed his usual backwoods costume of hunting-shirt and sword, and appeared as the old-time country gentleman—in three-cornered hat, powdered hair, ruffled shirt, and citizen's clothes generally. His demeanor in church was grave and reverential, and he never failed to give respectful attention to the services; but the strong Calvinism of the pastor, the Rev. Samuel Carrick, was not to his liking. He was too democratic in feeling to accept a creed which elects a few to happiness, and consigns all the rest of the human race to eternal reprobation, which doctrine at that time was the popular one throughout the country. He could not credit such a faith, and it may be that for this reason he was never a church-member; for he could not be a hypocrite—professing what he did not believe. And yet he had a firm faith in Providence, and was a man of deeply religious feeling — which grew deeper as old age stole upon him, and he came nearer to the end of his earthly journey. Once, after the expiration of his last term as Governor, he said to a gentleman who had reminded him of his great services to the country and to Western civilization : "I am not entitled to the credit, sir; I have been merely an instrument—led, and guided, and guarded by the INFINITE GOODNESS."

Near the close of his term in Congress he was asked by President Monroe to act as United States commissioner in running the boundary-line between Georgia and the Creek nation. Though much enfeebled by age and infirmity, he accepted the appointment. The labor was too great for his strength, and, worn out with his work, he succumbed in the summer heat to the fever incident to the season in that climate, and died in his tent, surrounded only by soldiers and a few Indian chieftains, on the 24th of September, 1815, in his seventy-first year. There they made his grave, and there his body lies to-day; over it merely a simple slab, on which is rudely cut the name "JOHN SEVIER."

When tidings of his death reached Tennessee, the whole State went into mourning. For the space of thirty days every public building was draped in black, and all the State officials wore crape upon their arms. A general sorrow was diffused throughout Tennessee and the whole Western country. And well might the people mourn, for "a great man had fallen in Israel." I have called him a hero, a soldier, and a statesman; but he was more than all these: he was a civilizer, a great organizer, a nation-builder. He found Tennessee a little cluster of log-houses, and he left it a great State, with happy homesteads, and smiling villages, and populous cities, in which were palatial dwellings and magnificent temples, and a population of nearly four hundred thousand souls.

To this day Tennessee has left him without a monument; and it may be said that no monument can so well proclaim his greatness as the great State which he builded. This may be true, and yet we do honor to ourselves and our common nature when we rear memorials to such men; and it is fitting that we should preserve their names and deeds in ever-during brass and marble, for they come to us only now and then through the centuries.

INDEX.

29

THE END.

THE TWO SPIES: NATHAN HALE AND JOHN ANDRÉ. By
BENSON J. LOSSING, LL. D. Illustrated with Pen-and-Ink Sketches. Containing also Anna Seward's "Monody on Major André." Square 8vo, cloth, gilt top, $2.00.

This work contains an outline sketch of the most prominent events in the lives of the two notable spies of the American Revolution—Nathan Hale and John André, illustrated by nearly thirty engravings of portraits, buildings, sketches by André, etc. Among these illustrations are pictures of commemorative monuments: one in memory of Hale at Coventry, Connecticut; of André in Westminster Abbey; one to mark the spot at Tarrytown where André was *captured;* and the memorial-stone at Tappaan set up by Mr. Field to mark the spot where André was *executed.* The volume also contains the full text and original notes of the famous "Monody on Major André," written by his friend Anna Seward, with a portrait and biographical sketch of Miss Seward, and letters to her by Major André.

THE REAR-GUARD OF THE REVOLUTION. By EDMUND
KIRKE, author of "Among the Pines," etc. With Portrait of John Sevier, and Map. 12mo, cloth, $1.50.

Many readers will recall a volume published during the war, entitled "Among the Pines," appearing under the pen-name of Edmund Kirke. This book attained a remarkable success, and all who have read it will recall its spirited and graphic delineations of life in the South. "The Rear-Guard of the Revolution," from the same hand, is a narrative of the adventures of the pioneers that first crossed the Alleghanies and settled in what is now Tennessee, under the leadership of two remarkable men, James Robertson and John Sevier. Sevier is notably the hero of the narrative. His career was certainly remarkable, as much so as that of Daniel Boone. The title of the book is derived from the fact that a body of hardy volunteers, under the leadership of Sevier, crossed the mountains to uphold the patriotic cause, and by their timely arrival secured the defeat of the British army at King's Mountain.

"Mr. Kirke has not only performed a real and lasting service to American historical literature in the production of this work, but has honored the memory and paid a tribute of richly-deserved praise to a band of men as brave and loyal and heroic as ever poured out their lives and treasure for their country's good."—*New York Observer.*

"No work of the kind that equals it in interest and importance has been published for many years. It is a distinct contribution to the history of the American Revolution, and even to the most industrious student of that period many of its facts will come as a revelation."—*Philadelphia Times.*

"The book is full of valuable information and historic wealth, while the gracefulness of style and the simplicity of the language make it one of the most useful and entertaining publications of the year."—*Boston Evening Gazette.*

New York: D. APPLETON & CO., 1, 3, & 5 Bond Street.

REMINISCENCES AND OPINIONS, 1813-1885. By Sir FRANCIS HASTINGS DOYLE, formerly Professor of Poetry at Oxford. Crown 8vo, cloth, $2.00.

"The author has known and appreciated some of the best among two generations of men, and he still holds his rank in the third. One of the pleasantest of recent publications is not the less instructive to those who are interested in present or recent history."—*Saturday Review.*

"The volume appears to fulfill in almost every respect the ideal of an agreeable, chatty book of anecdotal recollections. . . . The reminiscences are those of a genial man of wide culture and broad sympathies; and they form a collection of anecdotes which, as the production of a single man, is unrivaled in interest, in variety, and in novelty."—*London Athenæum.*

"For Sir Francis Doyle's book we have nothing to give but words of the strongest commendation. It is as pleasant a book as we have read for many a long day."—*London Spectator.*

"The volume teems with good stories, pleasant recollections, and happy sayings of famous men of a past generation."—*Illustrated London News.*

SKETCHES FROM MY LIFE. By the late ADMIRAL HOBART PASHA. With a Portrait. 12mo, paper cover, 50 cents; cloth, $1.00.

This brilliant and lively volume contains, in addition to numerous adventures of a general character, descriptions of slaver-hunting on the coast of Africa, blockade-running in the South during the Civil War, and experiences in the Turkish navy during the war with Russia.

"A memoir which enthralls by its interest and captivates by its ingenuous modesty. . . . A deeply interesting record of a very exceptional career."—*Pall Mall Gazette.*

"The sailor is nearly always an adventurous and enterprising variety of the human species, and Hobart Pasha was about as fine an example as one could wish to see. . . . The sketches of South American life are full of interest. The sport, the inevitable entanglements of susceptible middies with beautiful Spanish girls and the sometimes disastrous consequences, the duels, attempts at assassination, and other adventures and amusements, are described with much spirit. . . . The story of his slaver-hunting carries one back to boyish recollections of Captain Marryat's delightful tales. . . . The sketches abound in interesting details of the American war. It is impossible to abridge the account of these exciting rushes [blockade-running] through the line of cruisers—our readers must enjoy them for themselves."—*London Athenæum.*

"'Sketches from My Life,' by the late Admiral Hobart Pasha, provides very interesting reading. It relates in a frank and rough sailor fashion the principal events in its author's romantic and adventurous career, and is particularly attractive in its hunting incidents, its spirited accounts of chasing slave vessels, its stories of blockade-running during our Civil War, and its pictures of Turkish life, military, naval, and social. It is a bright and breezy book generally, and is full of entertainment."—*Boston Gazette.*

New York: D. APPLETON & CO., 1, 3, & 5 Bond Street.

THE GREVILLE MEMOIRS COMPLETE.

A JOURNAL OF THE REIGNS OF KING GEORGE IV AND KING WILLIAM IV. By the late CHARLES C. F. GREVILLE, Esq., Clerk of the Council to those Sovereigns. Edited by HENRY REEVE, Registrar of the Privy Council. Two vols. 12mo. Cloth, $4.00.

"Since the publication of Horace Walpole's Letters, no book of greater historical interest has seen the light than the Greville Memoirs. It throws a curious, and, we may almost say, a terrible light on the conduct and character of the public men in England under the reigns of George IV and William IV. Its descriptions of those kings and their kinsfolk are never likely to be forgotten."—*New York Times.*

A JOURNAL OF THE REIGN OF QUEEN VICTORIA, FROM 1837 TO 1852. The "Greville Memoirs," Second Part. By the late CHARLES GREVILLE, Clerk of the Council. Uniform with Part First. Two vols. 12mo. Cloth, $4.00.

"Mr. Greville's Diary is one of the most important contributions which have ever been made to the political history of the middle of the nineteenth century. He is a graphic and powerful writer; and his usual habit of making the record while the impression of the events was fresh upon his mind, gives his sketches of persons and places, and his accounts of conversations, great vividness. The volumes will be read with as much interest for their sketches of social life as for their political value."—*London Daily News.*

A JOURNAL OF THE REIGN OF QUEEN VICTORIA, FROM 1852 TO 1860. By the late CHARLES GREVILLE, Esq., Clerk of the Council. Being third and concluding part of the "Greville Memoirs." One vol. 12mo. Cloth, $2.00.

The preceding volumes of the " Greville Memoirs " consist of "A Journal of the Reign of King George IV and King William IV " in two vols.; and " A Journal of the Reign of Queen Victoria, from 1837 to 1852," in two vols. Price in each case, per vol., $2.00.

This volume, in addition to personal anecdotes, deals with many important events, such, for instance, as the re-establishment of the French Empire, the Crimean War, the Indian Mutiny, and the Italian War.

THE HISTORICAL REFERENCE-BOOK, COMPRISING A CHRONOLOGICAL TABLE OF UNIVERSAL HISTORY, A CHRONOLOGICAL DICTIONARY OF UNIVERSAL HISTORY, A BIOGRAPHICAL DICTIONARY. With Geographical Notes. For the Use of Students, Teachers, and Readers. Second edition. By LOUIS HEILPRIN. Crown 8vo, 579 pages. Half leather, $3.00.

"A second, revised edition of Mr. Louis Heilprin's 'Historical Reference-Book' has just appeared, marking the well-earned success of this admirable work—a dictionary of dates, a dictionary of events (with a special gazetteer for the places mentioned), and a concise biographical dictionary, all in one, and all in the highest degree trustworthy. Mr. Heilprin's revision is as thorough as his original work. Any one can test it by running over the list of persons deceased since this manual first appeared."—*Evening Post.*

BRAZIL: Its Condition and Prospects. By C. C. ANDREWS, ex-Consul-General to Brazil; formerly U. S. Minister to Norway and Sweden. 12mo. Cloth, $1.50.

"I hope I may be able to present some facts in respect to the present situation of Brazil which will be both instructive and entertaining to general readers. My means of acquaintance with that empire are principally derived from a residence of three years at Rio de Janeiro, its capital, while employed in the service of the United States Government, during which period I made a few journeys into the interior."—*From the Preface.*

A STUDY OF MEXICO. By DAVID A. WELLS, LL. D., D. C. L. 12mo. Cloth, $1.00; paper cover, 50 cents.

"The results of the 'Study of Mexico' were originally contributed, in the form of a series of papers, to 'The Popular Science Monthly.' . . . The interest and discussion they have excited, both in the United States and Mexico, have been such, and the desire on the part of the people of the former country, growing out of recent political complications, to know more about Mexico, has become so general and manifest, that it has been thought expedient to republish and offer them to the public in book-form—subject to careful revision and with extensive additions, especially in relation to the condition and wages of labor and the industrial resources and productions of Mexico."—*From the Preface.*

"Mr. Wells's showing is extremely interesting, and its value is great. Nothing like it has been published in many years."—*New York Times.*

"Mr. Wells sketches broadly but in firm lines Mexico's physical geography, her race inheritance, political history, social condition, and present government."—*New York Evening Post.*

"Several efforts have been made to satisfy the growing desire for information relating to Mexico since that country has become connected by railways with the United States. But we have seen no book upon the subject by an American writer which is so satisfactory on the score of knowledge and trustworthiness as 'A Study of Mexico,' by David A. Wells."—*New York Sun.*

FLORIDA FOR TOURISTS, INVALIDS, AND SETTLERS: containing Practical Information regarding Climate, Soil, and Productions; Scenery and Resorts; the Culture of the Orange and other Tropical Fruits; Sports; Routes of Travel, etc., etc. With Map and Illustrations. New edition, revised. 12mo. Cloth, $1.50.

APPLETONS' GUIDE TO MEXICO. By ALFRED R. CONKLING. With a Railway Map and numerous Illustrations. Third edition, thoroughly revised. 12mo. Cloth, $2.00.

APPLETONS' HAND-BOOK OF SUMMER RESORTS. Fully revised for the season. With Maps and numerous Illustrations. Large 12mo. Paper, 50 cents.

APPLETONS' HAND-BOOK OF AMERICAN WINTER RESORTS. Revised to date of issue. With Map and Illustrations. 12mo. Paper, 50 cents.

APPLETONS' DICTIONARY OF NEW YORK AND ITS VICINITY. New edition, revised and corrected. With Maps of New York and Vicinity. Paper, 30 cents.

A TREATISE ON SURVEYING. COMPRISING THE THEORY AND THE PRACTICE. By W. M. GILLESPIE, LL. D., formerly Professor of Civil Engineering in Union College. Revised and enlarged by CADY STALEY, President of the Case School of Applied Science. With numerous Illustrations, Diagrams, and various Tables. One vol., 8vo. 692 pages. Half leather, $3.50.

The two works by Dr. Gillespie, hitherto published separately, "Leveling and Higher Surveying," and "Practical Treatise on Surveying," have been thoroughly revised and enlarged, and are now united in this volume, which is a complete and systematic work, including Land Surveying, Leveling, Topography. Triangular Surveying, Hydrographical Surveying, and Underground or Mining Surveying. With Appendices on Plane Trigonometry, Transversals, etc., and full tables of Chords, Logarithms, Logarithmic and Natural Sines, Cosines, Tangents, etc., Stadia Tables, Transverse Tables, and Tables of Refraction in Declination, etc. The whole now in convenient and comprehensive form is specially adapted for class use in High-Schools and Colleges.

THE RISE AND EARLY CONSTITUTION OF UNIVERSITIES. WITH A SURVEY OF MEDIÆVAL EDUCATION. By S. S. LAURIE, LL. D., Professor of the Institutes and History of Education in the University of Edinburgh. Vol. III of "The International Education Series," edited by W. T. HARRIS, LL. D. 12mo. Cloth, $1.50.

"In the history of the rise and organization of universities, the student of education finds the most interesting and suggestive topics in the entire range of his specialty. For, in the history of the development of the higher and highest education, he sees the definite modes by which the contributions of the past to the well-being of the present have been transmitted."—*From Editor's Preface.*

The previous volumes of the series are:

Vol. I.—THE PHILOSOPHY OF EDUCATION. By JOHANN KARL FRIEDRICH ROSENKRANZ, Doctor of Theology and Professor of Philosophy at the University of Königsberg. Translated from the German by ANNA C. BRACKETT. 12mo. Cloth, $1.50.

Vol. II.—A HISTORY OF EDUCATION. By Professor F. V. N. PAINTER, of Roanoke College, Salem, Virginia. 12mo. Cloth, $1.50.

APPLIED GEOLOGY: A TREATISE ON THE INDUSTRIAL RELATIONS OF GEOLOGICAL STRUCTURE; AND ON THE NATURE, OCCURRENCE, AND USES OF SUBSTANCES DERIVED FROM GEOLOGICAL SOURCES. By SAMUEL G. WILLIAMS, Professor of General and Economic Geology in Cornell University. (Appletons' Science Text-Books.) 12mo. Cloth, $1.40.

This is the first work published in this country which aims to give a connected and systematic view of the applications of Geology to the various uses of mankind. It gives the classification of the rock-forming minerals, with a description of each, also the arrangement of rock masses, mineral fuels, illuminating materials, and metalliferous deposits. It treats of the relations of geology to agriculture and health, and presents, in an exhaustive manner, the properties and modes of occurrence of the different metals. It also discusses the substances adapted to chemical manufacture, fictile materials, etc., together with a description of ornamental stones and gems.

THE GEOGRAPHICAL AND GEOLOGICAL DISTRIBUTION OF ANIMALS. By ANGELO HEILPRIN, Professor of Invertebrate Paleontology at the Academy of Natural Sciences, Philadelphia, etc. 12mo. $2.00.

"An important contribution to physical science is Angelo Heilprin's 'Geographical and Geological Distribution of Animals.' The author has aimed to present to his readers such of the more significant facts connected with the past and present distribution of animal life as might lead to a proper conception of the relations of existing fauna, and also to furnish the student with a work of general reference, wherein the more salient features of the geography and geology of animal forms could be readily ascertained. While this book is addressed chiefly to the naturalist, it contains much information, particularly on the subject of the geographical distribution of animals, the rapidly increasing growth of some species and the gradual extinction of others, which will interest and instruct the general reader. Mr. Heilprin is no believer in the doctrine of independent creation, but holds that animate nature must be looked upon as a concrete whole."—*New York Sun*.

MICROBES, FERMENTS, AND MOULDS. By E. L. TROUESSART. With 107 Illustrations. 12mo. Cloth, $1.50.

"Microbes are everywhere; every species of plant has its special parasites, the vine having more than one hundred foes of this kind. Fungi of a microscopic size, they have their uses in nature, since they clear the surface of the earth from dead bodies and fecal matter, from all dead and useless substances which are the refuse of life, and return to the soil the soluble mineral substances from which plants are derived. All fermented liquors, wine, beer, vinegar, etc., are artificially produced by the species of microbes called ferments; they also cause bread to rise. Others are injurious to us, for in the shape of spores and seeds they enter our bodies with air and water and cause a large number of the diseases to which the flesh is heir. Many physicians do not accept the microbian theory, considering that when microbes are found in the blood they are neither the cause of the disease, nor the contagious element, nor the vehicle of contagion. In France the opponents of the microbian theory are Robin, Bechamp, and Jousset de Bellesme; in England, Lewis and Lionel Beale. The writer comes to the conclusion that Pasteur's microbian theory is the only one that explains all facts."—*New York Times*.

EARTHQUAKES AND OTHER EARTH MOVEMENTS. By JOHN MILNE, Professor of Mining and Geology in the Imperial College of Engineering, Tokio, Japan. With 38 Illustrations. 12mo. Cloth, $1.75.

"In this little book Professor Milne has endeavored to bring together all that is known concerning the nature and causes of earthquake movements. His task was one of much difficulty. Professor Milne's excellent work in the science of seismology has been done in Japan, in a region of incessant shocks of sufficient energy to make observation possible, yet, with rare exceptions, of no disastrous effects. He has had the good fortune to be aided by Mr. Thomas Gray, a gentleman of great constructive skill, as well as by Professors J. A. Ewing, W. S. Chaplin, and his other colleagues in the scientific colony which has gathered about the Imperial University of Japan. To these gentlemen we owe the best of our science of seismology, for before their achievements we had nothing of value concerning the physical conditions of earthquakes except the great works of Robert Mallet; and Mallet, with all his genius and devotion to the subject, had but few chances to observe the actual shocks, and so failed to understand many of their important features."—*The Nation*.

New York: D. APPLETON & CO., 1, 3, & 5 Bond Street.

CREATION OR EVOLUTION? A PHILOSOPHICAL IN-QUIRY. By GEORGE TICKNOR CURTIS. 12mo. Cloth, $2.00.

"I some years ago took up the study of the modern doctrine of animal evolution. Until after the death of Mr. Charles Darwin I had not given very close attention to this subject. The honor paid to his memory, and due to his indefatigable research and extensive knowledge, led me to examine his 'Descent of Man' and his 'Origin of Species,' both of which I studied with care, and I trust with candor. I was next induced to examine the writings of Mr. Herbert Spencer. . . . The result of my study of the hypothesis of evolution is that it is an ingenious but delusive mode of accounting for the existence of either the body or the mind of man; and that it employs a kind of reasoning which no person of sound judgment would apply to anything that might affect his welfare, his happiness, his estate, or his conduct in the practical affairs of life."—*From the Preface.*

LIFE AND LABOURS OF THE REV. W. E. BOARD-MAN. By Mrs. BOARDMAN. 12mo. Cloth, $1.25.

The life of the Rev. Mr. Boardman was full of varied incidents and experiences, both in this country and in Europe. It includes graphic pictures of life in California, and striking incidents of the civil war.

THE CENTENNIAL HISTORY OF THE PROTESTANT EPISCOPAL CHURCH OF THE DIOCESE OF NEW YORK, 1785-1885. Edited by Gen. JAMES GRANT WILSON. 8vo, 464 pages. Cloth, gilt top, $4.00; half calf extra, gilt top, $7.00.

WHY WE BELIEVE THE BIBLE. AN HOUR'S READING FOR BUSY PEOPLE. By J. P. T. INGRAHAM, S. T. D. 16mo. Cloth, 60 cents.

The dedication to this manual indicates briefly its purpose: "To the Jews, from whom the Bible came ; to the Gentiles, to whom it came; and to all who would like to confirm their faith in the Bible, but who have not leisure for large volumes, this book is respectfully inscribed."

NOTES ON THE PARABLES OF OUR LORD.
NOTES ON THE MIRACLES OF OUR LORD.

By the late Archbishop TRENCH. New revised editions. 12mo. Cloth, $1.50 each.

The present are entirely new editions of books that enjoyed great popularity during the lifetime of Archbishop Trench. The text has received the author's latest emendations, as made by him in his own copy during the last years of his life, and *the notes, in Latin and Greek, are translated,* carrying out an intention which had long been in the author's mind, thereby bringing the volumes within the reach of a larger circle of readers.

SERMONS NEW AND OLD. By Archbishop RICHARD CHENEVIX TRENCH, D. D. 12mo. Cloth, $1.50.

The late Archbishop Trench's "Notes on the Parables and the Miracles of Our Lord " have been widely read, and the admirers of those interesting and instructive essays will welcome the selections of the Archbishop's Sermons contained in the present volume.

New York: D. APPLETON & CO., 1, 3, & 5 Bond Street.

PHYSICAL EXPRESSION: Its Modes and Principles. By FRANCIS WARNER, M. D., Assistant Physician, and Lecturer on Botany, to the London Hospital, etc. With 51 Illustrations. 12mo. Cloth, $1.75.

"In the term 'Physical Expression,' Dr. Warner includes all those changes of form and feature occurring in the body which may be interpreted as evidences of mental action. At first thought it would seem that facial expression is the most important of these outward signs of inner processes; but a little observation will convince one that the posture assumed by the body—the poise of the head and, the position of the hands—as well as the many alternations of color and of general nutrition, are just as striking evidences of the course of thought. The subject thus developed by the author becomes quite extensive, and is exceedingly interesting. The work is fully up to the standard maintained in 'The International Scientific Series.'"—*Science.*

"Among those, besides physicians, dentists, and oculists, to whom Dr. Warner's book will be of benefit are actors and artists. The art of gesticulation and of postures is dealt with clearly from the scientific student's point of view. In the chapters concerning expression in the head, expression in the face, expression in the eyes, and in that on art criticism, the reader may find many new suggestions."—*Philadelphia Press.*

COMMON SENSE OF THE EXACT SCIENCES. By the late WILLIAM KINGDON CLIFFORD. With 100 Figures. 12mo. Cloth, $1.50.

"This is one of the volumes of 'The International Scientific Series,' and was originally planned by Mr. Clifford; but upon his death in 1879 the revision and completion of the work were intrusted to Mr. C. R. Rowe. He also died before accomplishing his purpose, and the book had to be finished by a third person. It is divided into five chapters, treating number, space, quantity, position, and motion, respectively. Each of these chapters is subdivided into sections, explaining in detail the principles underlying each. The whole volume is written in a masterful, scholarly manner, and the theories are illustrated by one hundred carefully prepared figures. To teachers especially is this volume valuable; and it is worthy of the most careful study."—*New York School Journal.*

JELLY-FISH, STAR-FISH, AND SEA-URCHINS. Being a Research on Primitive Nervous Systems. By G. J. ROMANES, F. R. S., author of "Mental Evolution in Animals," etc. 12mo. Cloth, $1.75.

"A profound research into the laws of primitive nervous systems conducted by one of the ablest English investigators. Mr. Romanes set up a tent on the beach and examined his beautiful pets for six summers in succession. Such patient and loving work has borne its fruits in a monograph which leaves nothing to be said about jelly-fish, star-fish, and sea-urchins. Every one who has studied the lowest forms of life on the sea-shore admires these objects. But few have any idea of the exquisite delicacy of their structure and their nice adaptation to their place in nature. Mr. Romanes brings out the subtile beauties of the rudimentary organisms, and shows the resemblances they bear to the higher types of creation. His explanations are made more clear by a large number of illustrations. While the book is well adapted for popular reading, it is of special value to working physiologists."—*New York Journal of Commerce.*

"A most admirable treatise on primitive nervous systems. The subject-matter is full of original investigations and experiments upon the animals mentioned as types of the lowest nervous developments."—*Boston Commercial Bulletin.*

A HISTORY OF ENGLAND IN THE EIGHTEENTH CENTURY. By WILLIAM E. H. LECKY, author of "History of the Rise and Influence of the Spirit of Rationalism in Europe," etc. Vols. I, II, III, and IV. Large 12mo. Cloth, $2.25 each; half calf, $4.50 each.

"On every ground which should render a history of eighteenth-century England precious to thinking men, Mr. Lecky's work may be commended. The materials accumulated in these volumes attest an industry more strenuous and comprehensive than that exhibited by Froude or by Macaulay. But it is his supreme merit that he leaves on the reader's mind a conviction that he not only possesses the acuteness which can discern the truth, but the unflinching purpose of truth-telling."—*New York Sun.*

"Lecky has not chosen to deal with events in chronological order, nor does he present the details of personal, party, or military affairs. The work is rather an attempt 'to disengage from the great mass of facts those which relate to the permanent forces of the nation, or which indicate some of the more enduring features of national life.' The author's manner has led him to treat of the power of monarchy, aristocracy, and democracy; of the history of political ideas; of manners and of beliefs, as well as of the increasing power of Parliament and of the press."—*Dr. C. K. Adams's Manual of Historical Literature.*

HISTORY OF THE RISE AND INFLUENCE OF THE SPIRIT OF RATIONALISM IN EUROPE. By WILLIAM E. H. LECKY. 2 vols. Small 8vo. Cloth, $4.00; half calf, extra, $8.00.

"The author defines his purpose as an attempt to trace that spirit which 'leads men on all occasions to subordinate dogmatic theology to the dictates of reason and of conscience, and, as a necessary consequence, to restrict its influence upon life'—which predisposes men, in history, to attribute all kinds of phenomena to natural rather than miraculous causes; in theology, to esteem succeeding systems the expressions of the wants and aspirations of that religious sentiment which is planted in all men; and, in ethics, to regard as duties only those which conscience reveals to be such."—*Dr. C. K. Adams's Manual of Historical Literature.*

THE LEADERS OF PUBLIC OPINION IN IRELAND: SWIFT, FLOOD, GRATTAN, O'CONNELL. By WILLIAM E. H. LECKY. 12mo. Cloth, $1.75.

"A writer of Lecky's mind, with his rich imagination, his fine ability to appreciate imagination in others, and his disposition to be himself an orator upon the written page, could hardly have found a period in British history more harmonious with his literary style than that which witnessed the rise, the ripening, and the fall of the four men whose impress upon the development of the national spirit of Ireland was not limited by the local questions whose discussion constituted their fame."—*New York Evening Post.*

HISTORY OF HENRY THE FIFTH: KING OF ENGLAND, LORD OF IRELAND, AND HEIR OF FRANCE. By GEORGE M. TOWLE. 8vo. Cloth, $2.50.

CAMEOS FROM ENGLISH HISTORY. By CHARLOTTE M. YONGE. 12mo. Cloth, $1.00.

THREE CENTURIES OF ENGLISH LITERATURE. By C. D. YONGE. 12mo. Cloth, $2.00.

HISTORY OF THE UNITED STATES OF AMERICA, FROM THE DISCOVERY OF THE CONTINENT TO THE ESTABLISHMENT OF THE CONSTITUTION IN 1789. By GEORGE BANCROFT. The author's last revision. Complete in six volumes 8vo. Price in sets: blue cloth, gilt top, uncut edge, $15.00; brown cloth, gilt top, uncut edge, paper titles, $15.00; sheep, marble edge, $21.00; half morocco, gilt top, uncut edge, $27.00; half calf, marble edge, $27.00; half grained morocco, gilt top, uncut edge, $27.00.

The six volumes of this new and fully revised edition of Bancroft's "History of the United States," now complete, comprise the twelve volumes of the original octavo edition, including the "History of the Formation of the Constitution" last published, and are issued at just half the price. Volume VI contains a new portrait of Bancroft engraved on steel.

HISTORY OF THE FORMATION OF THE CONSTITUTION OF THE UNITED STATES. By GEORGE BANCROFT. 1 vol. 8vo. Cloth, $2.50.

This volume includes the original two-volume edition of the work, with an Appendix, containing the Constitution and Amendments. It is designed for constitutional students, and is sold separately from the other volumes of Bancroft's History.

HISTORY OF THE PEOPLE OF THE UNITED STATES, FROM THE REVOLUTION TO THE CIVIL WAR. By JOHN B. McMASTER. 5 vols. 8vo. Vols. I and II now ready. Cloth, $2.50 each.

SCOPE OF THE WORK.—In the course of this narrative much is written of wars, conspiracies, and rebellions; of Presidents, of Congresses, of embassies, of treaties, of the ambition of political leaders, and of the rise of great parties in the nation. Yet the history of the people is the chief theme. At every stage of the splendid progress which separates the America of Washington and Adams from the America in which we live, it has been the author's purpose to describe the dress, the occupations, the amusements, the literary canons of the times; to note the change of manners and morals; to trace the growth of that humane spirit which abolished punishment for debt, and reformed the discipline of prisons and of jails; to recount the manifold improvements which, in a thousand ways, have multiplied the conveniences of life and ministered to the happiness of our race; to describe the rise and progress of that long series of mechanical inventions and discoveries which is now the admiration of the world, and our just pride and boast; to tell how, under the benign influence of liberty and peace, there sprang up, in the course of a single century, a prosperity unparalleled in the annals of human affairs.

New York: D. APPLETON & CO., 1, 3, & 5 Bond Street.